THE LONG
RIDERS' WINTER

By Frank Calkins

THE LONG RIDERS' WINTER
THE TAN-FACED CHILDREN
JACKSON HOLE
ROCKY MOUNTAIN WARDEN

THE LONG RIDERS' WINTER

FRANK CALKINS

DOUBLEDAY & COMPANY, INC.

GARDEN CITY, NEW YORK

1983

With the exception of actual historical persons, all of the
characters in this book are fictitious and any resemblance
to actual persons, living or dead, is purely coincidental.

Library of Congress Cataloging in Publication Data
Calkins, Frank, date
   The long riders' winter.
   (A Double D western)
   I. Title.
PS3505.A4215L6   1983   813'.54

First Edition

ISBN: 0-385-18877-3
Library of Congress Catalog Card Number 83–9058
Copyright © 1983 by Frank Calkins
All Rights Reserved
Printed in the United States of America

For Margaret

NOTE

This manuscript was written in 1924 by Thomas Lavering, a prominent ranchman of Dillon, Montana. Mr. Lavering's heirs placed the manuscript in the State Historical Society's archives with one provision: It must not be read by anyone, including Society officers, for a period of fifty years following the author's death.

The fifty years have long since passed. But, because of the sensational nature of some of Mr. Lavering's account, the Society has hesitated to make it public. Only this year was the decision made to publish. The Society urges that the criminal nature of portions of this account be read for what they are. The manuscript is presented for its historical value only.

THE LONG
RIDERS' WINTER

CHAPTER 1

The trouble started one night in October of 1882 when Frenchy Raymond shouted that he was "through eatin' with sheepherders!"

Frenchy had a winter's job breaking horses for the big Honeybee ranch on the edge of the western desert in Utah. It's hard, aggravating work, and Frenchy's hot temper didn't help. I'd seen him get bucked off twice that day.

The four other men at supper understood that was what Frenchy was really mad about. So we all kept still, ducked our heads, and continued eating. But everyone shot quick looks up to the head of the table, where Mr. Bob Lee sat. He was the top hand. He had been on the ranch nine years and drew ten dollars more a month than anyone else. We all thought he earned it. Bob Lee was a retired cavalry sergeant but still as tough and trim as a fire-cured brick. The men thought he should have been the foreman instead of Gladding Murdoch. Murdoch was more of a timekeeper than a ranchman.

Mr. Lee said, "Fall back, Frenchy. I seen you get bucked off today. Pickin' on us poor old shepherds won't gentle your broncs." Lee grinned. "And the Lord knows we're all too scared to ride 'em for you."

Usually that would have made Frenchy grin. But this night he was mad clear through. He glared at me, then said, "I do notice wipin' Tommy boy's nose is more important to you than doin' a man's job." Then Frenchy used a word that froze Mr. Lee's face and made him go white around the lips.

I idolized Bob Lee. He had taught me all I knew about the work. And I jumped when he ordered, "Tom! Help me move this table!"

As we lifted the table Frenchy grabbed a bowl of red gravy from it and threw it. We all knew Gladding Murdoch had an ironclad rule against fighting. But no one seemed to remember it. The gravy was still running down the wall when Bob Lee hit Frenchy.

I was just a green farm kid and was unprepared for the viciousness of Bob Lee's attack. When Frenchy lunged at him, swinging a left hand, Mr. Lee stepped inside it and hit the bronc rider. He hit him twice under the heart, bang! bang! Frenchy dropped as if hit with two slugs from Bob Lee's Colt revolver. He fell forward onto his hands and knees, then vomited.

No one said a word. I think we all felt distressed and embarrassed to have witnessed such slashing savagery. Most of us took what was left on our plates and scraped it into the slop barrel.

Perhaps I should have expected Bob Lee's manner of fighting. He was a Civil War veteran. He had joined the cavalry at twenty and fought for the Union at Antietam, Gettysburg, and in a score of deadly skirmishes. He was a sergeant with the Federal cavalry that surrounded the Army of Northern Virginia at Appomattox in April of 1865.

Of that he had said, "The South had Robert E. Lee an' the North had me, Bob Lee. My side won. Guess that says somethin' for the northern Lees." Then he had laughed and slapped me on the knee.

I was twenty years old and Bob Lee was forty-five but I had to hump to keep up with him. Mr. Murdoch had hired me as a camp tender. But without Bob Lee's guidance I would have made a poor job of it.

He made you respect him. He was not like some old soldiers you see loafing around towns with sagging bellies and puffy eyes. He was parade-ground trim, five feet ten and about 165 pounds. With his hat on you wouldn't suspect that he was losing his hair.

The man was a perfect specimen—except for one thing. The ring and little fingers were missing from his left hand. Once he'd raised his damaged hand for inspection. The old scars were still white against the tan of his skin.

"That's what put me out of the Army," he said. "Damned Injun knifed me. Can you beat it? Not a scratch in the war. Nigh on ten years in the Department of the Platte an' then a scurvy Snake Injun carves me up!"

He spoke bitterly when he said, "Soon as my hand healed they pensioned me off. I could've gone to Division and maybe clerked for West Point lieutenants. But I think they only offered that so's I'd retire. Now I draw four dollars and thirty-eight cents a month as a disabled veteran."

"How could they do that to you?" I asked.

"The Army can do anything to you it wants. I gave 'em the best fifteen years of my life. They said thanks and gave me a one-way ride to the railroad station."

Bob Lee's bitterness never affected his ranch work. Good hands were loyal to a ranch in those days; more loyal than some soldiers were to the Army of the Platte.

And those of us in the bunkhouse that October night had reason for showing extra loyalty. We all wanted to hold our winter jobs. Being paid off and sent down the road come fall wasn't funny.

Some hands rode the "grub line," bumming from ranch to ranch until spring. Others trapped fur or hunted for the market. Some men hung around the town odd-jobbing or gambling. And every winter there were good men who somehow got into trouble.

After the brief fight we were straightening up the bunkhouse when our foreman, Gladding Murdoch, appeared in the doorway. He probably had heard Frenchy yelling. Perhaps he even stood outside and watched the fight through the window.

He said, "You men know the rule about fighting. The company won't have it. Lee, you know better. Come up to the house in the morning and get your time."

"Yes, sir." Mr. Lee might have been taking orders to fix a gate, he was that calm.

The other men studied the floor or ceiling, all quiet as poisoned gophers. But I couldn't believe what was happening and blurted, "That's not fair! Mr. Lee didn't start the fight."

Murdoch looked at me coldly. "Keep still, son."

"To hell with you! You can figure my time, too." Perhaps I thought the other men would also stand up for Bob Lee. Whatever I thought was wrong. No one peeped.

Murdoch said, "As you wish, Lavering. Anyone else quitting?" He looked at the other men and each one looked away, sheepishly silent.

After Murdoch left, Bob Lee gave me a wondering smile. "Tom, you throw up a good job awful easy."

"I'll get by," I said but there were already doubts in my mind.

The next morning I was even less confident. I had about fifteen dollars in wages coming. Snow was already in the high country and I didn't have a guess as to what I'd do until spring.

Bob Lee must have sensed my growing worries, for, as we were dressing, he said, "Seein' you got today off, how about helpin' me catch my horses? I'm headin' for Salt Lake City. You can ride one of my bays if you're goin' that way yourself."

"Sure!"

Bob Lee grinned. He knew my predicament; I was afoot and Great Salt Lake City was more than fifty miles to the east. The way I'd been feeling that morning, Bob Lee could have led me into hell. Later on I was to think he had.

As soon as the other hands finished their breakfasts they hurried out to work. There is nothing like a firing to inspire ambition in a crew. The cook, Israel Chiles, poured boiling water over a pan filled with dirty dishes. Mr. Lee went out with Frenchy, who had sheepishly offered to catch us a couple of horses to use in rounding up Mr. Lee's horses. I rolled my bed and stuffed my few possessions into a canvas sack.

"Come an' have a coffee, Marse Tom," said Israel.

I sat in a chair beside the stove while the big black cook poured my coffee. "Here," he said, "you done lost you a good winter's job."

"I know. Frenchy's the one that should be leavin'."

"Why, Marse Tom, didn't you know Massah Murdoch had it in for Massah Lee?"

"No," I replied. "Why did he?"

"Massah Lee, he too good a hand. Don't pay to be *too* good. Makes some bosses nervous."

Bob Lee stuck his head in the door. "C'mon, kid. Let's saddle up and go find my horses. Might take us a while. Let's go in and draw our time first."

It was a fine morning. Too nice a day to be losing a job. Gladding Murdoch was waiting in his office, which occupied one corner of the foreman's home. We knocked, then entered when he called.

"Well, boys, they say a change is as good as a rest. I'm sure you will find new positions."

Bob Lee asked, "Can I use your name for a recommend?"

"Certainly, you have given good service here for . . ." Murdoch consulted his ledger. "For almost nine years. Of course, I would have to say you were discharged for fighting."

"Of course," said Bob Lee, pulling a mock frown.

Murdoch chose to ignore that. "You have three months' wages on the books. I reckon one hundred fifty dollars. Correct?"

"Correct and thanks." Bob Lee picked up seven twenty-dollar gold pieces and change from Murdoch's desk. He buttoned the coins into his shirt pocket.

"Lavering," Murdoch said to me, "you hired on at thirty a month. This is October sixteenth. I reckon fifteen dollars."

"Yes, sir."

Murdoch slid the coins across his desk with the end of a ruler. "Young man, I admire your loyalty if not your judgment. You have done well here. With some seasoning you should do well elsewhere."

Outside Mr. Lee put his hand on my shoulder. "Don't worry, there are other jobs. Come on, it could take half the day to find them horses."

Later I hoped Bob Lee guessed more accurately about finding jobs than horses. We were all day locating his three horses. They were spending the last warm days of fall loafing in the juniper.

The two bays were big, near 1,200 pounds. The third animal was a sleek, long-legged sorrel named Socks. Mr. Lee called him his "running horse." And the sorrel could beat anything in that valley. Eventually no one would race him, so Mr. Lee and Frenchy had spent most Sundays training the horse against a watch.

We left the Honeybee ranch early on the day after being paid off. The road led north along the gray-green foothills of the Stansbury Mountains. I rode one of Mr. Lee's bays and led the other, which was packing our outfits. The old sergeant was mounted on his high-spirited sorrel.

He handed me the packhorse's lead rope saying, "If I was to get a rope under this horse's tail he'd go crazy."

Actually, there was no more chance of Bob Lee getting a rope under a horse's tail than there was of teaching a ewe to count. He was letting me pay my way to Great Salt Lake City by leading the packhorse. I was glad to do it.

The day was warm with white clouds loafing in a blue sky. In an hour Mr. Lee's fast-moving sorrel had left me far behind. The horse and his rider alternately shimmered then faded from sight in the heat waves. I was alone with my thoughts.

The valley we rode through was called Skull Valley. In earlier days many buffalo had been caught here by a terrible winter and died. Some of the bones and skulls still could be seen bleaching on the light gray soil.

I was not sorry to be leaving. The valley was dusty-hot in summer and mild to miserable in winter. When it rained or the snow melted, the alkali bottoms turned boggy. I have spent many a half day getting my team and wagon two hundred yards.

Nevertheless, I was worried. Western Utah was a hardscrabble place for a single fellow on his own. Mr. Lee had made a vague reference to a winter's job. But when I questioned him, he said he needed more time to think on it. I guessed that was what he was doing now, riding up there alone and thinking.

CHAPTER 2

Our first destination was Timpie Springs at the point of the mountain range. A road ranch was located there where we could put up for the night. But before I tell what happened at the ranch I must mention those two big bays of Mr. Lee's. Although we had fallen far behind the sorrel, those bays were not plug horses. Mr. Lee would not have owned a shabby horse.

He once said, "A man can ride either of these big boys forty miles a day and then get on 'em in the mornin' and ride forty more. They've got bottom, not all horses do."

He told me about a cavalry captain he'd had. "That man knew cavalry and he knew history. He said that big horses like mine was what the old-time knights rode. Plowed 'em right through infantry, knockin' down men right and left. I've done it myself with Injuns. Them knights used bits with foot-long cheek bars. With an outfit like that a man could spur his horse down a cannon barrel.

"Course, if a horse is well trained and trusts you, he'll do things like that without needin' much force."

The road ranch at Timpie Springs was operated by a thickset middle-aged Hawaiian called Kanaka Bill. Additionally Bill was a brand inspector and a deputy sheriff. He was much better at those two jobs than he was at innkeeping.

The "ranch house" was a sagging conglomeration of crooked log walls and dilapidated chinking under a tarred canvas roof. None of the few windows matched in size but all were equally filthy. Inside, stale cooking smells mixed with the odors of sweat, dust, and livestock.

Bill's cook was a bare-footed Gosiute Indian. The mainstay of her table was fat pork and beans. Some claimed that if an old sheep died anywhere in the surrounding scrub, Bill's menu changed to mutton and beans.

But the place had food and water for travelers and their livestock. Bill sold a local whiskey called Valley Tan. And he kept the gambling honest. But Kanaka Bill's real talents were as a tracker and stock detective. He was the best man and cow hunter since old Port Rockwell had died in a fit a few years before.

After the Union and Central Pacific railroads met at Promontory in 1869, the emigrant trails were less used. Still, there were enough stock drovers and freighters passing by to keep the ranch profitable. Kanaka Bill maintained a lucrative livestock trade, finding strays, buying worn-out horses and mules, then charging triple prices for fresh animals. At the Honeybee they told stories of Kanaka Bill tracking down rustlers. He showed them all the mercy Port Rockwell had—which was none.

By the time I dismounted in front of the weathered inn Mr. Lee had already unsaddled and put his horse into the big corral. He and Bill were sitting in homemade chairs on the porch, a quart of whiskey on the table between them.

"Turn the horses into the corral when you've unsaddled, Tom. Look 'em over good for sore backs, you know. And feed 'em good—Bill is charging us plenty."

There was a kid who helped in the corral. He tried to feed the bays salt-grass hay which was cut wild on the Great Salt Lake marshes. But I was wise to that. When I protested the boy grinned and furnished bright timothy hay and plenty of oats from a large bin.

After finishing with our horses I collected our duffel and went around to where Kanaka Bill and Bob Lee sat. In the twilight I saw that a third man had joined them, probably not by invitation. He was a stock drover called Captain Suggs. Suggs made a living by contracting to deliver beef cattle to mining districts in the desert.

"Howdy," he said.

"Evening." I was carrying our canvas duffel bags.

"Be careful whose bed ya put that stuff on. Smells of sheep." Suggs stared at me, trying to make me look away.

Bill said, "Cap'n, these men are customers. I say where they sleep, please." Kanaka Bill had a high, singsong voice but there was no mistaking his meaning.

Suggs was a stringy man, stooping into his mid-forties. He had beaver teeth and pale blue eyes. I had seen him several times on the desert. And I would not have trusted him with a dog's dinner.

He said, "Sheep are ruinin' the country. Any fool can see it."

Mr. Lee, who had been sitting quietly, now spoke. "I don't see it. And if that bunch of played-out rail fences is your idea of cattle, don't brag on 'em."

A small herd of miserable-looking cattle was holding about a half mile off in the dusty spring bottoms. Mr. Lee continued, "I've seen better-lookin' beef cattle lying dead in dry washes."

Suggs's yellowed front teeth showed. "That stock is consigned to the mines out at Pinto and Deep Crick. Fat cattle couldn't make that drive."

The men fell silent and I entered the building and set our duffel on the bunks indicated by the Indian cook. The room had a low, smoke-stained pole ceiling. At one end was a rusty range with lump coal piled on the dirt floor beside it. Standing between that and the bunks was a long dining table with benches on either side. A round card table with numerous burns in the green felt covering stood nearby.

Placed along the walls were six double-decked bunks. Boards had been nailed to the uprights to serve as ladders to the upper bunks. On a busy night Bill could sleep two men to a bunk and more on the floor. I was glad Mr. Lee and I had our own bedrolls and would not have to rent one of Bill's dirty blankets for twenty cents a night.

While I watched, the Indian lit three kerosene lamps that hung from the ceiling. They did not give much light, which was probably an asset to the food we were about to eat.

Cap Suggs had two tired-looking young drovers with his herd. The men came in alternately to eat so that the stock was never left alone. Not only was grass sparse, thus encouraging the animals to roam, but there were Digger Indians out in that sage who were not above stealing. For those miserable people, who ate such things as sagebrush tops and rodents, a beefsteak would have been an unimaginable luxury.

After dinner Mr. Lee crawled into his bunk with a quart of Valley Tan. I lay back on the straw tick and determined to keep watch through the night. All my money, a twenty-dollar gold piece and some cartwheels, was tied up in a pouch that hung from a cord around my neck. My companions appeared to be the sort who were ready to relieve me of that pouch.

After we had been in bed for an hour Mr. Lee asked me, "Kid, what's your opinion of Chinamen?"

At first I thought he was talking through the Valley Tan. Then I realized he was serious. But he might as well have asked me what I thought about the Clayton-Bulwer Treaty. Nevertheless, I tried to answer. "Chinese are good workers. Built the railroad and all. Some people say they work too cheap and get jobs Americans should have." I stopped, having already said more about the Chinese than I truly knew.

Bob Lee resumed the conversation. "You can buy one in Frisco. Did you know that?"

I had not known it.

Mr. Lee continued, "We killed a lotta good men in the war fightin' slavery. But the Chinese go right on sellin' each other. Pretty little gal can bring two thousand dollars."

"If I ever had that much," I said, "I'd buy a farm. Did you ever know someone who bought a girl?"

I heard Bob Lee roll on his straw mattress. "There was a time when I tried to." Then he fell silent and, in a few minutes, began snoring.

I lay awake thinking until one of Suggs's drovers came clumping in and woke his boss. "After eleven, Cap. Your turn with the herd."

Suggs grumbled, "All O.K.?"

"They're sure hungry. Feed's so poor they want to wander."

Suggs, seemingly trying to wake the house, clumped around getting his boots on. Finally, after clapping on his low-crowned hat, he banged out the door.

The drover was a red-eyed kid about my age with patchy, blond whiskers. He sat down at the table with a mug of coffee. He saw me watching him and nodded. "No sleep?"

"No."

"Christmas, I can! Old Suggs's idee of takin' turns with the herd is about four to one. One hour for him and four for us."

"Why don't you say something?"

"Hell no! This is the only job I could find. It sure beats eatin' jackrabbits and sleepin' in haystacks."

His coffee finished, the young drover fell into an empty bunk and slept soundly for two hours. At 1 A.M. he got up and left. I felt sorry for him. Cap Suggs made Gladding Murdoch look like a saint.

Eventually I fell asleep and was awakened by Mr. Lee bumping my bunk with his knee. It was daylight. "Tom, get up! We got trouble. Our horses is gone!"

I tumbled out of bed, feeling for the money pouch around my neck. It was still there. I asked Bob Lee, "Did they stray? I'm sure we closed the corral gate."

He said, "It was open this mornin'. They could be headin' for the ranch. But Suggs left early and run his stock down the same road. Bill an' I tracked 'em for a half mile but even he couldn't make much sense outta all them tracks."

"What'll we do?"

Lee said, "Bill's got a mule you can borrow. Take a couple of halters and head south toward the Honeybee ranch. Bill an' me will follow Suggs's herd. He might've stole 'em."

"I thought of that," I said.

"If the horses just strayed and you find 'em, catch 'em. But if Cap or one of his riders has them, lay back. Bill an' I will be comin'."

We agreed to meet at Pinyon Springs that night. The springs were on the far side of the Cedar Mountains, which formed the western wall of Skull Valley. Mr. Lee had shown them to me the year before.

My borrowed mule was the hardest-riding creature in Utah. But I stayed with him and five miles from Timpie Springs I found the tracks of three horses going in the direction of the Honeybee. It appeared that the horses had traveled ahead of the cattle until the herd was turned southwest. The horses had continued south and I hoped to catch them before they made it all the way back to the ranch.

Although the animals were moving south, their tracks sometimes wandered off the trail and into the juniper foothills. It was difficult to follow them there. Approaching the Honeybee I found the tracks of other horses. And, by midday, I was walking as much as riding, slowly trying to sort out the tracks of our strays.

At one point our horses veered onto a broad, rocky flat. If one of them hadn't obligingly lifted his tail and left me a fresh trail marker, I might have missed their change of direction.

That turn bothered me. I'd assumed I was tracking strays. But straying horses do not head out over rocks by themselves. They'll take the dirt trail every time. Someone was with Bob Lee's horses.

He had taken the animals over the rocks to throw off a tracker. And he might have fooled me were it not for the road apples. There was something else, too; when a shod horse steps on a rock he often leaves a tiny white scratch. I dismounted and began following the faint scratches. It was slow work and I wished an expert like Kanaka Bill had been there to do the job properly. But I persisted and by late afternoon traced the horses across the flat. They were now heading southwest and, I was sure, to a rendezvous with Cap Suggs.

Ahead lay the Cedar Mountains, a desert range whose lower slopes were a mixture of dry gullies and rough, juniper-dotted foothills. At a clump of the twisted trees I saw that the horses had stopped. This time there was a fourth track. A man had dismounted among the trees.

As I stood there examining the tracks a chilling thought arose. I could have been easily ambushed by a man hidden in those trees. Plodding along in my heavy canvas coat, my hat pulled low as shade against the setting sun, I'd have been as easy as a turkey in a dead tree.

I became more watchful. Whenever that old mule threw his ears forward I slid off him quick. And I held him between me and whatever it was his ears pointed at. All I had for weapons were a stockman's knife and an empty salt sack I'd put a rock in. Some might laugh but that loaded salt sack made a good sap. Mr. Lee told me about it. He'd watched a drunken trooper clean out a "hog ranch" with just such a weapon. Still, it was no defense against a sniper.

After checking his back trail the horse thief was apparently satisfied that his wanderings had thrown off any pursuers. Because, when he remounted, he made a beeline for the old Canon Station Trail.

The trail led out to the Deep Creek Mountains on the Utah-Nevada border. There were mining districts scattered all up and down that country. I knew Cap Suggs's herd of cattle was being driven in that direction. Our horses were probably going to be sold to a miner heading into Nevada.

Pinyon Springs, our meeting place, was a half mile off the main trail, up a little draw. Even though they had been dug out and a small tank built to store the flow, the springs weren't generous.

It was nearly sunset when I reached the mouth of the draw. I had not eaten since morning. All I could think to do was to ride up there and wait for Mr. Lee and Kanaka Bill.

Days end fast on the desert. The sun drops over the far horizon and it's suddenly dark. It was full dark when I entered the draw. My mule smelled the water and began braying and walking quickly for the first time all day. At the spring box he jerked impatiently on the reins and thrust his muzzle deep into the water.

"Take it easy. I want some, too." I was tired and out of sorts.

"Ease up, he only wants a drink." Someone had spoken from behind the mountain willows bordering the spring. To suddenly hear a voice when I thought I was alone scared the green tar out of me.

"Who's there?" I whipped out my salt-bag sap and whirled it. "Is that you, Bob Lee?"

"It ain't the railroad Chinese."

Relief washed over me and I stuffed the sap back into my pocket. "I'm sure glad it's you. I didn't see any tracks come in here."

"You weren't s'posed to. With stock thieves wanderin' the country a man's better off if he don't tell 'em where he's at." He added, "Like you just done ridin' in here."

I felt foolish and was too ashamed of my carelessness to mention the tracking I'd done.

"Did you find the horses?" I asked.

"Sure did. Got 'em tied back in the juniper."

I asked, "Who had 'em?"

"One of Suggs's drovers. The guy with the skimpy beard."

That was the young fellow I'd talked to only the night before. I had much to learn about human nature.

Mr. Lee said, "That ol' Kanaka had 'em wired all the way, knew where they'd be before they did. Bill was down in some greasewood. He was sittin' on a rock, waitin' and lookin' sleepy, when the thief rode up."

"I'll bet he was surprised." I pictured that plump Hawaiian sitting there under his big hat and grinning up at the horse thief. "What happened then?" I asked.

"Feller whirled and started to call Bill a son of a somethin'. Which is when I raised up out of the brush and blew him into the arms of St. Peter."

"He's dead?" I was astonished.

"Want to see him?"

"No!"

Mr. Lee laughed. "Kanaka Bill's a deputy. Feller had a gun and resisted arrest—which was a great convenience to the taxpayers of Utah. Bill's out now watchin' Cap Suggs and his crowbaits. Cap may try trailin' at night."

"What are you gonna do with them?" I was still shaken by the ferocity of desert justice. A man I'd talked with last night lay dead in the sage tonight.

"Not much we can do with Suggs. He'll claim the drover quit last night. He won't know a thing about my horses bein' stole. So we'll just meet him tomorrow mornin', tip our hats, and hand over the dear departed."

Mr. Lee had bacon and coffee in his saddlebags. We made a light supper and then curled up under our saddle blankets. I hoped I wasn't lying near the corpse.

Sometime in the night Kanaka Bill came in. He moved so quietly that it wasn't until I heard him talking with Mr. Lee that I knew he was there.

Bill said, "They bedded the herd by Jennings Springs. Feed's poor, so they'll have to let the cattle move early."

Mr. Lee asked, "When do you figure to meet 'em?"

"Oh, we'll have time for coffee. Then we'll pack up the goods and hand him over to Suggs. I'd like to meet him 'bout where that fella resisted arrest." Kanaka Bill sounded like a foreman lining out a routine day's work.

Mr. Lee replied, "Sounds good. Tom got in about dark. Said that kid had wandered all around Robin Hood's barn throwin' us off'n his trail."

I heard Bill flop down and break wind. "Man that dumb shouldn't steal," he said.

It was cold in the morning and we all three crowded around the fire while the bacon and coffee cooked. I stood with my back to the fire and watched two magpies hop from limb to limb in a juniper. They were building up courage to flutter down on the corpse lying under the tree.

Bill saw me looking and asked, "Ever seed a dead guy before?"

"Yes, but never a horse thief." The drover was lying on his back. He was pale under the scrubby beard and his mouth and eyes were open. The eyes were China blue.

Mr. Lee finished his coffee and bacon, then walked to where the horses and my mule were tethered. "Hello, boys," he said. He walked among the horses, brushing off their backs, looking for injuries, then rubbing each between the ears. He fed them the last of some oats he'd carried from Timpie Springs.

"Bill," he called, "will your mule pack a stiff?"

"Sure. He's gonna snort and roll his eyes first but he'll do it, you bet."

After the mule was saddled I helped Mr. Lee swing the corpse across the saddle. I held him by the wrists and thought they felt like thin splints of wood. Some people believe a corpse is always stiff with rigor mortis.

They are stiff for a while but in a few hours they'll loosen up. The dead cowboy was loose. After the mule put on his predicted show we loaded the corpse. Mr. Lee balanced the load like you would a deer, then tied the arms and legs to the cinch rings.

Kanaka Bill supervised. "I guess you packed lotta stiffs, Bob? In the war and all."

"Yep. Lots of 'em dirties theirselves. Buster here sure filled his britches. That's how the world last seen this trash; gone to glory with his pants full and his mouth hangin' open."

I began to get sick. "C'mon, let's *go.*" The two men sounded like hunters talking about game they'd shot.

Leaving the draw, we rode through the sage until we reached the Canon Springs Trail. We turned onto it heading for Timpie Springs and our meeting with Captain Suggs.

The sky was overcast and shaded furrows of gray cloud lay roped overhead. A cold wind blew from the northwest and we turned our collars up against it.

"Maybe snow," said Bill.

"She's overdue now." Mr. Lee had a pipe stuck in his mouth, gloved hands resting on the saddle horn. He might have been riding across a pasture to close a gate. But I was very nervous about meeting Cap Suggs.

Mr. Lee said, "Bill, I think Tom ought to be in the middle. Suggs will be ridin' drag. Tom can go right up to him and hand him the package. You an' me'll flank him, right and left. Keepin' about sixty yards off. That way, if he or the other drover shows fight we can put 'em down with our rifles."

"Good," said Bill. "Take the man closest to you?"

"Right."

"Wait a minute!" I said, "All I've got is a sack with a rock in it. What am I supposed to do?" I pictured myself being used as bait in a shooting.

"Tom," said Mr. Lee, "I don't think Suggs will do a thing. You're gonna be safe as church."

CHAPTER 3

I may have been safe that morning but I have never been more scared. Suggs and his cattle were still miles away when we located them. The distance gave me time to worry. Was Suggs pulling his rifle from the scabbard and levering a shell into the chamber?

No. He wasn't expecting us. On the other hand, a man who had just stolen three horses from Bob Lee wouldn't take chances with anyone.

All these worries raced through my mind again and again. Then Cap Suggs was there, sitting on his horse six feet in front of me. My chest tightened and my spit turned to alum. Suggs said, "What is this, a holdup?" His voice was scratchy and his rabbit teeth showed. He was afraid, too!

"Your drover," I said, "he stole our horses. Kanaka Bill and Bob Lee caught him."

Suggs screamed at the other drover, "Damn it, can't you see the herd's scatterin'? Head 'em up. Keep 'em on the trail!"

Then he said to me, "That feller quit me at Timpie Springs. Left in the night. He's nothin' to me. You kill him?"

Mr. Lee had ridden up, carrying his rifle with its butt resting on his thigh. He said, "Man sacrificed himself for you, Cap."

"He never, you're crazy!"

Mr. Lee looked at the barrel of his Winchester and then at Suggs. The drover dismounted, carefully. He walked to the laden mule and looked into the corpse's face. Next he turned to Mr. Lee. "He was just a kid. I warned him when he hired on. He was a damn fool goin' agin you and the Kanaka. Well, you prob'ly done the country a favor and I say, 'Good riddance.'"

Suggs left the mule and remounted his horse. He grinned. He had no more chin than a rabbit; and even less courage. "Well, ya showed me. I'm convinced; never shoulda hired the bugger in the first place." He tugged at his hat brim.

I couldn't believe it. Captain Suggs was tipping his hat to Mr. Lee!

"Whoa, Cap. We think you're responsible for him. What about his people?" Bob Lee asked. "There wasn't much on him. He had a name. You owed him wages."

"I don't owe nothin' to a quitter horse thief," Cap was whining.

"Well now, Cap, that's not so," said Bob Lee. "It took three men the best part of two days to catch this feller and recover stolen stock. I'd think you'd want to do the right thing."

Kanaka Bill had come up and was listening. He said, "Cap'n Suggs, you owe fifty dollar. Our wages, court costs an' all." He nodded toward the corpse. "That's got to be buried."

"You can pay that outta his back wages," said Lee.

Cap Suggs did not reply. His face got white and his hands shook as he pulled five yellow-backed bills from the money belt under his shirt. "Here." He shoved the currency into Kanaka Bill's outstretched hand. Bill's fingers closed tightly over the money as the wind threatened to tear away the fluttering bills.

No sooner was the money paid than Cap Suggs sunk spurs into his horse and galloped away, sawing hard on the reins and bawling, "Damn it . . ." The wind carried off the rest of his oath.

I said, "He's the guilty one and you both know it. Are you going to let him off?"

Kanaka Bill was laughing. "Noo, he just pay me fifty dollar fine."

Bob Lee was laughing, too. "Yep an' we scared about a year off'n his life. Did you see his hand shakin' when he counted out the money?"

The two men grinned. Kanaka Bill handed two of the yellowbacks to Mr. Lee. "Here's twenty," he said. "I figure twenty for me and ten for the kid. I get his boots."

"Sure." Mr. Lee tucked the bills into his money belt. I folded my ten twice and put it carefully into the leather pouch hanging around my neck.

We set out again. The smoke from Mr. Lee's pipe left a fine scent in the air until the wind whipped it away. At the first deep gully the two older men left the trail and rode up the gully a half mile. We all dismounted. While I held the horses the men untied the corpse's arms and legs and flung it onto the ground. Kanaka Bill pulled off the boots, then shook each to see if any money had been hidden in them. The thief's pants, coat, and shirt were also stripped off. Mr. Lee placed his booted foot under the corpse and rolled it into the gully as one might roll a log. There was a soft thud as the body landed. None of us looked down after it. I imagined the dead drover lying there in his filthy underwear. But I tried to forget it.

Bill rolled the boots, pants, and shirt inside the man's coat and tied them behind his saddle. He said, "Shirt's pretty bloody. Injuns won't care. I'll sell everythin' for three, four dollar."

It was dark and wind-driven snowflakes were scattering across the sagebrush when the three of us rode into Timpie Springs. Mr. Lee and I were the only guests that night. The Indian woman served us greasy beans and fried bread. I was so hungry that I had three helpings. Bill felt complimented and beamed. Mr. Lee washed down his supper with some of the quart of whiskey he'd bought from the bar.

After eating he took the bottle with him to his bunk. He said, "Tom, you might be too tired to sleep. Take yourself a cup of this Tan."

"I don't think so, thanks."

"Today bothered you, didn't it?"

"Yes, it did."

"What was it?"

I said, "There should have been some sorrow. I know that man was a horse thief. But the people I come from are sorry when a man dies or gets killed. We accept it but we feel bad for him and his family."

"Look at this." Mr. Lee rummaged under the duffel he used for a pillow. He pulled out a large revolver and said, "That's a Navy Colt; thirty-six caliber, cap-an'-ball. I had one durin' the war. This one looks like it's went through two wars. That feller had it hangin' from a cord on his belt."

I accepted the old revolver gingerly because I wasn't familiar with handguns and mistrusted them.

"Know how it works?" Mr. Lee raised himself up on one elbow.

"Not for sure."

"Give it here. I'll show you. Want to show you somethin' else, too."

Mr. Lee explained how the revolver was loaded by putting black powder, greased wads, and a ball in each chamber. The loads were then seated with a rammer which was attached under the barrel. The gun was primed by placing a percussion cap over the nipple at the rear of each cylinder.

"When she's loaded, just cock the hammer and pull the trigger for each shot."

Knowing that the revolver was loaded made me even more reluctant to handle it. But Mr. Lee insisted that I draw the hammer back to half cock and examine the percussion caps.

"See," he said, "two caps have been busted but the gun misfired."

"What about it?"

"Ever think that turkeyneck might've popped them caps tryin' to shoot you? This gun was in his hand when I plugged him." I looked at the rusty old weapon. The rough grips felt like the scales of a rattlesnake. Had that flat-topped front sight wavered across my chest?

Mr. Lee removed the two fired caps and found one had misfired because of a broken nipple on the chamber. The other cap had simply been defective.

He explained, "Sometimes oil gets into the cap and makes a dud. But this old six-shooter prob'ly ain't seen oil since sixty-five. My guess it was just a bum cap." He warned me about the folly of trying to economize by buying cheap ammunition. The old cavalry sergeant's lecture concluded when he gave me the gun.

I was pleased. "It will make a fine souvenir when I'm old."

"Might come in handy long before that. Man never knows when a howlin' Injun may jump him or a doped-up Chinaman might try to chop him with a hatchet."

Mr. Lee said this with a grin. But there was another of his references to Chinese. These dark and always belligerent remarks seemed to be following a pattern. But it was a pattern I could not yet see.

The old gun would need repairs before I could count on it for protection. I resolved to take it to a gunsmith when we reached Great Salt Lake City.

Then, despite the day's excitements, I fell asleep and didn't awaken until morning. Kanaka Bill did that when he scolded his Indian cook. It had been a cold night and she had not gotten up and built a fire. Bill could curl up and sleep under a bush on the trail. But he wanted his comforts when they were available.

Outside Mr. Lee was already in the corral and looking at his horses. "See," he said, "I told you—we can ride these bays forty miles day after day. They got bottom the runnin' horse ain't. A wore-out horse will get sore lots faster than a fresh, well-fed one. If horses was smart enough to know their own strength we'd be workin' for them."

It was thirty-five miles to the city. We borrowed Kanaka Bill's mule to pack our outfits. Mr. Lee wanted his running sorrel to have as easy a trip as possible. The horses were fed big rations of oats and hay before we went in to breakfast.

With Mr. Lee's help, Kanaka Bill wrote a letter to the United States marshal in Salt Lake describing the capture of the horse thief. "Don't say too much," Lee advised. "A guv'mint man don't want to think too hard on such matters. Don't get him stirred up."

As it happened, Kanaka Bill's report was read, filed, and never referred to again. The young drover became just one of many who went into the Great American Desert and stayed there.

Our route lay around the southern tip of the Great Salt Lake. The day was stormy. Gray waves rolled up on the salt-crusted shore while, above, a few gulls rode the strong winds. The lake was a great dead sea where nothing could drown and nothing could live.

Mr. Lee cast a bleak look out across the water. "On a sunny day it's kind of purty, blue an' all. But except for floatin' everything from dead sheep to fat ladies that can't swim, I can't see as it's worth much."

The city named after it was different. I had come from the Sacramento River country a couple of years earlier looking for a ranch job. This was the first time I'd been far enough east to see the famous Mormon city.

The stories about its inhabitants were widely known. How randy old men kept herds of young girls as wives. And how everyone defied Federal law in Utah. We knew that old wolf Brigham Young had outsmarted General Johnston and stood off his army in 1857. We also knew Utah was being kept a territory in reprisal. But I didn't know if it was true, as Frenchy claimed, that Mormons had horns.

As we entered the city I examined the citizens closely. But as I had suspected all along, I saw no horns. What I did see, however, was one of the prettiest cities there ever was. Upwards of 40,000 people were living in a great valley at the foot of the Wasatch Mountains. There was snow on the peaks and clear water running out of the canyons. The wide streets were clean and lacked the usual collection of vagrants and drunks. No painted women hung from second-story windows.

"This is a nice town!" I said to Mr. Lee. We were riding up Main Street to where he said there was a livery barn and lodging for us.

He said, "It sure beats Denver." He was excited, too. I saw him looking over the town and the pretty female shoppers on the sidewalks.

"I was stationed at Fort Douglas," he said, "on the foothills. The Mormons didn't much like us except on paydays. And even then they didn't suffer a trooper who got out of line. He'd get thrown in jail, which is a sight dirtier than these streets, or at least delivered back to camp. They expect us to blow the dust out of our ears. Just don't do it in public."

Like any young buck, I felt mysterious yearnings to "blow the dust out of my ears." But I was just a gangling youth and ignorant of city ways. Bob Lee would have to serve as my guide here, too.

After we had put up the horses and arranged to have Bill's mule returned, Mr. Lee asked, "What's your pleasure, Tom?"

"Why, look for work."

Lee's blue eyes twinkled but he stifled the laugh I saw behind them. "Why, Tom, the day's shot but the night's young. We been a year in the desert. One look at us now an' the girls'll think we pack road apples in our pockets. We need to clean up an' get new duds. Only job you could find now is scarin' little kids. Best way to get a job is to look like you don't need it."

We put up at the Salt Lake House in the center of town. Our room was upstairs over a busy saloon. Leaving our duffel in the room, we found a barbershop. After I'd had my bath the barber fussed loudly about the black ring I'd left in his tub. Mr. Lee had me tip the man a nickel and he was all smiles after that.

While Bob Lee was getting himself a shave and haircut, he sent the boy who heated bath water out to find us a haberdasher. When the man arrived we both ordered new shirts, coats, and California pants. I chose a black plug hat. Mr. Lee took a wide-brimmed Stetson of a fawn color. We learned the location of a good bootmaker and vowed to visit him the next day. In the meantime the water boy did his best to shine our old boots.

At 9 P.M. we stepped out of that barbershop looking like the gold dust twins. Bob Lee handed me a green panatela cigar. We both lit up and stood there appraising the town.

"How much do you weigh, Tom?"

I hesitated to answer, wondering if Mr. Lee was trying the old joke about six feet of cow chips. But his expression was serious, so I replied, "One sixty-five, last summer."

"I was afraid of that, you're way too heavy."

Overweight had never been my problem. And we had done some long riding on short rations since leaving the ranch. I said, "That clothing salesman just said I had a thirty-inch waist."

"You're too heavy to jock my runnin' horse. We got to get him some matches, but first we need a jockey."

Mr. Lee didn't say much more on the subject while we walked back to the Salt Lake House. I wondered about horse racing. The season was over. The blustery weather we had been riding with proved that.

In the room Mr. Lee announced, "We need three weeks. I've seen good weather hold in this valley till Christmas. Can't depend on it, though. We've got to be ready to leave by Thanksgiving."

"Thanksgiving!" I cried. "I can't afford more than three more nights in this room. I've got to find a job."

Bob Lee paced around the room puffing on his cigar. "All right," he said. "You look for your job. But first, take your gun to the gunsmith and have it fixed."

"I will."

"Did you ever visit a house of ill fame?"

"No." The cigar I'd tried to smoke and then thrown away was as near to vice as I'd been.

"They've got some dandy places here."

"I've only got a few dollars between me and vagrancy."

Mr. Lee said, "We're partners, aren't we? I'll stake you."

The green cigar had made me light-headed. Whiskey and women would only make me sick. I said, "No, thanks." But being called Bob Lee's partner made me feel good.

He put on his new hat and left. I didn't see him again until he came in to breakfast the next morning. He was freshly shaved and neatly dressed. To this day I have never understood how that man could drink a quart of whiskey after supper, do God knows what else, then be clearheaded and ready for work the next morning.

He sat down and ordered breakfast. "What's your plan of attack, Tom?"

"Guess I'll just look. I'll take anything. Want me to ask for you, too?"

"I'd be pleased to hear of somethin' really good. But I'm goin' to concentrate on runnin' my horse. I got a line on a jock last night."

"Isn't racing done for the year?"

"Horse racing's never done. But it's true; a lot of the fellows ain't raced since September at the fairs. Pulled the shoes off their horses, took 'em off grain, and pastured 'em. A horse will go soft in three weeks. I'm countin' on that."

"I don't follow you, Bob."

"Never mind, leave this to me. Go hunt a job and I'll see you here tonight."

The first places I tried were the horse barns and livery stables. But so many out-of-work ranch hands had already asked there that some of the establishments displayed NO HELP WANTED signs.

I walked to the edge of the city and asked for work at some farms. The farmers just laughed. Most of them had herds of strapping sons to do all the work.

One kindly farmer did give me some bread and milk. He advised me to try the mines. "It's hard, dangerous work. Our brother Brigham Young advised the Saints not to dig mines. We are farmers and herdsmen."

The nearest mines, however, were miles back in the canyons of the Wasatch Mountains. It would require two days to walk there and back. I walked back into the city with a heavy heart.

Bob Lee was sitting in the saloon of the Salt Lake House when I walked in that evening. "Hello, Tom. What luck?"

"Not a thing. I'll try the mines."

Bob Lee said, "If there is a job there you'll find ten Chinamen lined up ahead of you. They'll work for nothin' and eat less. If a blast goes off too soon and kills one, the Chink bosses will have another coolie in his place before the blood's dry on the timbers."

"In that case I'll hold up the Zion's Trust. I did take my pistol to the gunsmith."

Bob Lee gave me a strange look before replying, "Don't pick on Zion's Trust. Every sheriff in Utah would be after you. But before the law got you, the Danites would've strung you up by the heels."

"What are Danites?" The name was strange to me.

"Old Brigham's private army. Don't think 'cause the old feller passed on that the muscle's gone. These people made fools of the U.S. Army. Don't ever try robbin' 'em. Rob somebody no one likes."

I shook my head. "I was just fooling. I heard there was muskrat trappin' out by the Salt Lake. I'd try that before robbing somebody."

After supper I spent some of my small supply of dollars on a new pair of boots. The walking I'd done had finished my old pair.

When I returned to our room I asked Mr. Lee if I could borrow one of his bay horses to ride to the Alta mines.

"Sure," he said. "Take either one, they need the work. Just be sure you grain 'em good and don't sore 'em up."

Early the next morning I set out for the Alta mining district high in the mountains southeast of the city. It was a fine day. The canyon was beautiful with towering walls and a clear stream splashing at the bottom. But my reception at the mines was ice cold.

I was advised to try the Brighton district in the next canyon. Mr. Lee's horse and I spent the night in an alpine livery barn where the darkness was torn by the clamor of tipples and the thud of underground blasting. The board for one horse was two dollars. Mr. Lee's bay dined on expensive hay and grain while I mooched some of the liveryman's lunch. There were no jobs at any of the mines. I was back in the city the next afternoon.

At the livery barn I found Mr. Lee and a small fellow about my age whose hair hung down in his eyes. He chain-smoked cigarettes; as Mr. Lee explained, "It keeps his weight down, stunts his growth, too. Which is what a jock wants. Tom, this here is Hummingbird Terhune, our jock."

I shook hands with Terhune. He did not appear pleased to meet me.

Mr. Lee said, "We have been working the horse. There's a man down from Layton with a buggy horse he thinks can run. We have a race." Bob Lee was grinning.

Hummingbird Terhune, I soon learned, was a vile little man. He was cruel and absolutely ruthless on the racecourse. He knew every dirty trick there was to win races. He was to win one race for us by spitting tobacco juice in the other horse's eye. He crowded, cut off, and swung wide on the turns. I suspect he even doped horses. But whatever his means, they worked. He and Mr. Lee's running horse won every match.

Some fine-looking horses began arriving in the city from outlying areas. On one day we raced three times. All the horse owners in town became eager to try their horses against Bob Lee's fleet sorrel.

These races weren't fancy thoroughbred races reported in the papers. Matches were made in bars or tobacco shops and the races were run on the dirt streets of Salt Lake City. It was against the law but no one cared. The stakes were usually small and if a big crowd gathered I would circulate through it booking wagers. If the other man's horse looked good I laid off some of the bets by placing the money on our opponent's horse. We didn't win a lot of money and what we did win was split with Hummingbird.

When I observed that our competition was improving all the time, Mr. Lee said, "Tom, we're in a campaign. You fight it two ways; with tactics to win each race but strategy to win the campaign."

I didn't fully understand. But we continued winning, so I did as I was told and kept quiet. After two weeks we had won over a dozen matches and almost five hundred dollars. Hummingbird took two hundred of that. But the little imp was worth every penny. He used some of his winnings to bribe a jock whose horse we knew could beat us. Hummingbird won that match by a head. People talked about it for a week—our most exciting race yet. I felt embarrassed by people's gullibility.

On November 15, 1882, Bob Lee was eating breakfast in the Salt Lake House when a well-dressed older man came to his table. He introduced himself as Damon Meservy. Meservy was an associate of several members of the Mormon Church's Council of the Twelve. And as such he was one of the richest and most powerful men in Utah. He also loved to race horses.

He told Mr. Lee, "I hold gambling a sin. But I would like to test one of my ponies against that fine horse of yours. I propose that we race. The winner shall have the option of buying the loser's horse for five hundred dollars."

Mr. Lee told me about this later and how he had talked Meservy into raising the option to seven hundred fifty dollars. He said, "I know Damon Meservy's 'pony.' He's taken every match race and county fair he ever ran in. We haven't a chance. Which means we're gonna clean up."

At last I understood Mr. Lee's "strategy." "You want me to bet Meservy's horse."

"Right, every cent. I've got about four hundred and he'll be buyin' Socks after the race for seven-fifty. Bet that, too, on the cuff."

Race day was on a brisk fall afternoon. Damon Meservy's horse arrived at the appointed place in a padded horse van. When they unloaded him even I gasped. He was a big black thoroughbred with a white star and a pelt as shiny as ice in the sun.

As we prepared to race, two of Meservy's men stood beside Hummingbird and watched him like bailiffs. They never said a word but our little bandit ducked his head into his collar and spit out his chew. He knew we were whipped.

Terhune tried, however, and raced fair and square. Socks gave his best and, thanks to Terhune's superb ride, we only lost by a length.

The odds had not been good. Many in the crowd were wise to the horses and we only made four bits on each dollar bet. But that was nearly six hundred dollars' profit. Mr. Lee came out of that race with seventeen hundred dollars; three hundred of that went to Hummingbird and another hundred paid our expenses.

In the room that night Mr. Lee counted out over thirteen hundred dollars. I held my breath. "That is more money than I ever saw before. You're set for the winter. You can live right here in the Salt Lake House."

"No. This is our war chest, Tom. First thing in the mornin' we are gonna buy two more good horses. Horses as big as my bays and I hope half as good. Afterwards we're all getting on the train to Evanston, Wyoming. It's about a five-hour ride. And then, my young friend, if you're game, we are gonna see a rich Chinaman and collect about ten thousand dollars."

"Ten thousand!" I whooped.

"Maybe more. It'll be a nice winter's job for you." Bob Lee lay down on the bed and took a long drink from the whiskey bottle that stood on the bedside table.

CHAPTER 4

It was an education to watch Bob Lee buying horses. He peered into their eyes, ran his hands down their legs and across their backs. He examined their mouths. In three days we must have looked at over a hundred horses. Out of that bunch he rode a dozen himself, galloping them up the streets, turning hard, then slapping them in the face with his hat. He shouted at them and mounted from the wrong side.

"No way to treat good horses, Tom," he said. "But we got to be certain they're steady. The combination we need in our horses ain't common. Wish I could shoot over 'em but that might be too obvious."

"Shoot!" I was alarmed but Mr. Lee ignored me.

In the end he chose two fine horses, both close enough in color and size to Lee's bays to be their twins. Lee partially explained, "Everyone rides bay horses."

Despite my misgivings, the preparations for our trip were great fun. We bought additional tack and saw to the shoeing of the horses. Mr. Lee bought four boxes of .45 cartridges for his Colt revolver and four additional boxes of .44-40s for his Winchester. I got a tin of percussion caps, wadding, and a can of powder for my .36 cap-and-ball. Mr. Lee bought me enough lead bullets to ballast a schooner.

I am probably the only gunman who got his first lessons by shooting from the open door of a moving boxcar. No sooner had we bought the horses than Mr. Lee hired a railroad car to carry us and the animals to Evanston, Wyoming Territory.

"Private railroad car, eh, Tom?" Bob Lee grinned as we sweet-talked the apprehensive horses into stalls jerry-built at either end of the boxcar. We loaded at Salt Lake, then were shunted onto the main U.P. line at Ogden. The yardmen there added two extra locomotives to push and pull the train up the long, eighty-mile grade to Evanston.

Amidst all the banging and jerking of making up the freight train Mr.

Lee and I stood with the horses. We said, "Soo, boys, it's all right," and fed them oats on the palms of our hands. The important thing to remember in handling a horse is to stop trouble before it starts rather than try to calm it after hell has broken loose.

Once the train started up the canyon grade we left the horses and stood by the open car door eating box lunches. The sun shone brilliantly on the tan-colored cliffs. All the leaves had fallen from the oak brush and chokecherries, making the hills look bleak and unwelcoming. Only the gray-green sagebrush appeared to be living.

"Sun shines but don't warm much this time of year," Mr. Lee said. He tossed an apple core onto the right-of-way and watched it bounce along the grade. Suddenly there was a boom and the core disintegrated.

I jumped, so startled I nearly tumbled out the open car door. Bob Lee stood across the opening from me smiling and with his revolver hanging loose in his hand.

"You scared me!" I blurted. I was embarrassed to have been so startled.

"The element of surprise, Tom. Never forget it. A shot that scares the whey out of somebody is almost as good as the one that hits him—for a few seconds anyway."

I nodded, my surprise giving way to admiration for any man who could shoot like that. "Didn't you aim or anything?" I asked. "I thought you just let drive and centered that apple core in mid-bounce."

Lee thumbed the Colt's hammer back to the second click, then swung open the loading gate. He turned the cylinder and ejected the empty cartridge. "Yes, Tom. I aimed. But you do it all so fast it can look like pointin' and shootin'."

We had shared a can of peaches for our dessert and Bob Lee had me toss the empty tin can out of the car door. "Throw it as far and as high as you can," he said.

He drew and hit the can at the top of its rise. He hit it again as it fell and finally bounced it all over the railroad grade with his last three bullets. With five .45 slugs passing through it, the empty can ended up a scrap of metallic glitter.

"You never missed." I was in awe.

"I've had lots of practice. I used to be better."

"I don't see how."

"I used to bust big dough-babe marbles fast as I could toss 'em up. Come on, get out that pistola of yours and I'll show you something."

Compared with Mr. Lee's trim and polished Colt with its four-and-three-quarter-inch barrel and walnut grips, my old cap-and-ball was shabby. It had a long barrel and the last of its bluing had disappeared years before. Still, it had been carefully repaired and timed by the gunsmith in Salt Lake. He said the weapon should last me another twenty years.

Mr. Lee took the ungainly old revolver in his muscular hand. "I carried one of these for years. It ain't the stopper my forty-five is. And a cap-and-ball is slow to reload. But it'll kill 'em just as dead as the new cartridge guns. Shoot off your toe or kneecap, too, if you ain't careful."

Mr. Lee loaded the gun, first charging the chambers with powder, then ramming the patched balls into the cylinder chambers. He said, "Never cap a gun until it's all loaded." As he spoke he placed copper-colored primer caps on the nipples at the end of each chamber. In the next instant he had selected a whitish chunk of rock ballast along the grade, then driven it crazily across the ground. He hit it six shots out of six.

"Old gun shoots true," he said, handing the weapon to me for reloading.

Once I'd loaded it Mr. Lee had me shoot at the telegraph poles that appeared along the right-of-way. He showed me how to seat the revolver in my right hand. When I aimed, the barrel was supposed to be in line with my extended forearm.

"Hold it straight out. Don't bend your wrist. Look right down your arm to the front sight. Good, now hit that pole!"

I missed the first twenty-five poles before I was able to graze one, the ball leaving a splintered yellow furrow in the wood.

"Now you're gettin' the lead." Bob Lee was an enthusiastic coach.

But I missed five more poles in succession before hitting the second. At last, however, I learned to anticipate and then follow my shots into the poles. By that time my hand ached. Black powder residue was buried in my flesh, turning my hand a bluish gray.

"That's enough." Mr. Lee took my revolver and blew through the empty chambers before handing it back. "Man can overdo and start to flinchin'. Won't hit a thing and it's a hard habit to break. Let's wait and see if the jackrabbits don't start showin' up around sundown."

At times the freight climbed the grade so slowly that I thought a running man could have kept pace. And there was little in the long miles between Ogden and Evanston but sage and cold, blue sky.

This lonely picture made what happened next all the more startling. A pair of battered boots suddenly hung down in the open doorway. Then the boots swung out of sight and a gray, cadaverous face replaced them, looking at us upside down.

"Howdy, gents," said the face. "Target practice over?"

"For now." Mr. Lee wore a bemused expression. "Come in," he said, "get outta that wind."

The face grinned and disappeared. Then it reappeared as its owner scrabbled his way down the ladder beside the door and swung clumsily into the doorway. Mr. Lee caught him before he tumbled out onto the rocky grade.

The man was gaunt, over six feet, and with a ten-day beard. He had watery blue eyes with yellowish whites. He was breathing so hard from his exertions that he could not speak but sat humped and pale against the car wall.

Finally he said, "You're Sergeant Lee, ain't ya?"

"I was. Been Mr. Lee for some years. Don't I know you?"

"You should. I was in your company at Camp Medicine Buttes for six months. When I seen that shootin' I thought it might be you. But then there was a lot of bangin' and no hittin', so I wan't sure."

I blushed. It was I who had done the "banging." I said, "I'm learning to shoot a new gun."

The man nodded. "Sarge, you remember Toby Gates? Used to call 'im Tanglefoot."

Bob Lee smiled. "Sure, Gates. I never had a recruit so clumsy. Had you walking punishment tours every week, didn't I?"

"Yep." Gates grinned, showing yellowed teeth, separated by black voids. "I never made a sojer."

"Deserted, didn't you?" Mr. Lee said this without heat.

"Well, I did forget to come back. Woke up in a crib down in Corinne an' never bothered goin' back."

Mr. Lee had told me that desertion took far more troopers than the Indians ever had. The men couldn't stand the lonely posts, harsh discipline, and cold bivouacs.

Mr. Lee said, "You made a mistake. Sounds like you've got consumption now."

"Don't everybody?" Gates replied. "I ain't got the strength of a cottontail. I was hopin' to find a watchman's job on the railroad line. Maybe a lookout for ol' Chun Kwo's Fan-Tan Parlor. I'd be good at that an' still not have to do much. Hell, I can't do much."

Mr. Lee grew more interested. "You been in Chun Kwo's place lately?"

"Six months ago. He's tore out a wall an' made the place bigger 'n ever. You know, girls upstairs and tables an' all downstairs with waiters runnin' drinks up and down."

All of this left me puzzled. But it didn't take genius to guess that Chun Kwo was the man Mr. Lee was going to take ten thousand dollars from.

Bob Lee spoke. "Tell me about Chun Kwo."

"Not much to tell, Sarge. They threw me out the minute I reached for the free lunch. But, like always, a man could go around the back and get a bowl of soup. Chun might be a crook but he don't turn us old sojers away from a meal."

"The miners still hooraw on payday?" Mr. Lee asked.

"Sure, you know miners. But there's more Chink miners now. Most of 'em are savin' up stakes and don't gamble too much. The rest sort of loses it slow, making the pain last." Toby grimaced. "But you're right, payday is still the big one, must be thousands of dollars spent in there the first couple of days of each month."

"What's the setup?"

"Huh?" Gates didn't understand.

"Where are the lookouts? How many dealers, bouncers, bartenders; what's upstairs besides the girls?"

Toby grinned. "Like I said, they throwed me out pretty fast. I did see that one bouncer."

Then he pondered a moment, trying to use a portion of his ravaged brain that had not often been called upon recently. He said, "Lemme think. There's a Chinese lookout on the balcony. I think he's got a shotgun up there. You can't tell for sure because there's paper decorations on the railings that hide it. But I think there's a gun all right. There's at least two bartenders, probably more on paydays. There's seven, eight tables, maybe more. Some white dealers, some Chinks. But, gosh, Sarge, I never paid that much attention. I wasn't fixin' to hold up the place."

Mr. Lee looked hard at Toby. "Neither am I. I just like to know what I might be walkin' into. We've been doin' some horse racin' down in Salt Lake. Season's over but we might do some inside gamblin' this winter."

Toby Gates nodded. He wanted to believe everything Mr. Lee said. He rambled on about the Fan-Tan Parlor. Much of it was incoherent but Bob Lee listened intently to it all.

Gates said, "I don't know nothin' about the girls upstairs." A sickly smile played over his cracked lips. "Chun's got an old man and woman livin' with him. Maybe his folks. I seen 'em in the kitchen when I asked for somethin' to eat."

"What do they do?" asked Bob Lee.

"They do pretty damn well; fat old buggers, the both of 'em. The old lady is dressed real nice. So is the old man—silk."

Bob Lee smiled and slapped Toby on the shoulder. He gave the wrecked old soldier our last sandwich and a cup of whiskey from the bottle in his war bag. When Gates finished eating and drinking he rolled over on his side and fell asleep.

While Gates snored Mr. Lee drew me into the far end of the car. He said, "We'll be in Evanston soon. It'll be dark. I'll take the horses and move them to a place I know. Here's a hundred dollars. I want you to spend it this way: Put ol' Toby in the Railroad Hotel. Keep him fed, slightly drunk, and out of trouble for the next three nights. You go to Chun Kwo's every night. Don't lose no more than fifteen a night. Quit if you lose that much and go back the next night. But play slow an' take it all in. I want to know how that show operates, top to bottom."

Had he tried, Bob Lee could not have picked a less experienced scout. I had a passing knowledge of poker. But I knew nothing of the game's odds, how to read the other players' hands or make smart bets. At blackjack I hit thirteen and stood on fourteen. And that was what I knew about gambling.

When I reached the Fan-Tan Parlor I headed for a penny-ante poker game. Playing there, although I lost steadily, gave me the time to size up the place before Bob Lee's money ran out.

There was one thing about Chun Kwo's I had not expected to learn. *It was a nice place.* I had grown up on sermons about the dangers of gambling hells, deadfalls, and dance houses. Such degraded places surely existed but I didn't think Chun Kwo's was one of them. The Fan-Tan Parlor's dealers were probably crooked but they were also polite. If some miner or U.P. hogger got drunk and loud, two muscular bouncers swept up to him and put him out gently and quietly.

There was an armed lookout on the balcony. He watched the games to make sure no patron cheated or tried to break the bank with a six-shooter. I was told he used a rifle. A shotgun blast from that distance would spread out too much.

Sometimes Chun Kwo's girls came down and sat in on the games. I knew what they were but they seemed very nice. The woman who ran this line of women looked like Miss Parr, an old maid who played our church organ.

Chun Kwo warmly welcomed his customers at the front door. He called many of them by name and was always signaling for free drinks for his customers. I guessed him at about forty-five, medium tall, with slicked-back hair the color of jet. He wore dark suits and a red and yellow checked vest. On his fingers were several flashy-looking rings. I imagined him using them to read or mark cards. For all his good humor, Chun Kwo had eyes as warm as a rattlesnake's.

Carrying guns was prohibited on the streets of Evanston. But if some drover wandered into Chun's wearing a Colt he was immediately required to check it. Somehow Chun could tell if a fellow was carrying a hideout or sleeve gun. I saw a red-faced drummer sheepishly hand over a derringer that Chun had somehow spotted.

If Bob Lee was going to hold up this place he would first have to figure out how to get a gun past the front door. I told him that the night he came to my room.

It was after midnight. I'd had some unusually good luck and actually won five dollars. I'd continued playing until the last sodden john stumbled downstairs and the last busted cowhand stamped out the front door.

Lee was sitting in my room when I entered. "Evenin', Tom. Been enjoyin' yourself?"

"Not much. I lost thirty the first two nights but won five of it back tonight." I handed him the silver cartwheels.

Lee handed them back. "You keep 'em. They were just makin' sure you'd be back tomorrow night."

I reached inside my shirt and removed the notes I had taken each night after leaving Chun Kwo's.

Mr. Lee read them carefully. "He's a smart one. Man walks in and Chun slaps him on the back and frisks at the same time. Lookout in the balcony with a rifle has the drop all the time—on everybody. You know there's at least one shotgun under the bar. And Chun's behind you, maybe with a wire but probably a knife and a sleeve gun, too."

I said, "The Chinese waiters are slipping around through the crowd as smooth as weasels. They're always scattered. No way to get the drop on them."

Mr. Lee had many questions about the Fan-Tan Parlor. I had drawn a floor plan from memory after returning to my room the first night.

He pointed to the kitchen door. "What's back there?"

I shook my head. "I don't know exactly. There's a kitchen. They serve some meals out of there. The free lunch comes from there, too. But I think there's too much room back there for just a kitchen. When the door swings open I see a Chinese guy in a white apron."

"Is he the old man Toby talked about?" Mr. Lee asked.

I replied, "No, this fellow's young, with a pigtail hanging down his back."

Mr. Lee grunted and returned to my floor plan. I had drawn it indicating the kitchen and back bar area where beer barrels and cases of liquor were stored. The two rooms were side by side but I doubted that they ran the whole length of that part of the building.

"Where does Chun stay?"

"He's on the floor all night. Sometimes he spells the dealers. Tonight he went into the kitchen and stayed about twenty minutes."

"Do you know what he was doing?"

"No. I thought he might be eating his supper."

"Damn it, Tom. This is important. We've got to figure out what's back there. I think it's our key to the door."

Bob Lee was running far ahead of me. The planning fascinated me and became more of a game than a crime. I found Bob Lee could get information from me I didn't realize I had. For instance, Chun didn't live downstairs behind the bar. He had an apartment upstairs with a Chinese girl.

All night long he and his bouncers circulated from table to table, checking the take. He never let much cash accumulate at a table. Instead he collected all surplus cash and took it into the mysterious rooms behind the bar.

"All right!" Bob Lee was smiling. "He must have a safe or strongbox back there. I'll bet those old people are his folks. He'd trust them to look out for his dough."

I pulled off my boots and lay down on the bed. "I don't see how you're going to get into that strongbox with all those people around all the time."

Bob Lee rose and slapped me affectionately on the knee. "Don't worry, kid. Old Chun's gulled soldiers and fleeced miners around here for twenty years. But now he's gonna step in a badger hole—yes, sir, a big one!"

CHAPTER 5

Toby Gates was seated against one wall in the Railroad Hotel bar. It was 8 A.M. and his eyes were filmed and smoke-reddened.

I sat down beside him, preparing to lead him through the instructions Mr. Lee had given me the previous night. "Morning, Toby."

"Oh! Hello there."

"I'm Tom Lavering, remember?"

"Sure. Sarge Lee's pal. Right?"

"That's right. The sarge sent me. He needs your help." I gave Toby the simple duties he would have to perform.

"Where do I get the horse?" he asked.

"I'll rent one for you at the livery stable."

"An' that's all I got to do? Well, I'd do that for nothin' just to see the look on old Chun's puss."

"You won't forget?"

"Count on me, ah, ah, kid."

If he couldn't remember my name I wondered how we could expect him to do as he was told. But Mr. Lee had said Toby would come through if I kept after him and repeated what he had to do right up to the time he did it.

It was on for tonight. Chun Kwo's Fan-Tan Parlor was going to be robbed. Mr. Lee had promised that if I did my part his plan could not fail.

He had said, "At eleven o'clock get up from your card game and go out through the kitchen to the privy. When you get in there, lock the door. There's a hook. Now stand on the seat and reach up under the eaves on the right-hand side. Feel around. Your six-shooter will be there."

"Mr. Lee, I don't mind being in this with you. I want to help you fix Chun's wagon. But I don't want to shoot anybody."

"If you and Toby do your jobs nobody's gonna get hurt. Now listen. Take your gun and stick it under your belt. Pull your coat over it and go back in through the kitchen. When you get there, stop and ask the cook a question or order dinner—do whatever it takes to stay in there a few minutes."

"Yes, sir. I understand."

I pulled the cap-and-ball from my war bag, carefully loaded it, and handed it to Bob Lee. He stuck it under his coat.

"Now, you know what to do next?"

"Yes, sir. As soon as I hear the commotion I'm to pull my gun and cover everyone in the kitchen."

"Right. Herd 'em into a bunch and be damn sure none of 'em slips out on you. Specially not that old couple."

On the day of the holdup time dragged terribly. I took a walk up the railroad tracks and out of town. When I came back I looked at the clock in front of the jewelry store and found I'd only been gone an hour.

Toby was now sitting in the hotel lobby. By design, his allowance had run out the night before and he was in need of a beer. I led him into the bar and bought him one. Then I had him go over his part of the action again.

"Oh, hell . . . ah, ah."

"It's Tom," I said.

"Yeah. Tom. I told you my part fifty times already. When I was in the cavalry I used to do this for nothin'."

"Well, tonight you'll be doin' it for all the troopers Chun Kwo ever cheated. We're going to play him a trick he'll never forget. It'll drive him wild."

Toby grinned. "You bet . . . ah, ah . . ."

"Tom."

"Yeah."

That evening I sat in my room and tried to read the Bible. At seven o'clock I gave up and left for the Fan-Tan Parlor. It had been open since midmorning but the day's more serious customers were only now beginning to arrive.

"Greeting, Tom." Chun Kwo smiled and bowed.

"Evening, guess I'll try that poker game again. It owes me."

Chun motioned for me to follow him. It was silly that he thought it necessary to lead me to the table I'd been playing at every night. It was another reason for me not to like the slick-haired gambler.

At the table he said, "Gen'lemen, Tom comes back to even up the pots. I wish you all good luck." Chun bowed and backed away from the table.

I sat down and watched the desultory play move around the table. The dealer was playing with two other men and I suspected that one of them was a shill.

When the hand was called and the pot raked in, the dealer nodded at me. "Ante up, sir."

I tossed a nickel into the meager pot and was dealt a hand of draw. It was seven-twenty.

By eight forty-five all the seats were filled; seven men were at the table. At five past nine I said, "Deal me out of this one. Nature calls." I looked at the dealer. "Can I get to the privy through your kitchen?"

"Sure, tell the cook you're goin' for a music lesson."

The players chuckled briefly but never took their eyes from the cards. In the kitchen the Chinese cook looked at me sharply until I signed and stated I was heading for the privy.

I sauntered through the kitchen, noticing a door that led off the kitchen opposite from the doorway into the back-bar storeroom. That had to be the room where Chun took his collections.

The kitchen was L-shaped, the short leg being a pantry containing a potato bin and barrels of flour, sugar, and lard. Seated in there was an old Chinese woman peeling potatoes. She glared at me as I passed.

Outside, a wintry freeze had replaced the earlier chill of fall nights. I waited in the privy a few minutes, then went back across the barren lot and re-entered the kitchen. This had not been in Bob Lee's plan but I wanted to see the place before the action began.

I did not see any more than I have already described. The old lady was still peeling potatoes when I returned. The door leading off the kitchen remained closed.

When I sat down at the card table again it was nine-twenty. The play was routine and only the bantering back and forth kept the game from being a bore. I stayed about even, winning enough good pots to make up for the many hands when I only fed the kitty. I ordered a steak from a passing waiter. When it was served I ate it from a little side table the waiter placed beside my chair.

An old railroader said, "Son, you're gettin' hooked on the game when you can't even sit out to eat."

I grinned but said nothing. Privately I agreed with the man. I was becoming so nervous I could barely swallow the food. At ten-thirty I ordered a cup of coffee.

At ten-forty I finished the coffee and said, "Let's deal a winner here; I'm awake again." But my two pairs were beaten by a small straight. I should have known better.

Then I won a pot of five dollars and the dealer said, "Along toward mornin' the old hog found an acorn." It was ten fifty-five.

"Yes," I said, "and now he's gotta go again. Deal me out till I come back." The dealer nodded, never dreaming that I was not coming back.

In the kitchen the cook was sleeping on some sacks of flour. The old woman was seated at a small table drinking tea. She looked at me with hard little eyes set in a face that looked like a relief map of China. I said, "Evening!" but the woman did not reply.

In the privy I latched the door shut and stepped up on the seat. My gun was wrapped in a piece of butcher paper and hidden under the eaves just as Mr. Lee promised. I unwrapped the gun and struck a sulphur match. The percussion caps were all in place and the patched balls set square in the cylinder mouths. I took a deep breath. I was about to become an outlaw.

I slipped the gun under my belt and buttoned my coat over it. The scene in the kitchen was unchanged. The cook was still asleep and the old woman sat over her tea. Beyond, in the gambling hall, there was the mutter of voices, glasses clinking, and hurdy-gurdy music. I helped myself to a mug from the rack and filled it with coffee.

My heart was beating too wildly to swallow much of it. I stood there trying to sip from my cup and hoped that old woman with the shoe-button eyes wouldn't see my hand was shaking.

Although I knew what was about to happen I would have liked to see it. It went about like this: First came a loud bang and then a surprised outcry from the crowd. Then followed some ragged cheers, more bangs, and the loud footfalls of men scuttling for cover.

Toby Gates, wearing only a plug hat, his long red underwear, and seam-burst boots, had ridden a bronc into the center of the room. Someone fired a shot. I learned later that the pony's hind leg had broken through the flooring and then there was hell to pay: Chinese waiters fleeing, bouncers trying to rush the plunging horse, and bartenders hurriedly trying to protect their glassware and mirrors.

In the midst of the pandemonium I drew my revolver and herded the surprised cook and the old woman through the mysterious door. Once through I found nothing mysterious at all. We were in a large and lavishly furnished room. At one end there was an arrangement of red-plush parlor furniture. Beyond that, at the far end, was a big walnut bed with an astonished-looking old Chinese man sitting up in it. His surprise was made all the greater by my aiming my revolver at him.

"Come on, mister, out of the bed." I motioned for the old man to get up. Momentarily he did not move but jabbered something to the old woman, who rattled off an excited reply. Then I saw the old fellow's hand slipping under his pillow.

"No, sir!" I sprang to the bedside and with one hand dragged the old man out onto the floor. I threw aside the pillow. There on the sheet lay a nickel-plated .32-caliber, top-break revolver. That old man had been going to shoot me!

"Damn you!" I gave him a shake, then jerked him across the room to stand by my other two captives. For a long moment we all just stood there staring at each other. My orders only went this far; I was to hold everyone from the kitchen.

In the gambling room there was still a tumult of excited voices mixed with raucous laughter and the sounds of splintering wood. At that moment Chun Kwo, closely followed by Bob Lee, stumbled into the room.

"Good job! Now put your pistol to the old man's head." To Chun he said, "Get up the cash or see Dad's brains on the wall!" For emphasis he prodded Chun with a vicious-looking knife.

The ashen-faced gambler didn't move. He appeared dazed. Bob Lee commanded, "Quit stallin'!" He stepped beside the old man and held his knife to the man's throat. Chun still did not move and Lee ticked the old man's throat. A small rivulet of blood ran down his neck.

"If you want to see the rest, just keep standin' there." Bob Lee's hard features were taut and if murder was ever in a man's eyes I saw it in his.

Chun stared about him frantically, then headed for the walnut bed. Kneeling beside it, he slid out a heavy chest bound with strap iron and opened it with a key.

"Here." He handed out bills and sacks of coins while Bob Lee carefully packed them into a canvas bag he'd had hidden under his coat.

"That's more like it. Don't forget any."

The next thing happened so fast that I barely saw it. But there was the old lady with a knife flashing in her hand. In the next instant I saw blood on Bob Lee's left sleeve. The room erupted. I hit Chun over the head with my gun. He dropped. The cook darted for the door and I tackled him, clubbing him with my revolver even as we fell.

As I stood up Bob Lee was looking down at the old woman. She was lying on the floor clutching her stomach. The old man knelt beside her, his mouth gaping with a silent scream. I saw bright red blood on Lee's knife.

He shoved me. "Move, kid! Through the kitchen!"

Outside the cold air struck my face like a dash of ice water. I was too excited to think. Bob Lee kept shoving me and I stumbled blindly through the darkness in the direction I was being pushed. I put my hand out and felt a horse's shoulder.

Bob Lee ordered, "Go!"

Somehow the reins were in my hand and my foot hit the stirrup. I could see a little better. Bob Lee swung aboard his horse and broke away running. I booted my horse and he leaped away. We thundered down an alley, jumped a ditch, crossed the main street, then skidded down the grade overlooking the river. Now we were on the road east.

My God! What a wild ride! We rode five miles, going all out, on two of the best horses in the territory. When Bob Lee suddenly pulled up behind a blind curve in the road I nearly shot over my horse's head.

"Whoa!" The horses were excited and still ready to run. It was then I realized that I still had the cap-and-ball in my hand. I made sure the hammer was safely down, then tucked the weapon into my saddlebag.

Bob Lee was tying the canvas money sack to the pommel of his saddle. I asked, "How's your arm?"

"Not too bad. I should have known that old woman would have tried anything to help her men. She had the knife under her blouse. The minute I took my eye off'n her she cut me."

"Is she dead, do you think?"

"No. I just cut through the fat on her belly. But she'll think twice before she cuts a white man again."

I said nothing. The reality that we could have been murderers, not just outlaws, pounded in my brain. I should have known this winter's job would have its risks.

"C'mon, Tom. Half the Chinamen in Wyoming will be after us by daylight." Bob Lee swung his horse off the road and into a long swale that had a spring at its top.

We rode at the trot, the dried grass crackling under the horses' hooves. In the darkness my confusion was complete. All I could see were some shadowy junipers on the surrounding foothills. But Mr. Lee led the way confidently, stopping to water the horses at the spring and then riding on into the junipers.

The trees' scaly branches scratched and tore at my face and hands. I finally put my face against the horse's neck and held up my right arm to ward off the oncoming branches. How Bob Lee ever set such a pace through that tangle without having his eyes scratched out, I'll never know.

Although it seemed we rode through those cursed trees forever, it was probably just a couple of miles. We stopped and Bob Lee whispered, "O.K., Tom?"

"I hope."

"There's an old blind trail through here. Rustlers made it. I trimmed it some while you played cards."

Dimly outlined ahead I saw a narrow opening through the trees. It was an old trick. If an outlaw planned a job and wanted to throw off his pursuers he rode into the brush beforehand and cut out a trail. But he began his trail in the middle of the thicket. There was almost no chance of a posse picking up our trail until daylight. I hasten to add, however, that Bob Lee's blind trail was no highway. The ground was rough and there were countless limbs left to reach out and slash at us.

Nevertheless, we loped our horses along this trail. If we gained just an hour on any pursuers, Mr. Lee said, his trail clearing was worth the effort. He also said that if we gained a half day our race with any pursuers was as good as won.

Bob Lee was unbelievable. To this day I have never understood how he led us away from Evanston that night. It seemed he knew every inch of the route and we moved faster in the dark than many men would have in daylight.

The blind trail was nearly five miles long, rising up through juniper-clad foothills, then breaking out onto rolling land covered with sage-brush. In the early-morning grayness traces of snow shone weakly under the sage. They were the last vestiges of fall snow that would soon be replaced by deep, lasting winter snow.

Our route lay southeast through broken country as wild as the Indians who once roamed it. We seldom crossed a trail and never saw a road in all those empty miles.

The eastern sky was a dull pink as we single-filed up a ridge. We kept below the crest to avoid skylining ourselves. At one point the ridge curved to form a small basin. Chokecherries, fifteen feet high, were growing there. Mr. Lee rode into the center of the brush and dismounted. It was only then that I saw the corral and our other two horses standing inside it.

"Injuns used to camp here. We're changing horses." Bob Lee slid from his horse, his left arm held stiffly at his side.

"Let's tend to your arm before we go on," I said.

The sleeve of Bob Lee's canvas coat was stiff with blood. I helped him remove the coat and, after that, his blue wool shirt. He unbuttoned his underwear and let it hang from his waist. I had to marvel at the man. He was nearing fifty but he had the chest and shoulders of a thirty-year-old.

Bob Lee looked down his left arm at the angry gash that ran from the biceps to below his elbow. "I seen worse," he said. "Good thing I had all those clothes on."

He was right, the cut was painful but not serious. Still, if he bent his arm the wound would break open. And, serious or not, his arm hurt.

I said, "I'd better do the saddling. The less you bend that arm, the better."

"You're right. Sure am sorry about this, Tom. I'd best take care. There's no dispensary where we're headin'."

"Where is that?"

"Brown's Hole, our first stop anyway. It's down on the Green River. Been a hideout for years."

I had never heard of Brown's Hole. And now, on the edge of that desolate ridge, hiding in the brush from God only knew what, I was not enthusiastic. I shrugged and asked, "What do we do here?"

"There's a sack of oats back in those ledges above the corral. You unsaddle the horses and grain 'em and I'll get ready to ride."

The horses in the corral whinnied loudly at my approach. They'd had ample water from the spring that was inside the corral. There had been enough grass for them, too. But they were lonesome and eager for some grain.

The horses we had ridden rolled happily after I'd pulled their saddles and turned them loose in the corral. We had talked of riding them forty miles in a day but these marvelous animals had carried us sixty miles. I rubbed their sweat-caked backs with the empty grain sack. My heart was filled with a mixture of gratitude and sadness for these fine animals. Their fate was no more certain than my own.

Bob Lee was counting the money when I returned. "Not as much as I hoped. But not bad for a few minutes' work. It sure beats any winter's job I ever had."

"How much?"

"Five thousand four hundred and eighty-six dollars plus change." Lee grinned. "That's two thousand seven hundred and forty-three dollars for you, kid. Want to count it yourself?"

"No, sir, your word's good." I looked at the pile of bills. "I never saw that much money before—let alone owned some of it."

"Sure puts tendin' sheep camps in the shade, don't it?" Bob Lee smiled at me. "Here, the money's divided. Take your share."

"What will I do with it?"

"You might strap it down in your saddlebags. But I'm puttin' mine in my money belt. If it's around my waist it's not goin' far without me."

I didn't own a money belt, just a salt sack. But I fastened a thong to it, tied the sack tightly shut, then hung it down my back, inside my shirt.

Mr. Lee looked up at the sun. "We daren't stay here any longer."

"I thought you might rest up here, then go on after dark."

Lee frowned. "Our tracks is too fresh. The next men in here are gonna be talkin' Chinese."

I began saddling the fresh horses while Mr. Lee climbed to the top of the ridge for a look around.

The horses were ready when he returned. "See anything?" I asked.

"I saw a wee puff of somethin' way off yonder." Mr. Lee pointed toward the west and Evanston.

"What was it?"

"I think it was dust. It could have been antelope but, bein' a prudent man, I'm getting out of here like it was a division of cavalry."

We didn't gallop the horses but pushed them steadily, breaking into a lope whenever the terrain permitted it. Each of us led one of the horses we'd ridden in on. That always slows you down.

At one place the ground was bare and flinty hard. We rode stirrup to stirrup, the horses loping easily. I asked, "What's in Brown's Hole?"

"Can't say for sure. It's been years since I was there. Used to be a lot of cattle with the wagon-wheel brand. Nobody'd claim 'em when strangers were around."

"A wagon wheel?"

"Yeah. There's not many brands can't be covered up with a nice big wagon wheel. Picture it."

I did and saw in my mind's eye that Bob Lee was right, as usual. So Brown's Hole was a rustlers' den. When I went into the holdup business I never anticipated the company I would have to keep.

We rode steadily all the rest of the day. Mr. Lee checked our back trail frequently but saw no one. At one point I said, "I think we've gotten clean away."

"Don't be dumb. That was Chun's ma that I cut. He'll never forget that."

I began having visions of our being caught by a posse, of being shot down in the dirt, or dragged back to Evanston in handcuffs. All I could do now was ride and hope that the old cavalryman in front of me knew what he was doing.

Lee never appeared to tire. And he never mentioned that we hadn't eaten for nearly sixteen hours. I was hungry and cursed myself for not having brought along so much as a chunk of jerky to gnaw on. Then I saw a juniper branch rub cruelly along Bob Lee's wounded arm and he never flinched. I told myself that if he could stand that I could stand a little gnawing in the belly.

I concentrated on keeping up with Mr. Lee. The land we were traveling through was rolling and covered with sagebrush. There were low buttes in the middle distance and deep washes scattered in between. Far to the south loomed the Uinta Mountains. Their tops were snow-capped and somewhere in the intervening haze lay Brown's Hole.

In late afternoon, with weak sunlight shining on the butte tops, Mr. Lee halted. "Yonder is Brown's Hole."

All that I saw through my swollen eyes was an indistinct void near the distant mountains. I did not care. All I wanted was to get somewhere where it was warm and I could lie down and sleep for a week.

CHAPTER 6

Throughout our daring flight from Evanston my admiration for Robert Lee often changed to hatred. Except to change horses, he never stopped until far into the next night. I found myself falling asleep in the saddle. Even the cramped ache in my knees and feet was at least dulled by fatigue.

It was nearly midnight before we stopped. A cold wind was blowing and an occasional snowflake hit my face. We hid in a draw where a spring ran down from the rocks and watered a patch of grass maybe a half acre in size. I unsaddled and staked all of the horses in the grass. They mowed it like the hungry devils they were.

We were not as well off. Mr. Lee wouldn't allow a fire, although that didn't matter too much since we had nothing to cook and nothing to cook with if we'd had food.

"Mr. Lee, I could eat the rear out of a skunk."

"I was hopin' we'd see a porcupine. Make a nice roast of that. Guess we'll just have to notch in our belts."

I had a slicker tied behind my saddle and wrapped myself in it before lying down on the frozen ground. I hunched up on my saddle trying to keep the chill out of my shoulders and covered my legs and feet with a saddle blanket.

Mr. Lee bedded down against some boulders where the grass was thick. In the gloom I could see his outline humped against the cold. I supposed he was sitting up with his last chew of tobacco for the night. I momentarily wished I chewed tobacco, just to have something in my mouth.

"Hard day?" Mr. Lee asked softly.

"We hardly stopped in twenty-four hours."

"When I campaigned we was on Injun trails for thirty-six hours many a time. Them that couldn't keep up got left. But they kept up. Men knew a squaw would soon be carving her initials in their bellies if they straggled."

"But we haven't seen a thing since you thought you saw dust way back there on the ridge. Are you sure we're bein' followed?"

"I'm sure. Maybe the law and most folks don't care a damn that we held up the Fan-Tan Parlor. But Chun Kwo cares and he'll care even more that I cut his ma. He knows there's only a few places we can hide out. An' he's got more friends in any one of them places than you and I got in the whole world."

I said nothing but wished Bob Lee had told me all this *before* I went out to that privy and found my gun. Even sleeping in haystacks was heaps better than this.

Mr. Lee continued, "Chun's gonna have men look in Jackson's Hole, Star Valley, Pierre's Hole, and, maybe, as far south as the Henry Mountains in Utah."

All of this was a new and unpleasant part of our winter's work. I said, "You told me that the law wouldn't care what we did to a Chinaman."

"That's true. Every so often someone gets riled and rubs out some Chinese that're taking their jobs. Nothin' much is done." Bob Lee spat. Then he said, "I'm bettin' that Chun will put a price on us. The sort of fellers that tries to collect it will make the crookedest sheriffs look like saints by comparison."

In the darkness I found my saddlebag and took out the cap-and-ball. Then I rolled over on my side, stuck the gun under my left arm, and fell asleep.

"Tom!" I woke with a start. It was just breaking day and there was an inch of snow on me and everything else. Mr. Lee was up and looking after the horses. He was walking stiffly himself.

"Mornin'," I said. "Guess no Chinese found us in the night."

"Nope an' this snow will be a real help coverin' our tracks. They'll have to follow road apples now."

I got up and stretched. The only part of my body that wasn't sore was my mouth. And it tasted like Lee's army had camped inside it for a week.

"Sure am hungry," I said.

Mr. Lee came to stand beside me. He said, "When I campaigned with General Crook we ate our horses—just before the poor critters died of starvation. But mind what the Little Corporal said . . ."

I guessed that the "Little Corporal" was some fellow the old sergeant had known in the Army. "What did he say?"

"He said, 'An army travels on its stomach.'" With that Mr. Lee handed me a big can of peaches, saying, "Somebody else said, 'A general's only as good as his reserves.'"

We stood in the snow, cold and wet-footed, and ate peaches, passing the can and spearing the halved fruit with our jackknives. That still sticks in my mind as one of the finest meals I ever ate. I said so.

Bob Lee replied, "Yes, but you wouldn't've thought a thing about 'em yesterday when you just thought you was hungry. Man's got to learn to pace himself. Know your limits but don't give yourself nothin', either."

The sweet peaches did the trick for me. I was ready to ride again and said so.

"Good. I want you to ride down to the river and get us an outfit."

Lee directed me south by southeast to where I would find the head of a red rock canyon that led down into Brown's Hole. He warned, "Be careful all the way. Some of the Lord's worst mistakes live down there."

With that cheery send-off I began the long ride into Brown's Hole. The trail was well used. I had hung my revolver on a cord that went around my neck, somewhat in the manner Canadian Mounties carried their weapons. My gun was under my coat, however. I wasn't a fast draw, but with the gun hanging handy I could whip it out in a hurry.

Partway down the canyon I smelled wood smoke. I kept my eyes busy on the surrounding cliffs and patches of timber, looking for the source of that smoke. And, rounding a sharp bend, I found it. A low-roofed cabin lay couched in a narrow terrace on the side of the canyon. Smoke trailed lazily from a rock-and-mud chimney. With its mantle of snow, the scene before me was picturesque.

But spoiling that peaceful scene was a bearded man crouching behind a boulder and aiming a rifle at me. Mr. Lee had warned that there were men in Brown's Hole who would readily kill a man for his horse.

"Mean no harm," I said, hoping my voice didn't crack too much. "I'm just passin' through. Was told there's a trading post down on the Green River. We run out of bacon; we're camped back up the country a few miles."

The bearded rifleman never replied. He just stayed behind his boulder with a bead on me. I rode forward, keeping my hands in sight and looking straight ahead. I was as pious-looking as an altar boy going down the aisle with a frog in his pocket.

"Probably see you later, when I've got our supplies." The words were said over my shoulder and I never knew whether or not they were heard. There was no answer. And at the first bend in the trail I kicked my startled horse around it and out of sight.

With that scare behind me I figured the day ahead should be an easy pull. Which shows how little I knew about the folks down in Brown's Hole.

It was another hour before I emerged from the canyon. The valley, for that's what Brown's Hole really is, is surrounded by mountains. The Green River runs through the middle of it. Beside the roily-looking stream there were meadows but the grass had been well used. On the benches there was sage that gave way to patches of juniper higher up. In the summer, with sunshine on the river, this must be a pretty place. But in November, with the land fed off and bleak and the river the color of pork gravy, it wasn't pretty at all. Mr. Lee had said that in the valley's lower end the river entered a deep canyon filled with rocks and rapids.

I followed the main trail and finally saw a trading post near the river. The place was low-roofed with walls of twisted cottonwood logs. A mangy-looking dog lay beside the front door and growled as I got down and tied my horse.

There were two other horses at the hitching rail, long-haired, shaggy-hocked beasts that blew at me through their noses and showed the whites of their eyes as I passed.

Inside, the place was so gloomy that it was several seconds before I could see where I was. There was a gray-bearded man in leather pants and a beaded vest standing in front of the smoky fireplace. He was wearing a filthy shirt. Nearby and seated on homemade chairs on either side of the fireplace were two men. One was a Negro with a sombrero pushed back on his head. His companion was a wolfish-looking white man of about forty with bloodshot eyes.

"Hello," I said, nodding to the men.

"Well, young feller, don't think I've seed you before." The bearded man half smiled through his stained whiskers.

I replied, "Just passing through. We're camped above here. Our packhorse left us. Came to buy an outfit."

"Must be real dudes to lose your outfit in this country at this time of year." The wolfish-looking man stared at me expectantly. He obviously wanted an argument.

But I wouldn't accommodate him, saying, "Sure was. Put a bad crimp in our plans. We were heading over to Lily Park. Have friends there and we planned to spend the winter huntin' wolves and lions for the ranchers."

"From the looks of you, you couldn't handle nothin' bigger 'n a wood rat." The wolf-face sneered and the black man put his hand to his lips and made a slobbery, kissing sound.

The storekeeper said, "Now, boys, let's not job this stranger too hard. What can I get you, son?"

I gave him the short list: blankets, cooking utensils, some bacon, coffee, flour, and a sack of beans.

The storekeeper set about filling the order. The two blankets he set out looked as if they'd been stolen off dead men and I said so.

"Take 'em or leave 'em, they're all I got."

I took them. And I took measly-looking bacon, weevil-filled flour, and beans which looked wormy. I was almost relieved when he said he was out of coffee. I took tea instead.

"That'll be forty dollars."

"Forty dollars!" I was flabbergasted. Forty dollars should have loaded two packhorses with food. These purchases could be tied to my saddle with room left for me. I reached into my pocket, fingering the money I had there. "How about thirty-five dollars?"

"Have to take back the beans."

"Oh, hell, here." I handed him forty dollars and stood by as he dumped my grub into a canvas sack and rolled the blankets so I could fasten them on my saddle.

As I turned to leave, my purchases tucked under my arms, I noticed that only the Negro was still seated by the fire. He grinned at me, pursing his lips. "Bye-bye, darlin'."

Outside I stood squinting in the harsh light. And then I swore. My horse was gone!

I stormed back into the building and tossed my purchases on the hewn-plank counter. "That son of a bitch stole my horse."

The storekeeper looked indignant. "What son of a bitch was it you meant?"

"You know, the one that jobbed me. He was sitting right beside the fireplace." I pointed to the now-empty seat.

The Negro grinned at me. "I din't see no horse. An' we don't call no man names here 'less we can back it up."

Of the two men left in the store the black was clearly the more dangerous. If I went up against him he would kill me: probably not even getting off his chair to do it.

"Then I want my money back. Here, you can have the blanket." I tossed one of the blankets to the black and in the same instant swung around the counter and shoved my cap-and-ball into the storekeeper's ear.

For a moment there wasn't a sound except the click of the revolver as I drew it to full cock. I had hold of the old man's collar and twisted it tight.

"You're chokin' me!"

"Relax. I'll blow out your brains long before you choke."

The Negro sat with his hands on his knees. I saw his dark eyes flitting nervously. He wouldn't sit still for long.

"Isom, damn it. This ain't a joke. You get Denby back here with this feller's horse. He'll drill me."

Slowly and with mocking deliberation the Negro rose from his seat. "Why, Uncle Dick, if that boy's pistol goes off, I'll be out from under your bill."

"Isom, you better listen. He's chokin' me. Have Denby return that horse!"

Isom, I learned later, was Isom Dart, a known murderer. Now he sauntered toward the door, grinning. His big hat was still resting on the back of his head. It was then that I took one of the biggest chances of my life. I aimed and, thanks to great luck, put a ball through the brim of Dart's hat, about two inches above his skull.

He caterwauled but I outshouted him. "Don't turn around. Just drop your gun belt and go get my horse."

After I saw Dart trot away on his horse I released my grip on Uncle Dick's collar. He said, "You're dead. I hope you know that, sonny."

"If I am, you are, too."

"Isom Dart is way too much for you, you're just a punk. He's dumped better men than you in the river and watched 'em float away."

While we waited I kept my revolver trained on Uncle Dick's potbelly. I didn't trust him as far as I'd trust a coyote with my dog's dinner. As I waited I could hardly believe what had just happened: Two men had stolen my horse and then been angry when I called them on it.

It seemed like hours but it was probably just a few minutes before Dart and Denby returned, leading my horse. "Hi-ho, hardcase," called Denby. "We brung your pony. Now come on out and take him."

I had expected something like this. Those two weren't going to let a kid face them down. But I'd had an idea while Uncle Dick and I waited for them to return. They didn't know I was no shooter. In fact, that hole through the brim of Dart's hat said otherwise. I pushed Uncle Dick ahead of me. "Now, if they don't shoot you, I will. Go out there and get my horse. Bring him right up to the door."

Uncle Dick may have had some good qualities but I was counting on his cowardice to save me. And it did. He went out and led my horse to the door. I was standing inside. He asked, "Now what?"

"You and the horse are going to stay between me and your friends. Load my horse, then stay between us until I'm two hundred yards off."

Dick tied on my blankets and I handed him the sack of food. He tied that on and then we began walking. Dick blubbered, "They're gonna get you, they're gonna get even."

But the two men didn't get me that day. They sat in their saddles and watched us walk away.

When we had gone two hundred yards I said, "That's it, storekeeper. Now I'll check my cinch to be sure it isn't cut half in two and then I'll let you go."

Everything was in order. Uncle Dick said, "Go on, what're you waitin' on?"

I just grinned at him and the two bandits in front of his store. Then, moving as fast as I knew how, I sprang into the saddle and kicked that good bay into a gallop. Within three jumps a shot rang out and I heard a bullet whiz by. I swung around and fired a wild shot in the outlaws' direction. Uncle Dick yelled, "Murder," and dropped in the dirt, hugging his legs to his belly.

They shot once more but I was leaving them far behind and the slug wasn't even close. Still, I was too frightened to do anything but run like the devil.

I didn't pull that bay in until I was halfway up the canyon. Then I reined him to a walk and continued at that pace all the way to the cabin.

The bearded rifleman was again there to meet me. This time he spoke. "Where you been?"

"I went to Uncle Dick's place and bought supplies." Then I added, "Had a run-in with two fellows there."

"I'll bet you it was Dart and that dog-face pard of his."

"It was." I tried to smile.

"Sure hope you killed 'em both."

"No. But I did put a bullet through Isom Dart's hat."

The strange man chortled. "Good work! That'll teach 'em. He's been shot before, so he knows how it feels. Don't want no more of that, though he talks awful tough. They're always sneakin' around here, trying to rob me."

"Well, now if they show up you know they're tracking me. Head them back the way they came." With that I waved to the old hermit and rode on up the trail.

Bob Lee was waiting, out of sight, near our camp. He came up behind me and asked, "Everything O.K., Tom?"

"I got the stuff but I had trouble." I proceeded to tell my friend what had happened down at Uncle Dick's store.

"Damn it! I was countin' on staying here for a few weeks. Can't risk it now. We'll have to leave tonight. Wish my arm wasn't so sore. I could've gone with you and we probably wouldn't have had trouble. But we've got enough mad Chinks on our tails without addin' Isom Dart."

"Do you know him?" I asked.

"I know of him. I think you were lucky to get out of there alive."

But Mr. Lee laughed when I told him about shooting a hole in Dart's hat brim. "Tom, don't ever depend on your luck with a gun. That kind of charity only comes once in a lifetime."

Lee's remark reminded me that I hadn't reloaded my Colt. I poured fresh powder into the chambers and set new balls in place. I wished Mr. Lee would let me practice with the gun but realized that unnecessary shooting was out of the question.

I settled for some "dry" practice, pulling the gun and throwing it on a target while squeezing off an imaginary round.

An image of Jack Denby's wolf-like features hung over the foresight as I practiced. That man was no one to have behind you.

But the way I fumbled and sometimes nearly dropped that old pistol when I drew quickly was discouraging. I saw Bob Lee watching me and his frown said volumes.

While I practiced with the revolver Mr. Lee boiled water for tea and made bannock in the new frying pan. The food was pretty bad but I was so starved it tasted like Mother's cooking. "There's no seasoning like hunger." Lee lay back against his saddle and sipped hot tea.

Suddenly his eyes narrowed and his hand flashed out for the Winchester at his side. "We got company."

I rolled behind a rock that wasn't nearly big enough to hide me and Lee vaulted behind a boulder. There wasn't a sound. I held my Colt in both hands and it was shaking like something alive. The blood pounded in my ears. Then, even above the pounding, I heard a click. It came from some brush that grew thickly on the steep slope across from our camp. Soon a big doe deer in winter gray stepped out from behind a clump of serviceberries.

There was a gunshot and she collapsed in a heap. I looked back at Bob Lee but he only shrugged and shook his head. He hadn't fired. We stayed low and watched. After a few moments there was a soft clatter from the slope and a hunter appeared, leading a saddle horse. The hunter went to the deer and tied his horse. Then he stooped over the deer and began to dress it.

Bob Lee whispered, "Go over there. I'll cover you."

I signaled my agreement, then stood up. The hunter knew what he was about. The deer was nearly gutted by the time I got close enough to say, "Hello."

"Huh! Damn it, mister, don't ever come up on a person like that!" The hunter straightened up, the bloody knife held ready. The really unexpected development then occurred. The hunter was a young woman. She was in her late twenties with skin the color of old gold. There were wisps of ash-blond hair sticking out from beneath her battered hat. She wore a man's canvas coat and pants. She was big-boned with long legs and square shoulders that filled out the coat.

"Didn't mean to scare you, ma'am. We were having a bite to eat over there and heard the shooting. Can I help you? My name's Thomas Lavering. My friend's Bob Lee. We were passing through on our way to Lily Park."

The woman was not pretty but neither was she homely. She had appraising gray eyes and a man's mouth, large but with thin lips.

"I'm Georgia Willets. You and your partner aren't rustlers or men on the lam?"

"No. But I might as well tell you. I just had a run-in with Isom Dart and his friend Denby. Uncle Dick at the trading post isn't too fond of me either."

Georgia grinned and stuck out a bloody hand. "We don't ask many questions in Brown's Hole. But any enemy of Denby and Dart is a friend of mine." We shook hands. Georgia had a smooth but strong hand.

"Tell you what, Tom Lavering, if you and your friend will help me pack this deer home, I'll give you dinner and a place to sleep."

It sounded good to me but I said, "I'll go ask him. We've got a couple of extra horses."

Lee was waiting for me. I said, "It's a woman. I think she's O.K. Said folks hereabout didn't ask many questions. She asked us to dinner. She has a place to sleep, too."

"Sure," said Bob Lee, "anything will beat sleeping on the ground again tonight."

We loaded the doe on my saddle horse. Then, with Georgia Willets leading the way, we rode out a little side canyon and into the Green River breaks where the Willetses had a ranch. On the way we passed many fat cattle and saw two punchers sitting horses on the knolls and keeping an eye on those cattle.

"You watch your stock pretty close, I see," said Lee.

"They have a way of disappearing if we don't. Dad got started branding mavericks, we still brand 'em. But once they're branded we take exception to having them stolen."

The Willets ranch consisted of some log buildings with dirt roofs. Except for a cow barn, the buildings were small. The main ranch house wasn't much larger than the bunkhouse, which stood on the other side of the barren yard.

We hung the doe in the barn and Mr. Lee sat beside Georgia Willets—I think he was trying to charm her—while I skinned the deer. The doe was fat, obviously dry, with no fawns left behind.

Once the carcass was skinned I hoisted it high into the barn's peak with a block and tackle. There it would age ten days. After that one of the men would be sent out with a butcher knife and the woodpile ax to cut off the amount of meat needed for the next couple of days. It was the way most rural people handled their meat. For reasons of economy, many ranchers served game meat instead of the beef they raised.

I slid the doe's heart and liver into a bucket of cold water to soak overnight. Georgia picked up the bucket and said, "Come to supper, men. In about two hours. Put your horses in the corral. We have plenty of hay and there's grain in the bin. Help yourselves to the bunkhouse."

At six Mr. Lee and I presented ourselves at the Willetses' home. We had met the two hands in the bunkhouse. They were old cowmen, pushing forty, with permanently windburned faces and stubble on their cheeks. We had found them polite but distant. Strangers were not automatically welcomed in Brown's Hole.

At the table we introduced ourselves to Sam Willets, Georgia's father, and to his brother and partner, Buck Willets. Georgia said, "You may as well know about me, too. I'm a grass widow. Married a cowboy when I was eighteen. But I guess he liked Rock Springs more than me. Anyway, he left one day and the last I knew he was a brakeman on the U.P."

"Good riddance, too," said Sam Willets. He was a big, bluff man with thinning gray hair and a walrus mustache.

Buck Willets said, "I don't think you're gonna have much luck findin' work at Lily Park. Things are slow this time of year."

Mr. Lee said, "You're right, sir. But I got a good pard and we'll do all right."

I beamed like a smitten fool.

CHAPTER 7

Supper was venison stew. Georgia said, "I grew up on wild meat. Hope you boys like it."

"Certainly do, ma'am." Bob Lee helped himself from the aromatic bowl that was being passed around the table. To see him now, all slicked up and smiling, a person would never guess what a dangerous man Bob Lee also was. I liked being with him. I felt safe.

But there was no getting around it, his stabbing that old Chinese lady bothered me. I tried to forget the Fan-Tan Parlor and not be a wet blanket at supper.

One of the cowhands said, "I heard a stranger shot a hole in Isom Dart's hat."

The men all looked at Bob Lee, who was holding his coffee mug with both hands. He shook his head. "Not me. I've never met Mr. Dart."

Georgia asked, "Tom, did you do that?"

I knew I was blushing and probably blushed all the more on account of it. "Yeah, I did."

"I'll be damned!" Sam Willets wiped his mouth expectantly. He almost willed me to tell what had happened at Uncle Dick's. So I told it, trying to get through it as fast as possible and without mentioning what a green gunman I really was.

Buck said, "You better sew some stove lids into the back of your coat, son."

"Uncle Buck!" Georgia put down her coffee. "I'm sure Tom knows all about handling Isom Dart."

"I didn't when I shot through his hat," I said.

"I know Isom well," said Sam Willets. "He's worked for us a few times. He was born a slave, you know. He don't see things the same way we do. He wouldn't give a man much chance. On the other hand, I don't think he'd dry-gulch a kid." Willets nodded at me. "Sorry, anyone under thirty-five is a kid to me."

"I'm twenty-three," I said.

For some reason Georgia blurted, "Well, I'm twenty-eight and I sure don't feel like a kid. C'mon, Tom, help me with the dishes. We'll let the old folks rest."

The hands and Mr. Lee made their thanks and ambled back to the bunkhouse. The Willets brothers pushed back from the table and rolled cigarettes.

Georgia clearly didn't like that but she said nothing except "You want to wash or dry?"

"I'll wash. What I miss you get with the towel, O.K.?"

"I know all about that," she laughed.

There were lots of dishes plus pots and pans, too. "Feeding four hungry men two and three times a day is hard on clean dishes," Georgia said.

"How do you get time to go hunting?" I asked.

"I have to make the time. It's work to me. I like the deer except when they get into our haystacks. I wouldn't have shot that doe if she'd had a fawn. The deer move into the Hole by the thousands every winter. Elk come, too. Some of these men should be horsewhipped the way they slaughter them."

I said, "I've hunted some, but mostly for ducks, geese, and rabbits. My folks had a farm in the Sacramento Valley. We got deer maybe a couple of times a year. They were scarce but the old-timers said they were thick in early days."

Georgia asked, "How did you team up with Mr. Lee? He's old enough to be your father."

"Bob Lee's my friend. I never had a better one. We worked on a big ranch in the desert together. He's the best hand you ever saw."

"What happened to his hand?"

"Indian cut him. He used to be a cavalry sergeant. You should see him shoot."

Georgia stood close beside me, our arms touching. She said, "I could get Dad and Uncle Buck to hire you this winter." Georgia looked up at me with those gray eyes and my insides turned a somersault.

"Gosh, Miss Willets, I couldn't let you do that, much as I'd like to. Mr. Lee and I are riding together, we're partners."

"You're in trouble, aren't you?"

A chill ran up my spine and my warm feeling gave way to a chill. I said, "I guess I am down at the store."

"No, I don't mean that. I have the feeling that you and your friend are in big trouble." Georgia put her strong hand on my bare arm and said, "That's all right, Tom. I don't expect an answer. Just remember, I'll be your friend—if you like."

"I'd like that, Georgia. I really would." I looked down at the soapy water in the dishpan. I felt like there was a flood of stars in my chest. I'd never felt that way before.

"It's too bad you must leave; there's a big Thanksgiving dance over at the Davenport ranch in a few days. People come from miles around. Why don't you come?"

I was still blushing. "I can't dance a lick. I'd be like a drunken bear."

Georgia laughed. "No, you wouldn't, I'd teach you." And with that she took me by the arm and gave me a hug and spin around the kitchen floor.

I pulled away and attacked the dishes with a fresh vigor. I said, "You're a fine lady, Georgia. I'd like to dance with you but I've got to go. You don't even know me."

"Tom, when I looked into your eyes up there in the canyon this afternoon I knew what you were. Now, I am through being a silly old maid. You finish these dishes and scoot out of here."

When I went to the bunkhouse a few minutes later my feet scarcely touched the ground. I didn't know what to think. Was I in love with Georgia Willets? She was the nicest woman I'd ever met and I wished I could wipe away those few minutes in Chun Kwo's back room. I fell asleep pondering that.

I awoke, I don't know what time, with Bob Lee's hand on my shoulder. He had a gun in his other hand and was looking out of the window. "They're here, Tom," he said.

In one jump I'd cleared my bed, taking my cap-and-ball with me. The ranch dogs were barking fiercely and the scene outside was lit by moonlight. There were two Chinese men standing by the front gate. I can see them yet; they wore floppy black clothes, felt-topped boots, and fur mittens that reached their elbows. One wore a large black fedora while the other had on a dark skullcap.

"What are we going to do?" My heart raced but my brain had stalled.

"They don't know where we are. If they did, they wouldn't be standin' out there." Bob Lee appeared nervous but from the way he held his revolver I knew those Chinese were in grave danger.

Both of us simultaneously dressed while keeping watch out the window. Then, as we discussed our chances, Georgia Willets made the decision for us. She and her father came out of the house and engaged the two men. As they talked and gestured I saw Georgia point west, toward Clay Basin. Sam Willets nodded and pointed in the same direction. Chun Kwo's trackers were being given a false trail.

The man in the fedora bowed, then tipped his hat. Then the pair mounted big, raw-boned horses and set out at a trot toward the west.

Mr. Lee and I immediately slipped out a back window and ran to the corral. Our horses were saddled and we were opening the corral gate when Georgia came.

"You saw them?" she asked.

"Yes," said Bob Lee. "Thanks for what you done, we saw that, too."

"Don't be too quick to thank me. Those are two of the hardest-looking men I ever saw. They picked up your trail late yesterday and followed it all night. It's a good thing for you there are so many tracks around the ranch. It might be an hour before they discover we put them on the wrong road."

"It might be less, too," said Bob Lee as he swung aboard his horse. "Those fellows are real trackers, they're not a bit dumb."

Georgia told us about a back trail through the breaks that would lead us to a ford on the Green. I stood beside her, listening carefully. Then, and I'll never know how I got the nerve, I took her in my arms and kissed her full on the mouth. I've never really gotten over it. After all these years I can still feel her warm breath and the eager response in her lips.

"Save a dance for me," I said, shoving a foot into my stirrup.

She said, "I will. Tom, be careful." But I was already reining my horse around and flicking the lead rope on the trail horse.

"So long, Georgia."

We rode quietly, walking the horses as fast as they could walk—which was fast. Then, a half mile out, we figured it was safe to speed up. With a lift of the reins both horses hit a high lope that carried us to the ford inside an hour.

The water was swimming deep for about sixty feet. "Keep an eye out, Tom," said Bob Lee, who was looking all around himself. "If they tumbled to us they'd have us dead to rights in the middle of the river. One of 'em had a rifle big enough to kill buffalo at seven hundred yards."

Again I thought: Winter's job, hell. This is the damnedest fool thing I ever did. I'd peck with barnyard chickens before ever robbing someone again.

But once you have stolen something and there was blood spilled, too, the injured parties never forget it. They want you any way they can get you. If I'd had any doubts about that the arrival of Chun Kwo's men sure set me straight.

After crossing the Green we rode through some rocky foothills. Every juniper we saw seemed to have a deer behind it. I was beginning to understand how they felt about being hunted.

"The deer are comin' down from the Uinta Mountains. An inch of snow here can mean a foot up there," said Mr. Lee.

"What's up there?" I wanted to know where we were going.

"This is Diamond Mountain. It's a big mountain with lots of breaks and open parks on top. There used to be a shack up in a place called the Lanes. If I can find it we'll hide up there, at least until we've decided what to do."

The cabin was easily twenty-five miles from the Willets ranch. It sat half hidden against the backbone of Diamond Mountain and looked out over a big park that must have covered a square mile. Out in the open the snow was nearly a foot deep.

The lack of tracks suggested the cabin was empty but we knocked anyway. No one answered and Bob Lee pushed open the door. "Somebody's been usin' the place. But they're gone now. Maybe a sheep outfit or rustlers."

I looked around. The one-room shack had a crumbling rock fireplace and pegs driven into the log walls for hanging things. A bed frame built of poles lay in one corner, partially collapsed.

"Home was never like this, huh, Tom?"

"No, sir. But it'll do. I'll go stake the horses." There was good mountain grass under the soft snow and the horses easily pawed down to it.

The last occupants had not left any firewood in the cabin. So I went into the patch of aspen behind the place and gathered enough wood to keep us warm—if we didn't want to be too warm. Aspen is poor firewood; the dry stuff burns too fast and the wet is already half rotten.

It was late afternoon by the time I had enough wood collected for the coming night. Mr. Lee's arm was still too sore for him to do much work, so he did the cooking. I was ready to eat when he called me. Neither of us had eaten since the night before at the Willets ranch.

"If we ever can light on one branch long enough I'll soak some of the beans you got. Cook 'em slow with meat all day."

I guess he said that because I was wearing a long face. I could not help worrying. "Mr. Lee, do you think we're ever going to get away from those Chinamen?"

"No point in lyin' to you, Tom. It sure would have been easier if that old lady hadn't butted in. Chinese put great store by their elders. Chun's not gonna forget this."

"Are we going to have to fight those two?"

"Maybe, but I hope not. We'll try to outdistance 'em. Our ponies are the best in the country. We can be in Vernal tomorrow and halfway into the Book Cliffs the day after."

"What about Isom Dart and Jack Denby?"

"They're bums. They'd kill you if they got the chance but they won't put themselves out any unless there's something in it for them. The only way they'd cause you trouble is if you was foolish enough to go into Brown's Hole again."

"I half promised Georgia I'd go to the Thanksgiving dance at Davenport's ranch."

"Don't do it, Tom. Dart and Denby will probably be there—even if they aren't invited. Those two Chink trackers might show up, too. In their place, I'd take a look."

Mr. Lee was right, as usual. But there was a fire raging in me to see Georgia Willets again. She was always in my thoughts now. I said, "I'd be careful. I could slip in, have a dance or two, then get out again."

"All right, Romeo. I know what it is to want a woman. Lord knows, it's about the strongest pull there is. Maybe I ought to tell you a story about a woman."

Mr. Lee dished up our meal. We'd killed a couple of grouse behind the cabin. They were fool hens; I'd knocked them both off a log with a stick.

But back to Bob Lee's story: He said, "Years back I was stationed at the Presidio in San Francisco. It's the prettiest post you ever saw and Frisco is sure the best town. It was rough around the edges but the folks there sure know how to live.

"Anyway, I was on a detail along the docks one day, lookin' for contraband, when an old Chinaman calls me over. You know they kinda singsong when they talk. He had a big basket, close to four feet high. When I was standing in front of him he opens the basket and up pops the sweetest, smilingest Chinese gal you ever saw.

"She had on a light blue dress with dark trim, I remember that. And the old man says, 'You buy her, three hunner dollah.'

"To make the short of it, I did buy her. Her name was Ching Lee Ping. But I didn't have the three hundred. So me an' that old slave trader worked out a deal. Ching Lee went into a house on Grant Street. An old woman there was a kind of chaperon. I paid on the house and I paid the old man. Every chance I got, I visited Ching Lee. I was crazy about her. She was a real beauty and as kind and considerate as I ever knew a woman to be. I believe she loved me."

As Mr. Lee talked about his Chinese girl it was with more affection than I'd ever heard him express about anything. He was still in love with Ching Lee.

He continued, "All of a sudden we got sent up the coast after some Modocs. We were gone three months. Ching Lee was gonna have a baby and I was half crazy with worry. She was such a little thing. Finally we got back to Frisco and I made a dash for Grant Street. Only Ching Lee wasn't there; just the old woman. I damn near went wild before I got the story out of her.

"Ching Lee had our baby; it came early and it was a little girl. That lousy slave trader came by one day and took the baby. The old woman wouldn't say for sure but I think he threw it in the bay. And because I hadn't been there to pay the bills, he came and took Ching Lee back.

"I scoured the town for her. It got me in trouble with the Army but I didn't care. I must have searched every low-life joint on the Barbary Coast. But I never found her or the old man. All I ever found was a rumor. Some people in one house thought they knew Ching Lee. They said, if it was the same girl, that she'd been sold to the captain of an opium ship."

When Mr. Lee looked at me I saw great sorrow in his eyes. But as he spoke the sadness was replaced by fury. "I never found her. I even went back to the coast after I was mustered out; ten years later that was. I searched again, everywhere. But Ching Lee was gone."

I said, "Now I understand why you feel the way you do about some Chinese."

"Those people are a puzzle. I loved that girl as much as I hated that old flesh merchant who killed our baby and took Ching Lee away. I never got over it."

I said, "Then you can understand why I want to see Georgia again?"

"Sure, Tom, I understand. You go to the dance. My damned arm still aches, so I'll lay up here and rest it. But be careful, mighty careful."

The dance was still two days off. And we needed meat, so I went hunting and shot a couple of young bucks. Then, on the day before Thanksgiving, I cleaned up as best I could, sponging my clothes with a damp rag and shaving with Bob Lee's knife. On Thanksgiving eve I saddled one of the horses and rode off to Davenport's ranch on the Green River.

People would come from miles around, bringing food, kids, maybe even a dog or two. They'd dance all night, or as far into the night as they could stay awake. The following day, Thanksgiving, they'd have a feast. The Davenports would have roasted a steer and cooked a fat lamb or two in big dutch ovens. Everyone was welcome to come and eat as much as he liked.

I could not stay long, just long enough to see Georgia. I was crazy to hold her in my arms again and have a dance or two. Maybe I could even get her aside for another kiss. Then I'd have to beat it for Diamond Mountain.

The Davenport ranch lay sprawled on the riverbank and there appeared to be lights in the windows of every building. The night was blue dark as I swung my horse down from the snowy bench and single-footed toward the ranch. Once through the front gate I veered away from the main house and slipped through the shadows to the bunkhouse. Most of the hands were gone—probably to the dance. But there were a couple of old cowpunchers at a table playing checkers.

"Evenin'," I said, knocking on the door and opening it at the same time.

"Hullo." One of the hands looked up. "You want the dance. It's over at the big house, spillin' out into the hay barn, too."

"Yes, I came to the dance. But I need to get cleaned up first. Could I borrow some hot water and a hairbrush?"

The two cowboys grinned and got up from their game. While one found a comb and razor the other took a metal wash basin off the wall and filled it with hot water. I took a spit bath, shaved the whiskers I'd missed with Bob Lee's knife, then toweled myself dry. One of the men found a clean shirt for me to wear.

I had my old gun hanging from the cord around my neck. The men noticed that as soon as I removed my coat.

One of them said, "No guns, son. That's a strict rule here. Now, you can either leave it with us or check it up at the house. The boss don't tolerate guns or knives at these here dances."

I handed the man my revolver and he tucked it under the straw tick on his bunk, saying, "Nobody'll touch it. Pick it up when you're ready to leave."

The dance was whooping when I eased up to the door and looked inside. On the back porch some men were smoking and drinking from several jugs and bottles that had been stuck in the snow. A man offered me a snort but I said later, maybe. I wanted to find Georgia.

And then I saw her. Her fair hair was done up in curls and gleamed in the lamplight. Georgia wore a silk dress of lime green that shimmered when she moved. It was certainly an improvement over the old canvas pants and coat she'd been wearing when we met. The dress also revealed Georgia's fine figure. Maybe she wasn't pretty but she was certainly striking. And the cowhands were eagerly lining up to dance with her.

I pushed my way through the sidelines wallflowers to stand where Georgia could see me. The little band was playing a reel and when Georgia danced by she saw me and nodded.

I raised one hand and probably grinned like a fool. The next time she whirled by she was in another fellow's arms and she motioned for me to cut in.

Not being a dancer, I doubted that I could manage that reel. But when the fiddler tapped his bow and began a waltz I did cut in.

"Hello, Tom. I'm so glad you made it."

"Me, too. Can't stay long, though."

"I understand."

"Thanks for putting those Chinamen on the wrong track."

She laughed. "They were back in an hour. And were they angry!"

At the moment I wanted to forget my troubles, so I said, "You sure are pretty tonight."

"Thank you. Daddy ordered this silk from Chicago. It's French."

I didn't know how to respond, so I said, "Never could hunt deer wearing that."

"Why, Tom, I wore it to hunt you, and you're a dear."

With a look and a few words Georgia Willets could make me feel better than I'd ever felt in my life. I held her hand tight, pumped her arm, and spun her around that floor like I'd been waltzing all my life. She laughed and whirled with me. Suddenly I remembered. "I never danced a waltz before in my life."

Georgia laughed, she had a pretty laugh! "I know, but you're doing fine. And here we go!" Around that floor we went again like two dust devils spinning across the plains.

"Georgia, I love you."

"Oh, Tom! You barely know me. But I am very fond of you, too."

"Just fond?" My heart sank into my boots.

Georgia's expression became serious and she looked me in the eyes. "You're in trouble. I am trying hard not to love you. I can't bear it if I lose you."

"You're not going to lose me. I'll square this trouble. I promise."

She pulled me close and put her head on my shoulder. "Oh, Tom, this is insane."

A fellow tried to cut in and I ignored him but Georgia said, "Not now, Jim. Please?"

The waltz ended and we stood there looking at each other. "I wish I'd headed for the Green River instead of Salt Lake," I said.

"I wish you had, too."

Then Georgia asked, "Where is Mr. Lee? I thought he'd be with you. Is he a good man?"

"He's giving his arm a rest. He hurt it. To answer your other question: yes, Bob Lee's a good man. He's had a hard life. He went into the war when he was young. Saw a lot of action. That and some other things made him hard, otherwise he wouldn't be alive today. He's pulled me out of some bad mistakes."

"Did you two hold up that gambling hall in Evanston?"

"That's what those Chinese trackers think."

"Don't be evasive," Georgia said sharply. "A man was killed during that robbery."

"Man killed!" I must have gone white, for my shock registered on Georgia's face.

"Didn't you know? An old Chinese woman was stabbed by one of the bandits. And the man who rode his horse into the casino was shot to death."

Toby dead! I thought of that harmless and pathetic consumptive. Clearly, he had been slowly dying when we met. But I never dreamed that he'd be shot. His part in the holdup was just to hooraw the gambling hall's occupants.

I said, "I didn't know about Toby. Maybe he wasn't much but he was harmless. He just did it for a lark and a few beers. He thought we were playing a joke."

Georgia replied, "The way it was told to me, his horse broke through the floor. And while the horse was struggling, trying to stand, the lookout shot Toby twice with a rifle. They said he was dead when he landed."

"Oh, Georgia, I can't dance just now. I'm sorry." We walked to the sidelines, where Georgia Willets was immediately swept away by a young cowhand in a boiled shirt. I saw her look back at me with an expression of great concern. I pushed my way outside. All I could see was Toby in his red underwear hanging to that saddle and then that fellow pulling down and killing him with a rifle.

Outside some men were standing, smoking and passing a gallon jug back and forth.

"Here, pardner, take a snort."

"Thanks." I took the jug and swallowed a big drink of whiskey. I immediately regretted that, for my stomach was in knots from the news of Toby. The liquor almost made me heave.

As I stood there inhaling the freezing air and trying to collect my thoughts someone moved to my side and jostled me. I looked at him. It was Jack Denby.

"Well, kid, doin' a little socializin'? I seen you dancin' with the Willets woman. Ain't she a tad old for you, sonny?"

That remark made me furious. "Who're you to make judgments? You're nothin' but a sneak horse thief."

Denby jostled me again, then stepped back a few inches. In his hand was a cocked derringer.

"Put that gun up and I'll fight you."

"Maybe you'll get that chance. But right now there's an old friend of yours waitin' in the horse barn. Go on." Denby jabbed me with the pistol and I moved in the direction he indicated.

There were several men in the horse barn. All of them looked drunk.

And then Isom Dart stepped out of the shadows. He was stripped to the waist and I noted with dismay his broad, flat chest and powerful biceps. There wasn't an ounce of fat on that gleaming torso.

"Well, sweetie, old Isom's gonna teach you a lesson 'bout shootin' up other folks' hats."

I took off my borrowed shirt and hung it carefully on a peg. I might get whipped but at least Dart was going to know he'd been in a fight.

"Let's do it," I said.

CHAPTER 8

Isom Dart lunged at me, swinging an overhand right that just missed. I could thank God it did miss, he was wearing brass knuckles on his right hand. I backed away. My only hope was to stay away from him. If I could tire him I'd have a chance. Dart lunged again but this time I didn't move fast enough. I avoided that lethal right fist but he got an arm around me. We wrestled clumsily, each trying to throw the other.

It was then that I heard it. Dart was wheezing. His breath rattled like dried weeds in a winter wind. I tore my right arm free and punched him in the chest as hard as I could. It was like stamping on an old bellows. Dart gasped for breath. But, at the same time, he ripped his brass knuckles across my cheek. The knuckles just missed my left eye but cut my cheek badly.

Somehow I broke free of him and looped a punch off his chest. Dart gasped again. I knew he had the cowboy's curse, consumption. It was the same disease that had ruined poor Toby.

For five minutes I literally ran around that horse barn, avoiding the flailing Dart. He did catch me a couple of times, pounding my arms and shoulders. The brass knuckles left bloody wounds and fearful bruises.

"Come on, kid," yelled a drunk, "stand up and fight! Quit your damned runnin'."

I ignored him. I was concentrating on parrying Isom Dart's mad rushes and his churning fists. But as I spun by the sparse audience, one of the drunks stuck out a foot and tripped me. Down I went in the dirt and straw with Dart charging after me. For an instant he stood over me grinning. Then he dived at me. I rolled away, kicking at him with both feet, and jumped up. Dart was on one knee, panting but still half laughing. He thought he had me.

But I had him. Before he could stand I booted him under the heart as hard as I could. Dart's mouth flew open and his eyes rolled back in his head. He gasped for air he didn't have. I stepped back and waited for him to stand up. Finally he rose slowly and with obvious pain.

"Enough?"

Dart managed a sneer and, his mouth hanging open, lifted his arms. They must have been like lead, for he could barely raise his fists above his waist. I moved quickly, feinting by dropping my right shoulder, then stepping in and jabbing a left that landed on Dart's eye. It began to swell immediately and he tried to cover up. I swung a roundhouse right that broke Dart's flat nose and sat him down, a rush of blood coming from his nostrils. Then, slowly, Isom Dart tipped on one side and rolled over on his back. I bent over him and removed his brass knuckles.

As I straightened up there was a bright flash and simultaneous bang. I saw Jack Denby. He had fired his derringer at me. Somehow the ball missed. For a moment I stood there, not quite believing what had just happened. Then I saw my would-be assassin, his single shot gone, turn to run.

But as he did so one of the drunks grabbed Denby's coat. Denby struck out at the man holding him until another bystander grabbed his arm.

"C'mon, kid, let's see you fight ol' Jack here." The drunks hurled Denby toward me. I waited as he stumbled forward, trying to check his momentum. I hit him flush on the mouth with my right hand.

I saw his beard parting, the lip splitting, and his yellowed teeth breaking. Denby pitched forward. But before he could fall I caught him by the collar with my left hand and punched him twice with my right. They were raking punches that skidded on his face. Then I let Denby drop and pulled Dart's brass knuckles off my right hand. Hitting someone with them hurts your hand almost as much as it does your opponent. Denby was on his hands and knees, his face dripping blood.

After wiping my face and hands on a bandana I went to where my coat and shirt were hanging. I put on the coat and carefully folded the shirt over my arm. I looked at the bleary-eyed drunks standing around. Then I threw the brass knuckles far back into the hayloft. No one tried to stop me as I left.

The two cowhands were still playing checkers in the bunkhouse. One said, when he saw me, "Whew! Looks like you had a big time at the dance."

"Isom Dart and Jack Denby laid for me in the horse barn."

"You picked two mighty mean boys to play with."

I nodded. "You're right. Now I've got to get out of here. Can I get cleaned up?"

"Sure." One of the men filled a basin with warm water while the other found a bottle of peroxide.

"Here, kid," he said. "Wash them cuts with peroxide. Damn! Looks like they hit you with a club full of spikes."

"Dart had brass knuckles," I said.

A plate of stew meat probably looked better than I did. The peroxide stung and I knew I would be terribly sore in a few hours. Mr. Lee had been right. I should have stayed out of Brown's Hole. Then, as I dabbed at the ragged cut on my cheek, I thought of Georgia and the dance I'd had with her. I was glad I'd come after all.

After I'd washed and peroxide had been liberally poured over all my cuts I dressed. One of the cowhands helped me on with my coat. He also hung my cap-and-ball around my neck and buttoned the coat. Before stepping away from me he patted the gun, saying, "Hope you taken care of all your enemies. You an' that ol' gun aren't up to much right now."

"No. I've got to leave. Thanks, men, until you're better paid."

"Glad to. Stay off the skylines around here for a while. You'd make too good a target for some folks."

My horse was tied in a corner of the corral where I'd left him. He had eaten his hay and grain and whinnied when he saw me coming. After saddling him I decided to give him a drink.

There was a small side gate in the corral and beyond that a watering trough. I led my horse in that direction. It was a lucky move, for, in so doing, I avoided the main route through the ranch yard. I stood in the darkness and watched a heavyset man lead a big pinto horse across the yard. I scarcely breathed as horse and rider passed by. The man was Kanaka Bill!

As soon as the desert tracker disappeared I made my own tracks for Diamond Mountain. Partway I had troubling second thoughts. Had Bill seen me? He was a man who missed very little.

Perhaps he had let me go in order to follow me to Bob Lee. If that was his plan I was cooperating perfectly. I turned my horse and rode him up a swale. From there I climbed a wooded knoll to a spot where I could watch my back trail.

I stayed there, watching, for an hour, growing colder and aching more every minute. There was a crescent moon and periodically it appeared from behind the scudding clouds. Higher up the mountain, near the divide, the clouds weren't scudding. They were piling in on top of each other, then spilling down the mountain's sides. It was snowing up there.

My deer hunts on the mountain now began paying off in another way. I recognized landmarks and, using them, could make a roundabout return to the cabin. I turned to check my back trail every few minutes. I saw no one and it began to snow. I was relieved; in two hours there would be no tracks to follow.

The horse suddenly pricked his ears as we came down a shallow draw. The draw opened onto the snowy meadow that lay before the cabin. Probably he was telling me about a deer behind a juniper ahead. But I got down anyway and walked forward with my revolver in hand.

"Almost, Tom." A voice cracked at me from the snowy grayness.

"Huh?" I looked around wildly.

Bob Lee stepped from behind a clump of brush. "You almost did it right."

I walked to where he stood. "What do you mean, 'almost'? What are you doing here?"

"First, you believed your horse when he told you there was somethin' ahead. You got off and pulled your gun. But then you made a bad mistake."

"What mistake?" I was impatient to tell him about seeing Kanaka Bill.

Lee replied, "You should have reconnoitered. Gone around, not walked on ahead to an ambush."

"Well, I am truly sorry." There was an edge on my words. I was too sore and tired to reconnoiter. I'd already been circling half the night. But I skipped that to say, "Kanaka Bill's at Davenport's ranch!"

Lee turned on me, grabbing my coat. He didn't say anything for a moment. I could hear him breathing. Finally he asked, "Were you followed?"

"I don't think so. I watched my back trail, rode all over the mountain getting this far." I was afraid to think of what Bob Lee had in his mind just then. He was a man who looked after himself first and foremost.

I told him what had happened, about the fight and then seeing the tracker. "Bill didn't act like he saw me. He just walked by, looking straight ahead."

"That Kanaka didn't get as old as he is by lookin' straight ahead. We have to think he saw you." Mr. Lee gave my coat lapel a friendly tug.

"The next time I give you some advice, take it. That damn dance of yours could get me ten years."

Neither of us spoke as we rode to the cabin. It wasn't very dark. When the sky is overcast and there is snow on the ground, the nights have a luminous glow. At the cabin we immediately packed and were ready to leave in fifteen minutes.

As we looked around, making sure we hadn't left anything, I asked, "Where are we going now?"

"I been thinkin' on it. Havin' the Kanaka in the picture changes it some."

I said, "Maybe he isn't looking for us. We're not rustlers."

Lee snorted. "You saw that Hawaiian operate. Don't you think Chun Kwo would hire the best? Bill's after us all right."

Outside, the snow was falling gently in tiny flakes. It can snow like that in the mountains for a week. If we didn't get across Diamond Mountain that night we might not be able to cross it before spring.

The longer we hung around the cabin, the more nervous I became. "Hadn't we better leave?"

"Yeah, Colonel. Where would you suggest?" Mr. Lee's sarcasm was uncharacteristic. I shrugged my shoulders. I didn't have any suggestions.

"I see. Well, this is what we'd better do . . ." As Bob Lee's escape plan unfolded I saw the sense in it but, at the same time, drew back from its realities. Without an alternative to suggest I climbed on my horse and followed Bob Lee back, toward Brown's Hole.

We followed the route I had taken from Davenport's ranch a few hours earlier. The snowfall was not yet heavy enough to cover my tracks. A blind man could have followed them.

After riding a few miles Mr. Lee turned abruptly and began climbing a low ridge that had dark patches of timber along its top. We climbed steadily, the horses slipping, then catching themselves on the slick rocks. Before breaking out on top I dismounted and led my two horses.

Bob Lee stayed in his saddle. He was fifty yards ahead and when I caught up with him he had forted up in some dense timber. Below him lay my back trail from the ranch, two hundred yards away. We were looking down on a open gap in the foothills. The slopes on either side were too steep for easy riding. The bottom of the gap was the natural route. And I saw now that it was the natural place for an ambush.

Our horses were tied well back in the timber where they were unlikely to whinny and alert someone riding through the gap. As we left the horses I asked, "We're not going to dry-gulch anyone, are we?"

"No. I doubt that they followed right on your tracks anyway. They'd ride parallel to them, keeping a couple of hundred yards off. Just to avoid this kind of thing. But right here they almost have to follow in your tracks."

Mr. Lee's plan was this: I was to climb down the ridge through some brush until I was within seventy-five yards of my old tracks. I was to hide there. If any pursuers appeared I was to let them pass me. Then, when they came within sure range of Bob Lee's rifle, he would shoot their horses. I was to close in behind and seal off the gap. I'd use my six-gun to hold anyone who tried to get back down the trail. Just what I'd do with them wasn't explained.

It was full daylight when they came up the trail. They rode just where Bob Lee had thought they would. There were two black-clad figures—easy targets against the snow. The two Chinese trackers were riding big, platter-hoofed horses, the kind sheep outfits use both to herd and to pull their wagons.

As they passed, one of the Chinese looked straight at the rocks where I was hiding. For a moment I was sure he'd seen me. But he had not; he turned his head and looked on up the ridge. These men were experienced hunters, they missed very little.

And, as had happened before, we underestimated the Chinese. Somehow, the man leading sensed the ambush seconds before it was to have happened. He suddenly jerked his horse around and broke away down the gap. His partner turned, too, while simultaneously snatching a revolver from under his coat.

I hesitated, not sure what to do. Then two quick shots rang out and the leader and his horse went down in a heap. I ran down the hill, thinking I'd seal the gap and capture the second horseman. But he saw me coming and fired from the saddle. The slug whined by over my head. I returned the fire, aiming at his horse. I missed badly. But my shot accomplished one thing; it made the second tracker hesitate.

The man threw down on me again with his revolver. I stood and yelled, "Stop!"

On reflection, it was a greenhorn stunt. But I couldn't think of anything better to do. As I yelled the plunging horse screamed and sat back on his haunches. My opponent's shot flew high. And, in the same moment, his face contorted in pained surprise. He pitched forward out of the saddle. As his body skidded across the snow it left behind a broad smear of crimson.

I approached him warily. The man's dark eyes met mine for a terrible instant, then rolled back in his head. He was dead.

His horse writhed in the snow with Bob Lee's rifle bullet in his lower spine. As he tried to get up I shot him through the head.

"Check the leader, Tom. I'll cover you," Bob Lee was calling from his position on the ridgetop.

Feeling stunned and sick, I trudged back to where the second horse and rider lay spilled in the snow. The horse was dead, its large eyes already glazed and blood clotting in the snow around its muzzle. But the rider was alive. He lay in the snow watching me but unable to move.

I knelt beside him. "Do you speak English?"

He said something but I couldn't understand it. He lay on his stomach and I saw that the lower half of his coat was blood-soaked. He had been shot in the back.

Tears welled in my eyes and I couldn't help it. Damn, damn! These men were not supposed to have been shot. Our plan was to shoot their horses and set them afoot. By the time they walked back to wherever Kanaka Bill waited we would be across the mountains to Vernal, Utah.

"What about it?" Mr. Lee called from the ridge.

"You shot 'em both. This one's still alive. You better come down."

The wounded man said something but I didn't know what to do. He must have spoken in Chinese. I knelt beside him and put his big fedora under his head for a pillow.

"Where did I hit him?" Bob Lee walked up carrying his rifle tucked under his arm hunter style.

"He's shot low in the back. I think he hurts pretty bad."

Bob Lee knelt beside the man and roughly, I thought, pulled up the back of his coat and jumper. "Damn, that gun makes a mean-lookin' hole. Look here," he said.

I looked. In the man's golden skin there was a dark, bloody wound, a hole oozing blood near the spine and above the hips.

"God Almighty! Mr. Lee, this is terrible. His back could be broken." I couldn't stop the tears running down my cheeks. I hated Bob Lee.

Lee said, "Probably is busted. He's shot in the guts to boot. This poor fish hasn't got even a Chinaman's chance."

"We've got to help him."

Mr. Lee looked at me, his face hard and showing anger, "Listen, Tom, this just happened. I didn't plan it. But you might remember, I probably saved your life a few minutes ago. That China boy was throwin' down on you. And you was just standin' there like a dumb prairie dog pup. He'd a killed you. Now quit your blubberin' and help me look these boys over."

I realized Mr. Lee had saved my life. I had stood up to that man's gun and done nothing. But these two dead horses and the men sprawled beside them with blood all over the snow was sickening. And none of it was supposed to have happened.

I unsaddled the man's dead horse and spread the thin blanket over him. He said something but he was too far gone to know what he was saying. Still, I felt better for having tried to do something for him.

He had been carrying a heavy Remington single-shot rifle in .45 caliber. It was a buffalo rifle but with the buffalo about gone such weapons could be had cheap. Mr. Lee handed me the rifle and a container of twelve fat cartridges he found in the man's pockets. Lee said, "I'll show you how to strap this on your saddle so you're not obliged to carry it all the time. Think you can handle it?"

I didn't want the damned gun. It was the second dead man's gun he'd given me. But I said, "I have shot a rifle a lot more than a pistol."

Lee laughed. "I hope it's a *whole* lot more. You missed that horse by ten feet. I seen the ball hit the snow."

The other tracker had been armed with an old cap-and-ball of foreign manufacture. Lee said, "Trade gun, more than likely. They sold 'em to the South durin' the war. Sold 'em to Injuns whenever they could. Not worth takin'." He flung the gun in a long arc and it landed in the snow.

Lee looked at the dying man. "Those two were travelin' on rice and dried fish. I don't know how they do it. You gotta give 'em credit. They're tough."

I looked at the wounded man. He hadn't moved but seemed to be watching us. I looked away. Everything we did was pulling me farther down. I hated it.

"Mr. Lee," I said, "I can't square this. Let's return the money and turn ourselves in."

Bob Lee then said something I've never forgotten. "Look, kid, I like you. You've got sand. But if you think for a second that I'm gonna rot in jail because of some Chink crooks, you better think again. This campaign didn't turn out the way I planned. But I never saw a campaign yet that did. Somethin' always happens you don't expect. But, overall, we've done good."

I replied, "But there are three people dead. You said there wouldn't be any. You said we'd pull this off and spend the winter in the sunshine with our feet up."

Lee's anger was showing when he said, "This is still fall. We will winter in the sunshine. That is, if you don't go soft on me. If you do, Tom, I'll rub you out."

I looked at Bob Lee. His dark eyes were filled with hatred. I knew a lot of that hatred was directed at me. The man was a trained killer. He had just killed to save my life. I did not seem to appreciate that. How did a man square those two very different things? I shook my head. I didn't have an answer.

I said, "What you say is true. You did save my life. But I'm so mixed up. I won't give up to anyone. Let's stay partners. But let's help this man. Could we get him back to the Willets place?"

"Hell, Tom, he can't ride. Put him in a travois and he'll bleed to death in thirty minutes. I tell you what; we'll drag him over in them trees and you can sit with him. Hold his hand if you want, he'll be dead in a couple of hours."

Although we tried not to hurt him the Chinese groaned horribly when we moved him. I built a fire and covered him with saddle blankets. Mr. Lee climbed back up the ridge to wait.

I reached out and took the man's hand but he pulled it away. After that I just sat beside him. After a while he coughed up blood. I wiped it off his face but he didn't know it. He was dead.

On the ridge Bob Lee was sipping tea and chewing on a chunk of deer jerky. "Up the flume?" he asked.

"Yeah. Poor guy heaved blood and that was it. I put some rocks over them both."

"I hope you didn't do such a good job the Kanaka won't find 'em."

I looked at Bob Lee, he was funning me. I replied, "You think Bill will come here?"

"No later than day after tomorrow. When his bloodhounds don't come in, he'll go lookin' for 'em."

"Do you think he has other men helping him?"

"A course. Wouldn't be surprised if there wasn't fifty bloodsuckers keepin' their eyes peeled for us around the country. Always sit with your back to the wall." Lee grinned but there was no humor in his smile.

After I'd had some tea and dried meat we saddled the horses. Snow was still drifting down, putting a haze over the silent hills. The flattish top of Diamond Mountain was smothered by thick clouds.

As we stood beside the horses adjusting cinches I asked, "Where to?"

"Vernal or thereabouts." Lee straightened up. "You got a choice. Do you want to ride there or float to it?"

"Huh?"

"We just bought a little time; maybe four hours, maybe twenty-four. But you know that Kanaka will be comin' sooner or later."

Momentarily I wished the Hawaiian man hunter had been in this ambush. Then I chided myself for thinking like a criminal. Bill would be justified in shooting either of us on sight. If I wanted to survive this I would have to concentrate on doing it more intensely than I'd ever done in my life.

Bob Lee had also been thinking. He said, "There isn't much choice now. If we want to get away, we'll have to split up."

"What!" The reality of that, of being alone against Kanaka Bill, was frightening. I said, "I thought we were partners. You know this country. Half the time I don't even know what state I'm in."

"Now, Tom. I didn't say split up for keeps. But if we can throw that old bird off our trail long enough to get a jump we might get away clean. He can't chase us forever."

Lee's reasoning was this: We had already confused Bill by moving north to ambush his trackers. They had assumed we would continue running south. Now they couldn't be sure we wouldn't continue heading north, jump on a U.P. train, and wake up in Omaha.

Mr. Lee said, "We'll give him some more to figure on. One of us will take the horses and cross over the mountain. The other will go to Hoy's ranch and buy a boat. Then he'll float down the Green to Split Mountain. The other guy will meet him there. Should take about a week."

As a boy I'd almost lived on the Sacramento River. Whenever I could I was out in our boat fishing, trapping, or hunting ducks and geese. A boat ride down the Green sounded like the fastest safe highway out of here. I said, "I know boats. I can float down."

"You never floated Lodore Canyon. It's a pistol sometimes. You better be sure, Tom. There's thousand-foot rock walls in there. The river'll be low, you may have to rope partway down. And once you go in, you stay in till you hit the other end."

At home we often rode logs down the creeks, playing we were Indians in canoes. I said, "Let me try it. You have a better chance of getting the horses across the divide than I do."

Later I felt that Bob Lee had suckered me on that part of our journey. He'd seen Lodore. But I had never even heard of it.

Leaving the bloody ridge, we rode south and east, keeping to the timber and the juniper-clad foothills. It was early evening when we came out of the trees and heard dogs barking at Hoy's ranch.

We did not ride straight in, however. We "reconnoitered," as Mr. Lee called it, to be sure that we wouldn't be ambushed. Kanaka Bill could be waiting beside the haymow door, rifle ready.

Finally satisfied, I rode in, hoping the coming darkness would shield me. At the ranch gate I called, "Coming in, one man."

"Who are ya?" a voice replied.

"Lavering out of California. I'm trappin' beaver. Want to buy your boat."

"Maybe my boat ain't for sale."

"My price will be right."

Mr. Lee had said the present proprietor of Hoy's ranch was a known harborer of wanted men. He had sold more than one rowboat to a lone rider come in from the night.

I tied my horse at the gate. Then, shouldering my rifle and saddlebags filled with jerked venison, I walked to where a lamp burned in one window. Mr. Lee was waiting in the darkness. If I didn't return for my horse in a half hour he would ride in and lead him away. We would meet in a week's time at Split Mountain Gorge.

Whoever it was that sold me the boat was a short man with a gray-streaked beard and a bear's breath. When he sold me a boat he was also selling me a week in hell.

CHAPTER 9

"Figurin' on trappin' beaver, are you?" The man at the Hoy ranch had a whiny, insinuating voice.

I replied, "That's it."

"I got a fine boat. Built last summer, seasoned wood, an' none better for a trapper."

He charged me two hundred dollars for a double-ended, flat-bottomed boat built of rough-sawn planking. At home, on the Sacramento, it wouldn't have been worth ten dollars. Just sitting there on the streambank the boat looked cranky. Of course, I had to buy it and the fellow knew it. He sold me a pair of homemade oars for another fifty dollars. When I protested he threw in an eight-foot tarp, two lariats, and a half sack of potatoes. Had I known about this boat business on the Green, I might have spent a profitable winter just building boats for men on the dodge.

"You goin' downriver tonight?" the man asked as I secured my few possessions under one of the craft's two seats.

"No," I lied. "I'll row upriver to where I cached my traps; wouldn't want to have them stolen."

"Well, young feller, if you don't want your traps stole you come to the wrong country."

I replied that I was already personally aware of the thieving habits of some Brown's Hole residents.

The man cackled. "They're bein' careful right now. The law's here. Big feller come lookin' for a man about my age an' a kid about yours. Said they stuck up a joint in Evanston an' knifed a Chink woman."

"That so?" I replied. "Guess the man's that big Kanaka who rides a black-and-white pinto. I saw him the other night."

"That's the one. He know you?"

"Not me. I've never been in Evanston."

"Uh, huh. Well, boy, you're gonna need lots of luck." He turned and walked off, taking his lantern with him. I was left alone in the dark.

The snow had stopped. The three-inch accumulation was just enough to make doing things unpleasant. I wiped out the boat, then walked the riverbank until I found a water-soaked log about four feet long and eight inches in diameter. I tied one of the lariats to the log and fastened the rope's other end to the iron ring set in one end of the boat. In an emergency I could pitch the log overboard to serve as a sea anchor. It should help me to avoid broaching in rough water.

It was a gloomy night, not too cold because of the overcast and not too dark because of the reflecting snow cover. I decided to float downstream far enough to get away from the Hoy place, then pitch a secure camp for the night.

No sooner was I in the boat and underway than I discovered a leak. It wasn't bad, just a slow seep that soon had the floorboards awash in a half inch of water. My boots grew even wetter. I avoided thinking about the likelihood of being soaking wet for a solid week in late November.

But my mental picture of Kanaka Bill, relentlessly tracking me, was even more discouraging. I pulled hard on the oars and the boat wallowed sluggishly across the eddying current. I guessed my boat had been built by an unemployed sheepherder who never left dry land himself.

In the dim light my first perception of Lodore Canyon was one of deep foreboding. I could hear an ominous rumbling. And, looking up, I saw sheer rock walls that were hundreds of feet high. What light reached the bottom of the canyon was not enough to steer by. I pulled hard for the near shore. But even as I rowed the rumbling became a roar whose intensity grew with every passing second. I bent into those oars until they groaned with the strain. I became afraid that they would break at each stroke.

There were a few advantages. My boat, being double-ended, allowed me to go downstream bow first and thus sit facing forward. This made it easier to maneuver and to see oncoming danger.

The danger wasn't long in coming. The river was low and ahead it appeared to be paved with sharp rocks, some of them rising two and three feet out of the water. No boat, especially not my wallowing scow, could venture among those rocks and keep its bottom.

The chop on the water increased and spray began breaking in over the gunwales. Although I was rowing with all my might the shore only inched nearer. The boat nudged a rock and half spun in the current. With this for inspiration I braced my feet against a cross member and stroked with a strength I never knew I had.

Somehow I made it. Scant feet before entering the rapids the boat grounded on a tiny beach. I jumped ashore, going to my ankles in the slop of the waves. With a great heave I pulled the heavy boat as far up on shore as I could. Then I dropped to my knees trying to catch my breath.

My clothes were soaked with a combination of sweat and river spray. The driftwood I counted on finding for fuel didn't litter the tiny beach. In three steps I had crossed the beach and stood facing a sheer rock wall so tall I couldn't see its top. But when I began feeling around in the wall's crevices, I did find enough wood for a fire.

I carried an armload of it to the boat, then dropped it on the clammy ground. Then I tipped the boat on its side, making a crude shelter, and propped it there with my sea-anchor log.

I had only twenty matches in an oilskin pouch. And although I prepared the kindling carefully, the first match guttered out in the breeze. But on my second try the fire did take hold and in fifteen minutes I had a fine blaze. Its heat was trapped under the inverted boat and I was able to remove my wet clothes and dry them and myself.

I placed one of my potatoes at the fire's edge and heated water in an enamelware cup. Mr. Lee had divided our tea, giving each of us enough for two cups per day; ten cups would have been better. Next I attended to my guns; both were wet. I carefully wiped each one, then set them to dry under the overturned boat.

After a hot cup of tea and a chunk of venison jerky eaten with a baked potato I felt better. I was on my way to hoped-for safety although I had learned never to try floating this river at night. I expected that it would appear far less harrowing in the calm light of morning.

When I awoke next morning the river did look different. It was worse than I had ever imagined. Downstream it was extremely choppy from bank to bank and every chop could conceal a sharp rock. I was less than a mile into the depths of Lodore and, already, there was no hope of returning.

The waters of the Green River are not green. The river resembles dirty dishwater with greasy swirls covering the eddies. And always there was that low, ominous rumble foretelling God only knew what perils ahead.

At that bleak moment I would have sold my fortune for a nickel to be free of that awful place.

Nevertheless, I was hungry, so I rekindled my fire from the coals and boiled tea. Later, sipping the hot liquid, I recalled the fried mush, eggs, and thick strips of bacon we breakfasted on back at the Honeybee. It was painful to realize that that part of my life was now forever ended.

The rapids ahead were five hundred yards long. I removed my soggy boots and tied them to the boat seat. Then with my bare feet going numb in the cold water, I began roping the boat downstream.

As in performing many tasks, mine was not as terrible as it had first appeared. Without my weight the boat rode high on the water's surface. And although it banged against countless rocks, no damage resulted. By midmorning I had passed the first set of rapids and was again afloat and underway. The murky water was deep and the sound of the current was nearly inaudible.

I tried to let the current do the work in such places. I sat with the oars lifted and only dipped them into the water to alter course. If it had not been so dank and cold that part of the voyage might have been enjoyable.

Just after noon there was a noticeable change in the current. Around the boat the eddying waters were straightening out and I began moving faster. Below me began rising the dreaded roar of more white water.

This time I pulled to shore well upstream of the rapids. Beaching the boat, I walked down the narrow shore until I found the source of the roaring. My heart sank. Ahead were not rapids but a series of cataracts formed by many wagon-sized boulders.

Again I had to use the lariat to lower the boat downstream. But this time the current was too powerful and all I could do was try to guide the boat into a safe channel and then let it surge ahead over the waves. It struck some boulders but, again, its unladen weight allowed it to bounce off, rather than smash into the rocks.

My own progress wasn't so easy. My bare feet were numb. I was also soaked and battered by rocks as I clambered over and around them. The boat moved with heavy force and I tried to play it as one might play and slow a huge fish.

Apart from the worry of saving my boat I also worried about the lariat's strength. It was old and had already been under great strain. In certain places I looped the rope around my waist. In that way, I reasoned, even if I fell and lost my grip I would not be separated from the boat. I would also be less likely to break the rope.

This tactic saved my life and then nearly took it, all within a few minutes. Throughout the day I had riveted my attention on the canyon and its menacing river. The thought of danger from another source never occurred to me. I felt completely alone.

The last cataract in the series was a long one. A fifty-foot chute of white water gushed through a corridor of huge boulders. At the chute's tail there was a pool of calm-looking water. I looked forward to the relief of reaching that relative haven. There was firewood on the beach and ample room to stop, rest, and dry out.

I got the boat down the white-water chute mostly by luck. Trying to keep within a lariat's length of the boat while clambering around boulders, I fell repeatedly. After each fall I somehow got up again.

Then, in the last rush of water above the big pool, I was jerked down. The boat had cleared the cataract but the pool wasn't as calm as it had appeared. A strong current swept through it. This current unexpectedly seized the boat and sent it hurtling downriver. I was jerked off my feet. Suddenly, instead of me roping the boat, it had roped me and was now towing me downstream.

But as I was jerked from my feet something even more frightening happened. A large chip suddenly flew off the boulder beside me and pieces of it struck my cheek.

The bullet had been fired from high on the canyon rim. I even imagined seeing powder smoke rising over the gorge. My thoughts were a jumble as I was almost keelhauled by the blundering boat. Even so, I saw other slugs plunking into the water, making small geysers that sent their spray over my head.

I let the boat tow me several hundred yards downstream, half drowning me in the process. Then, under an overhanging cliff, I touched bottom. I braced my feet and slewed the boat. As it came under control I guided it toward the shore, wading in after it. I was too tired and frightened to be cold. Still, I realized that a fire was necessary immediately. Without warmth I could die.

Providentially, my matches were safe in their oilskin. I soon had a friendly blaze burning. Then, propping the boat for shelter, I stripped and tried to get warm and to dry my soaking clothes. I was too exhausted to be unhappy.

The boat and its few contents had passed the cataracts intact. I got my long-barreled rifle. Then, blue with cold, I stood and surveyed the canyon rim far above me.

My first coherent thoughts after getting warm were of Kanaka Bill. Was it he who had tried to shoot me? Although I was disgusted with myself for what I had done I did not think I deserved being ambushed. The person who tried it was good. He nearly got me the first shot. Having to bob along behind my boat was all that saved me. Now, as I studied the rimrock, I wished for a chance to square things.

But there was no chance. I saw no one and no more shots were fired. Perhaps it had not been Kanaka Bill. There were lots of people back upriver who didn't like me. Even the man at Hoy's ranch might have decided to reclaim his boat and sell it to another outlaw. For a moment I even wondered if Mr. Lee might have tried to get rid of me. Then I was ashamed of myself for having such a thought.

Instead, I did what he might have done—I studied the situation. I now had a sneak killer to worry about in addition to getting myself down a monstrous river. It was a depressing study.

A winter's day in a deep canyon adds to such feelings. The sun passes overhead quickly and well to the south. Certainly there is no chance of its drying you or your wet clothing. I sat under my tarp naked while my little fire alternately smoked then blazed.

I was cold, hungry, and even worse, I was afraid. The river was a mounting horror that could not be escaped. And somewhere, lurking above me, was an unseen killer.

So, when the shale on the steep slope behind me rattled, I bolted. With speed I didn't know I possessed I grabbed my revolver and swung it toward the sound.

It was not a man, it was a young buck deer. His big ears flared wide and he snorted as he tried to determine what I was. A deer in this canyon had probably never seen a human before. And especially not a human who stood before it buck naked.

The Colt's flat-topped front sight trained across the deer and, almost without my being conscious of it, stopped. It stopped on the deer's neck. I pressed the trigger and a yellowish flame streaked out across the gloom. As the gun recoiled I saw the deer collapse.

My shot had struck the animal flush on the neck and it was stone dead by the time I'd dressed and gone to where it lay. I ate broiled deer liver that night. And before turning in I roasted strips of the fresh venison over the fire until I'd had my fill. The fresh meat gave me a bellyache in the night but it was the ache of a full belly and I tried to ignore it.

Next day I jerked most of the venison, cutting it into thin strips and drying it over a smoky fire. The delay would put me even further behind schedule. But I knew that without more food I could fall permanently behind schedule. I cut the green deer hide into pokes. The first thing next morning I packed the jerky into these bags and carefully tied them into the boat.

That day was a repetition of the first day on the river. Within an hour I had been soaked to the waist and nearly overturned the boat. The entire morning was spent roping the boat a mile downstream. When I stopped to eat and have a rest a recurring worry dominated my thoughts. I was traveling so slowly that Mr. Lee might not wait for me.

At midafternoon I reached smoother water where I was able to float. It was a good thing, too, for I was nearly exhausted. I had stomach cramps and dysentery from eating too much fresh meat. My eyes burned from smoky fires and straining to see a hidden sniper or the next set of rapids.

Later that afternoon I encountered one set of rapids after another. In one place the water wasn't deep enough to float the boat. I had to drag it across one hundred yards of cobble rocks. I would pull the heavy boat five yards, then fall across its bow to rest. It was during one of those rests when I wondered if a sniper's bullet through the head would be so bad after all.

My clothes were falling apart from all the wettings and rough usage. The bench-made boots I had purchased in Salt Lake City were bleached and the heavy leather was swollen. The boots were either gummy from wetness or curled and hard from being too near the fire. I feared they would fall apart long before my journey had ended.

Somehow I kept my matches and bankroll dry. My gunpowder and percussion caps were in watertight cans with screw caps. The center-fire ammunition for my rifle was packed in heavily waxed cardboard boxes holding five rounds each. The cartridge brass might turn green but I believed each one would fire if I ever had a chance to return the hidden sniper's fire. On the other hand, my jerked venison molded in its green buckskin pouches. I ate it anyway. I would never have made it as far down the Green River as I did without that jerky.

Each day was so hard that I could not accurately gauge my progress.

Today I think I spent full days going less than a mile. All I knew then was that I was far behind schedule. By the sixth day I began having hallucinations and chills.

The canyon's cruelties were both unrelenting and unending. The boat began to leak badly, and while I attempted to plug the cracks with moss and dried grasses, the water continued to enter. At those precious times when I could float downstream I did so with my feet in ice water up to the ankles.

Eventually I lost track of the days. My guess is that I had been in the canyon for over a week when I collapsed on a sandspit below another rapid. Whether I fell asleep or passed out I don't know.

I awoke once in the night, wet and shivering but too weak to move. I had a piece of jerky in my pocket but chewing it was too much work. I lost consciousness again.

The morning came with chilling rain mixed with snow. But it didn't fall on me. I looked around. The boat was propped up and I lay under it wrapped in a blanket. My clothes were drying before a brisk fire and my guns had been carefully set out to dry, visible but out of reach.

For the life of me I couldn't remember making this camp. Where had the blanket come from? It wasn't mine. I glanced around. Had Bob Lee again come to my rescue?

I croaked, "Hello?"

From behind the boat, clad in a dripping old poncho, came one of the most peculiar human beings I had ever seen. To say he was ugly was understatement.

"Good morning. I am Yancey DeRoot. You appeared to be in a bad way last night and I took the liberty of making camp for you."

"I'm Tom Lavering. That was no liberty, you probably saved my life."

Yancey nodded. "Probably."

"How did you find me?" I asked.

"You washed up on my beach—so to speak. I have a cabin back in this canyon." Yancey indicated the steep canyon behind us.

"You live down here?" I could not conceive of anyone living in this forsaken hole by choice.

"It's been home for more than twenty years." Yancey DeRoot smiled at me.

I guess it was a smile. His face was leathery brown with small and deep-set eyes above a nub of a nose. His wide mouth turned down at the corners and there was only a suggestion of lips. His face appeared to have been skinned or seared. I was ashamed to think it but my benefactor looked more like a monkey than a man.

He saw me wondering and said, "I am the son of a Cherokee mother and Negro father. He was a sergeant major in a black regiment. I began my life as a bastard, unwanted by black, red, or white men. A kindly chaplain saw some worth in me, however, and got me a place at an eastern boys' school. I was a good student, especially of the classics. When I graduated I was given a scholarship to Harvard University."

I had heard of Harvard. "Isn't that back East, too?"

"Yes, Cambridge, Massachusetts. I loved the university if not the town. Some of the Puritans did not approve of me or of the color of my skin."

DeRoot handed me a bowl of rich soup. "Mountain sheep stock," he said. "It will soon have you back on your feet."

For the life of me I had to look away. DeRoot's face was one great scar —a tightening mask that pulled at his features, or rather what was left of them.

"I see that I make you uneasy."

"You got a bad burn, I guess?"

"Yes. A schoolboys' prank gone too far." DeRoot's face was incapable of much expression but I heard the sorrow in his voice.

"My Harvard scholarship didn't provide for spending money, so I did odd jobs around the campus and in town. One of my jobs was to tend the boilers that heated some of the university buildings. A few of my classmates, thinking to frighten me, placed what they thought was a harmless gas bomb in one of the fireboxes. When I lit the fire, the bomb exploded and covered me with burning liquid. I was badly burned, as you see."

Not knowing what to say, I changed the subject. "How far am I from Split Mountain?"

"In your condition an eternity away. You'll never make it."

"I've got to. A man's waiting for me there and I'm already days late."

"In *Richard II,* the Bard wrote: 'The high wild hills and rough uneven ways Draw out our miles and make them wearisome.' " DeRoot stretched his mouth at me, his manner of smiling.

"You have some wearisome miles ahead, Mr. Lavering. I suggest you rest here today and I will guide you downriver to Split Mountain tomorrow."

"How long will it take?"

DeRoot said, "That depends. One never takes this river for granted; we could have an upset. And then there is the problem of your companion on the rim. He seems to want to shoot you."

"How did you know about him?"

DeRoot replied, "I am inordinately curious about what goes on in my canyon."

"I don't know who he is for sure. He shot at me a couple of times back up the canyon."

"The worst of that danger is past," said DeRoot. "There is only one more place where he can get to the river for a shot. There are two men, really—an Oriental gentleman and an Indian. I know the Indian. He occasionally guides travelers in the area."

If it was any consolation I knew who was after me: another of Chun Kwo's bloodhounds. I asked, "Is there any way around them?"

"No. The Indian will know where to go and I expect them to be waiting for you there. Can you hit anything with that big rifle?"

I replied, "I doubt it. I've never shot it."

"Pity," said DeRoot. "It happens that I have a fine Creedmore rifle, thirty-two-inch barrel and lethal up to one thousand yards. If you like, we can prepare a surprise for your two friends."

The next morning we set out downriver in two boats. DeRoot had a double-ended skiff that rode high and swept easily over rapids that I had to rope my way through. DeRoot stood in the center of his boat and handled the two long oars as if they were toothpicks. He was the craft's complete master. With him at the oars his boat skittered over the river like a water strider.

By early afternoon he had far outdistanced me. I was becoming worried until I rounded a bend and saw him standing on a sandbar beside his beached boat. I pulled in beside him.

"Your friends will be waiting around the next bend, about a mile from here."

"What will we do?" I asked.

"We'll lure them out, at least the gunman."

My heart began to pound and I asked, "And I am the lure?"

"You will be all right. We'll make a cross-stick dummy and put your hat and coat over it. You will be lying in the bottom of the boat, near the stern, and under your tarp. The shooter won't expect that and, early in the morning, he won't even see you."

DeRoot's plan was deadly simple. The next morning, as I floated down, he would hang back upstream and watch the rim. If I was fired on he would return the shots with his Creedmore.

The ambush occurred just where Yancey had predicted it. It was a place where a long stretch of smooth water ran below sheer canyon walls. With the dummy in place I lay hidden under the tarp.

The first shot splashed water into the boat and the second knocked a chunk from the gunwale. The current was so smooth and calm that I could hear the boom of the big rifle hundreds of feet overhead as if I was standing beside it. A third bullet tore through the boat's bottom. A plume of water geysered up in the boat. I threw the tarp over it as another slug whistled down, then popped as it passed through my coat on the stick dummy.

There was a fifth shot that sounded more like a dynamite blast than a rifle shot. It echoed through the canyon. Then there was an instant of silence followed by a great whoosh of air and a tremendous splash in the water.

I rowed to where the splash was now subsiding within concentric rings. In its center a dead Chinese lay floating, face up.

CHAPTER 10

Yancey DeRoot drew his boat abreast of mine and together we rowed to the nearest sandbar. After beaching our boats he asked, "Was it the Oriental gentleman?"

"Yeah. But he's had his last shot at me."

DeRoot said, "The Chinese are ordinarily placid people. Apparently you have earned the hatred of some of them. I presume there will be more?"

I stood there for a moment looking into those intelligent black eyes. There was no fooling Yancey DeRoot. So I sat on the gunwale of my boat and told him the full story. About Mr. Lee and the horse thieves, the one he shot, and about Kanaka Bill and holding up the Fan-Tan Parlor. I told him about Toby Gates and fighting Isom Dart back in Brown's Hole. I even included Georgia Willets.

When I finished DeRoot said, "You have acquired a surprising number of problems for a man so young. Perhaps I can help you. As your friend Mr. Lee has said, the law doesn't much care what went on in that gambling house. I don't care about it either. I think you've had the lesson of your lifetime. Now all that remains for you to do is get away from Kanaka Bill and his associates."

I said, "That's easier said than done."

"Not entirely," said DeRoot. "I will see you safely down the canyon to Split Mountain for one thousand dollars."

I was momentarily stunned and Yancey added, "There will be no additional charge for removing the Chinese marksman from the canyon rim. Should any others try to hamper you I will deal with them also."

I gave Yancey a rueful smile. "It's a deal." After handing over the money I had barely fifteen hundred dollars left.

Yancey said, "Your boat isn't worth much. That plank with the big bullet hole in it should be replaced. We'll finish the trip in my skiff."

Yancey DeRoot was the strangest yet most remarkable man I had met since Bob Lee. In retrospect he was even more remarkable in his way. I have no idea how old he was. He could have been anywhere from forty to sixty.

Yancey wore an old canvas hat with a washbasin brim. After the rain and snow stopped he had removed his poncho. Underneath he was wearing a tailored Norfolk jacket of heavy tweed, canvas trousers, and gum-rubber overshoes over his boots. He dressed like a mining engineer. He was slender, of medium height, and with sprigs of kinky black hair jutting from under his hat. For some reason I found it unusual that one so badly disfigured would have such smooth manners.

We placed my few remaining supplies in Yancey's boat and shoved off. Yancey stood amidships, manning the oars. In white water where I would have roped my boat downstream, Yancey shot the rapids. He often did so while singing at the top of his voice. He said it was opera. He sang in Italian and also in German and French. To me, the most remarkable thing about Yancey's singing was that he could remember all those foreign words. When he was not singing he was often giving me a lesson. He was expert on local geology, natural history, and Shakespeare: " 'Be not afeard: the isle is full of noises, Sounds and sweet airs, that give delight and hurt not.' "

Yancey explained, "That's from *The Tempest*."

For all I knew, it could have been from the Postal Regulations. But I guessed that Yancey was trying to show me I wasn't the first to be carrying around a bag of worries.

He said, "I find it appropriate to run over some lines when I am on the river."

"Do you know them all by heart?" I was stunned.

"I know some of them, surely not all, though I have read the plays many times. Here! Give us a pull on the right!"

A series of rocks loomed before us and Yancey had me help him avoid them by stroking a bow oar. We passed the glistening black rocks in a rush of spray and foaming water that splashed in over the gunwales. But with Yancey DeRoot at the oars, shooting rapids almost became fun.

Once, when we were in a long drift of smooth water, Yancey was leaning on the oars, resting. "Tell me more about your friend Mr. Lee."

I repeated some of Mr. Lee's stories of the Civil War and his later battles with Indians. Despite his ancestry, Yancey didn't remind me of any Indians I'd ever seen. Therefore, I recited the latter stories with relish.

When I had finished he said, "Doesn't it bother you that the government makes treaties with the tribes and then promptly violates them? My mother's people have been destroyed by a government they once supported and helped."

There was little I could say. Until then I'd never thought much about the Indians' side of things. I asked, "Is that why you live down in this canyon by yourself? Because of the way white people have treated you?"

"That's some of it. But I also grew tired of being stared at. Once I was offered a job in a circus. I was to wear a little red jacket and be billed as the Monkey Boy. I realized that if I lived among my 'fellow men' much longer I would surely kill some of them. I am well educated but I cannot get a job except swamping saloons or rubbing down horses in livery stables."

"What are you helping me for?"

"Maybe for the thousand dollars. I must buy supplies, you know. But I am also helping you because, when I found you on the sandbar, I also found a human being who was worse off than I."

Yancey's statement shocked me. I thought even I was better off than he. Still, he had a point.

Yancey said, "We shall reach Split Mountain safely. But what then, Tom? Will you continue your life of crime? Are you a match for Kanaka Bill or even Isom Dart?"

I felt I'd settled my troubles with Isom Dart but Kanaka Bill was another matter. I said, "We thought he'd give up if we rode far enough south. Our idea was to stay far enough ahead of him until he gave up and went home."

"Bill does not sound like the sort of man who will quit until his work is finished. In fact, I doubt that it is work for him. It is a hunt, a challenge that must be satisfied."

Yancey then stood to his oars and pulled hard. We crossed the dingy waters of the Green and entered a small estuary of clear water.

He said, "This is Jones' Creek. It heads in springs far back up this canyon. The canyon is called Jones' Hole. From here it's a half day's float down to Split Mountain."

I helped him beach the boat. Then we walked a few yards from the river to a grassy campsite beside the creek. It was the first really pleasant spot I had seen since entering Lodore Canyon.

Yancey said, "Cut a willow rod, you can catch some fine trout for our supper." He took a small box from his kit and opened it. Neatly packed inside were some hooks, leaders, and trout flies.

"I presume you know how to fish?"

"That's one thing I do know. I fished at home every chance."

Yancey handed me his fishing tackle and I quickly rigged up a willow pole.

He said, "There are some fine pools back up the creek a ways. You'll do well there." Yancey turned and began setting up a simple camp.

Jones' Hole, the part I saw, was a steep-walled canyon rather than a "hole." The canyon appeared narrow and the only access appeared to be from either the river or down over the rim of Diamond Mountain. It was a lonely, beautiful place.

The large creek that flowed through the canyon was clear and, being spring-fed, of a cool rather than cold temperature. Beside it I found tracks of deer, mountain sheep, bear, and, at one place, cougar. After the prison-wall grimness of Lodore, the low trees and grassy glades in this canyon were especially pleasant.

I found the first of the pools Yancey had mentioned and went to its top. From the tackle kit I selected a large, white-winged fly with a red body: a royal coachman. Tying it to the leader, I flipped the line out across the water. The fly landed, then sank, and I let the current carry it downstream. As the fly swung in the pool's depths I lowered the rod's tip and twitched it. From the blue-green depths I caught a glimpse of flashing gold. The willow was immediately bent double. I had to chase the fish to keep it from breaking the line.

I held the willow as high as I could, putting pressure on the trout to tire it. It surged back upstream, then dove deep into the pool. The pole vibrated as the current broke over the taut line. Another ounce of pressure on the line would break it. To move the fish I thumped the butt of the pole with the heel of my hand. This worked and the great trout rose to the surface and rolled. I held the rod high to keep the fish from throwing its thick body over the line and breaking it. When rolling failed, the trout dived again. But this time I was able to stop it. It made several more rushes but each one grew weaker. Finally I was able to lead the exhausted fish into shallow water and beach it.

That beautiful trout was one of the largest I have ever caught. It was as long as my arm and must have weighed eight pounds. It was a cutthroat with slashes of bright orange under its jaw and golden sides that paled quickly when I killed it. I dressed the fish on the creek bank and tossed the grayish-pink entrails back into the water. Looking again at the fish, I felt a mixture of pride and regret at having killed it.

The daylight had acquired the purple cast of evening and the air was cold as I walked back to camp. It would have been nice to stay on the creek and try for another huge trout. But this was no time for sport. We had to eat, rest, and be on the river again at daylight.

The smell of wood smoke was in the air as I entered the grove sheltering our camp. I hoped Yancey would be pleased when he saw my fish. I found him seated by the fire, his arms hugging his bent knees.

"Look!" I called happily, holding up the trout.

Yancey turned his head and I saw something that made me forget all about catching fish. Standing or kneeling in the gloom just beyond the firelight were five sullen-looking Indians. They all wore buckskin leggings and decorated shirts or leather vests. The decorations were worn and faded; these Indians were not in their Sunday best. I noted that two of them carried guns: a single-barreled, muzzle-loading shotgun with an eagle feather tied to its barrel and an old Springfield carbine with brass tacks decorating its stock. The other Indians held short hunting bows with evil-looking arrows nocked and ready.

Yancey DeRoot looked at me. There was a trickle of drying blood on the side of his face. "Ah, Tom, there has been a new development. These men feel we are trespassing on their hunting territory."

I stood there, stunned, with a fish in one hand and my willow pole in the other. The cap-and-ball hanging around my neck seemed a hundred miles away. I immediately thought of Bob Lee.

I asked, "Do they speak English?"

"Probably, but they choose not to. Their leader will speak Spanish." Yancey nodded toward a Ute with slitted eyes and a large brass ring in his ear. "He's the gentleman with the Springfield carbine."

"Are you hurt?"

"Mainly my pride. The leader struck me with his gun barrel to ensure my cooperation."

Our long guns were covered by a tarp. Apparently the Indians had not had time to discover them before I arrived.

I looked at the Indians, doing my best to smile. *"Buenos noches, amigos,"* I said.

I walked to the one nearest me and handed him my fishing pole. *"Mi casa, su casa,"* I said. Then I went across the firelit circle and handed the Ute's leader my beautiful trout. He sneered and slapped the fish aside, knocking it from my hand. I remembered certain Indians refused to eat fish; apparently he was one of them.

"Perdona me," I said. But as my left hand holding the trout was slapped, my right drew the Colt from under my coat. The hammer clicked back reassuringly and I jammed the gun's muzzle under the surprised man's heart. *"Arriba los manos!* Get your hands up!"

It was a dangerous move. I could have had more barbs in me than a porcupine. But the Utes, seeing their leader in peril, didn't move. Their faces were a blend of bewilderment and anger. The leader slowly raised his arms. With my free hand I grabbed his carbine and tossed it to Yancey. He caught it on the fly.

Yancey swung the weapon to cover the other men. "I hope we're not biting off too much, Tom. These fellows mean . . ." Even as Yancey spoke one of the Utes broke for the trees. I speared his leader under the heart with the muzzle of my Colt. The breath whistled from him as he sank to his knees.

Yancey fired and the runaway dropped, howling and hugging his right leg. The brave with the shotgun seized this opportunity to fire. The charge, which we found later was mostly pebbles, took Yancey full in the face and upper chest. His blood spattered on me and I fired a ball into the man at my feet.

My second shot clipped a bowman's leg, cutting some fringe from his legging. He yelled and his arrow went wild. The other two Utes did not loose their arrows but ran back into the trees. From the darkness they yelled what I assumed were insults.

Violence erupts so swiftly. The veteran uses it while the innocent suffer from it. In the next moment silence returned as suddenly as had the gunfire which displaced it. The Indian I had shot lay groaning at my feet, his right shoulder soaked with blood.

The man Yancey had hit in the leg was lying where he had fallen clutching his leg. I hurried to Yancey. His face and chest were wet with blood and I thought the blast had killed him. Then he moaned and lifted a hand to his face.

"Yancey?" I asked.

"Oh! This is the unkindest cut of all. Someone has set fire to my eyes."

With my bandana I wiped the blood from Yancey's face. I was particularly careful around his eyes. But they weren't eyes anymore, only bloody sockets.

"How bad are they?" Yancey asked.

"It's hard to tell," I lied.

"You mean it's hard to tell me, don't you?" Yancey DeRoot was no stranger to facial injuries. He asked, "Is there anything left of my eyes?"

"You've been badly wounded."

Opening Yancey's heavy tweed jacket, I found that the shotgun's charge had indeed contained gravel. Most of the pebbles had barely pierced the jacket's thick fabric, although a few had entered Yancey's chest.

"We'll be digging pea gravel out of you for a month."

"What's the situation here?" Yancey wanted to know.

"One, the leader, badly hurt. The buck you hit in the leg is out of it. He's just over there." I pointed and then felt foolish for not remembering that Yancey could not see him.

I continued, "I creased another one in the leg. He sure howled."

"So there are two perfectly healthy and probably angry Utes left out there?"

"Yes," I said.

"I suggest you get to the boat and go on. Those Indians will never let us get away." Yancey was trying to sit up.

Over his protests I lifted the wounded man and carried him to the beached boat. I said, "You hang in here. I'm going back to bring the rest of our gear."

We had left the rifles, ammunition, food, and other supplies in camp. Moving as quietly as I knew how, I slipped back to the campsite. The fire was still flickering, casting a crazy pattern of light and shadows over the surrounding trees. I stayed low, waiting and trying to see if any of the Utes were lying in wait for me.

The brave with the leg wound lay before the fire moaning softly. I crawled to where the man lay and, with my knife, cut open the blood-soaked legging. Seeing his wound almost made me gag. The heavy slug had splintered the thigh bone and the resulting fracture was ghastly. I took the man's bow and cut off the string to make a tourniquet. With a stout stick I made a windlass and put the brave's hand on the stick. I wasn't sure he knew what I was doing. But I guess he saw that the tourniquet did stop his bleeding. He kept the bowstring tight. It was all I could do for him. As I finished, an arrow sped from the darkness and grazed my hip.

"Ow!" My cry was answered by a cry of triumph from the darkness. Gun in hand, I lay curled beside the Indian. More arrows were shot at me. But the Utes, mindful of their stricken companion, aimed high. I heard the arrows whiz and saw their shafts flash passing over me but I wasn't hit.

Lying there, I tried to think of what Mr. Lee would have done. He once said, "Put yourself in your opponents' place, then act accordingly."

I decided the Utes would not risk a charge nor would they all lay waiting for me until morning. The one with the creased leg would probably stay and watch me. The other two were likely going to the boat. They'd cut Yancey's throat, burn the boat, and steal anything they found.

With a mental picture of Yancey lying there blind and helpless I rolled away from the Ute. I was alternately firing shots and grunting as my wounded rump hit the ground. An arrow whistled by and I fired once in reply. Then I was up and running to where our rifles and ammunition lay hidden. I tossed back the canvas. As I scooped up guns and ammunition another arrow clattered against the stock of one. I threw one last shot into the darkness and ran.

Yancey and the boat were no more than thirty-five yards away. But they were thirty-five dangerous yards. Once clear of the firelight I dropped to all fours and checked our rifles. Both were loaded. Then, working quickly in the darkness, I reloaded the cap-and-ball. Thanks to Bob Lee's insistence I had learned to do this with speed. I was soon moving again.

At the mouth of Jones' Creek the canyon widens. More light reaches the ground there. Once away from the fire my eyes adjusted themselves to the dim light. I was now only thirty yards from Yancey. But as the distance decreased, the danger increased. Tucking the heavy rifles under my left arm and carrying the bag of ammunition in my left hand, I gripped my revolver in my right hand. I dashed for a clump of brush five yards ahead. Nothing happened. I stood there listening. But all I heard was the gentle rush of the creek as it flowed into the more powerful current of the river.

Perhaps the Indians had not heard me. In five big strides I had reached a large cottonwood. From there I saw the boat dimly outlined beside the river. I tensed for another dash. And in that same instant I was slammed back against the tree. The rifles clattered down and I fired the Colt unintentionally. The Ute who had sprung on me was stripped to a breechclout and his dark skin had been veiled in darkness.

A knife glinted and I instinctively jerked away from it, driving my knee upward. Both knife and knee missed their marks. But my upraised leg did force a wedge between us. I parried the knife thrust with my left hand and simultaneously fired the Colt with my right. The Indian gasped but pressed his attack. Somehow I had missed him. We wrestled for a moment and then a blast of orange-and-yellow flame shot out of the darkness. It was the muzzle-loader and my assailant gasped with pain and astonishment as a charge of gravel hammered into his bare back. I kicked free and shot him twice with my revolver.

There was no time to examine the good luck that had made the Ute gunman fire that careless blast. He had inadvertently saved my life. I picked up our rifles and ammunition bag, then sprinted to the boat.

"Yancey?" I called.

"Yes, dear boy. I am just where you left me."

"There's still two of 'em out there. But the Lord is sure looking out for us. That Ute shot his partner in the back."

"It's still dark then? I lost consciousness. My face hurts so. I was hoping it was light so you could see to navigate."

"You weren't out very long. We'll go on now."

Yancey agreed and I slid the boat into the river and reloaded our gear. I had abandoned everything but our guns and ammunition back at the creek.

"We should reach Split Mountain by noon," said Yancey. "I hope you were paying attention as I brought you downriver."

"I hope I was, too." The navigation of our boat was up to me now.

Yancey DeRoot felt no heavier than a big boy as I carried him to the boat and carefully place him on a tarp bed I'd made for him in the stern.

We agreed that I should take us no farther that night than necessary. At the first possible site I would row ashore. Yancey said there was such a place about a half mile downstream.

"You must look out for some big rocks in the river between here and there," he said.

With Yancey settled aboard I pushed off the boat and we were immediately seized by the river's powerful current. "Remember, Tom," Yancey said, "allow the river to do some of the work. Use its strength to save your own."

My first tug on the oars sent a stabbing pain up my back. I felt where the arrow had grazed my hip and winced. There was blood on my hand. There was no choice but to let it hurt. As people said, my wound was "a long way from the heart." And considering Yancey's condition, I had nothing to complain of.

"Milton was blind, you know."

I replied, "Milton, who?"

"John Milton, the English poet."

"Never heard of him. Does he travel the circuits like some of those other writers and actors?"

Yancey hurt too much to laugh but there was a touch of amusement in his reply, "John Milton has been dead for two hundred years. But, tonight, I am painfully reminded of a line from his *Paradise Lost.* 'He cried aloud and all the hollow deep of Hell resounded.' "

"You really hurt, don't you?"

"Yes, Tom, I really hurt. But I have hurt before. My great pain tonight is knowing that I am blind. I am a blind black man with a burned face and no marketable trade."

"You could be a teacher or, like that Milton, a poet."

"In our great American West, Tom, there is very little demand for poets. When did you last buy a poem?"

"Guess I never did." Somehow I felt guilty about that but could not have explained why. I said, "Never mind. We're partners. I wouldn't go back on you after all you've done for me."

Despite his pain Yancey could hear the river's changes and he alerted me to its dangers before I saw them. Between us we steered and rowed the boat safely downstream to a bar, where I beached it.

I built a fire there and made Yancey as comfortable as I could—which, I hate to admit, wasn't very comfortable. Until he'd taken that charge from the shotgun I wouldn't have believed the man could have been more disfigured. In the firelight I now saw that I had been wrong. I will never forget that poor man lying there on the sandbar, cold and in pain yet never complaining.

Once I had taken care of him I pulled down my trousers and looked at my own wound. It is always a shock to see your own flesh purple and raw with blood oozing from a wound. Yancey had a quart of brandy in his kit and after giving him a large drink I bathed my own wound with it. The liquor burned like hellfire, so I knew it was doing me good. I also used some of the brandy to swab off Yancey's face and chest.

"Thanks, Tom. You say the shotgun was loaded with rocks? Salt, too, I suppose. The Indians don't understand firearms. Lead shot is far more effective. Lead has great density and therefore travels farther and penetrates more deeply."

I replied, "You should be glad the Indians don't know that. Your thick coat caught most of the charge."

Yancey said, "Perhaps, but being shot with the camp's garbage pile is far more likely to cause an infection."

I had not thought of that. But I had seen gangrene rotting human flesh. A new fear shot through me and I said, "I'm going to wash you down with that brandy again."

"No, but I will take a drink of it."

I gave Yancey the bottle and he lay there with it in his arms the rest of the night. When it was light enough to see the river, the brandy was nearly gone.

Yancey seemed feverish and weaker when I helped him get settled in the boat. I asked, "You all right?"

"Sail on," he said.

With a push we were off and again at the mercies of the treacherous Green. In the strained light of early morning the river's rocks rose up like black fangs, each one waiting to rip us apart. Perhaps Yancey DeRoot could have guided our boat through two of the rapids we faced that morning. But I could not do it. I had to unload Yancey, then rope the boat through the rapids. That done, I had to wade back and carry Yancey down on my back.

"I certainly regret this. My strength is gone," he said.

"Don't worry about it." My own wound ached but I said nothing. Yancey was so much worse off than I. Besides, I was getting us downriver. I finally could believe that we would soon be out of that damnable cold canyon. When the last rapids loomed ahead at Split Mountain, I ran them with some skill. After that it was just a few minutes' pleasant boat ride before we passed through the ragged gorge and emerged from the canyon.

I pulled the boat onto a sandy beach. As I was lifting Yancey DeRoot out of the boat Bob Lee rode up. He was mounted on one of his bays and led another with my saddle on it. Bob Lee looked at us and grinned.

"Did you win or lose?" he asked.

CHAPTER 11

"We won," I said, "but I'm not sure it was worth it. That Lodore Canyon nearly finished us both."

Bob Lee glanced at Yancey. "Who's the nigger?"

"He's my friend." I am sure my anger showed when I said, "He saved my life. He picked one of those Chinese off the canyon rim with one shot. Must have been six hundred yards. I'd never have made it down that river without him. He's been to college, too."

Mr. Lee dismounted and tied his horse to a willow bush. "Sorry, Tom," he said. Then he knelt beside Yancey and examined his wounds. Yancey was slipping in and out of consciousness as he did so.

Once, when he awoke, I said, "This is Mr. Lee, Yancey."

"How d'ye do?" Yancey's voice was thready and faint.

Mr. Lee grunted and then turned to me. "I think he's got blood poisoning. An' I also think one or two of those pebbles carried deeper than you thought."

"What does that mean?"

"Blood's gettin' into his lungs. He might drown in it."

I hated to believe this awful opinion. "Yancey needs a doctor. He's a fine man and I owe him."

"Kid, I've waited four days too long already. It's too quiet. Bill must know you come down the river."

"But Yancey needs a doctor," I said.

"There isn't a doctor within miles of this place who'd tend him. There is an Injun woman livin' back up the country. She tends the sick. She's got a warm cabin and could see to your friend till he kicks over."

I began to protest when Yancey interrupted. "Your friend is right. There isn't a doctor here I'd want. I know that Indian lady; take me there."

Lee said, "I am sorry, kid. But if we hang around here much longer we're all goin' down. I'm leavin' tonight, with you or without."

Yancey said, "Tom, you must go. This isn't the finish I might have chosen for myself. But it's a finish all the same."

We made a travois and took Yancey DeRoot to the Indian woman's cabin. She knew him and agreed to look after him.

Before leaving the cabin we made Yancey a bed and I cut a lot of firewood. Mr. Lee shot a deer down in the river bottoms and hung it on the north side of the cabin.

As we left he said, "Don't give up on that one. He's a tough old bird to have made it this far. The Injuns have ways of curing folks we never heard of."

I said, "I hope you're right." But I was not optimistic, because as I was taking my leave of Yancey DeRoot he returned my thousand dollars.

In the cold twilight we swam our horses across the Green River, heading south. Before we stopped that night we had left Yancey DeRoot and the Green fifteen miles behind us. The country we rode through was dry and dusty: a cold desert of sparse greasewood and shadscale. My clothes were in rags. There were rips in my water-ruined boots I might have seen my stockings through—if I'd had stockings.

We camped that night in a thicket of juniper. There was no water and the horses had to eat snow. Mr. Lee let me build a fire and we also used snow to get water for tea.

"How was it coming over the mountain?" I asked after we had finished plates of beans and venison.

"The snow on top was up to the horses' bellies. You couldn't see the gullies where it drifted and we bogged in some; snow there was up to my shoulders."

Mr. Lee said he had rotated the lead horse every half hour as they broke a path through the deep snow. At one point he had broken trail himself to rest his tired animals.

He said, "My arm was hurting and we were all give out. So I put up with some of the Wild Bunch."

I had heard of a loosely knit robber gang that went by this name. But there were so many rumors; every missing horse and rifled sugar bowl was attributed to the Wild Bunch. The gang couldn't have done all the stealing.

"One of them's got a place on the mountain," said Lee. "He claims it's a horse ranch. I suppose it is but it's a little too good, all the mares have two and three foals a year. Some of 'em full-growed. And fellows come in after dark an' sleep in the loft with guns in their hands to keep them warm." Bob Lee spat into the campfire.

"We're outlaws, too," I reminded him.

"Maybe, but I don't see it that way. We relieved a crooked Chinaman of money he'd stolen from hardworkin' men. He couldn't even get a sheriff to look for us. Had to hire him some bounty hunters."

"You said Kanaka Bill is the best."

"Damn it, Tom. Don't be so all-fired technical. Bill *is* the best but he'll work for anyone. Those boys up in the horse camp had some hellishin' stories about Kanaka Bill."

"What did they say?" The Hawaiian tracker had become a subject of morbid fascination to me. Thoughts of him dominated my waking, and sleeping, moments.

"They told about him goin' after some cattle that was rustled up in Cache Valley a while back. It was in the fall and three fellers dressed up like Injuns and took forty fat steers out of a pasture. They was headin' for the Montana gold camps. They banked on winter weather comin' in and blockin' the passes before anyone started after 'em."

Mr. Lee poured himself a cup of whiskey from a quart bottle. "Anyway, these rustlers was pretty stupid. They headed straight for Virginia City. They used the main roads and sold a steer here and there to buy their traveling whiskey. Once, when their snoots were full, they told some folks how they snookered some old Mormon down in Cache Valley.

"Well, those folks was Mormon, too. They didn't think rustlin' was all that funny. Word got back to Kanaka Bill."

Bob Lee replenished his cup. "Bill threw off their trail and took the train north. He was waitin' in Virginia City when the three bozos came in with the steers. Bill had him a room in the hotel and a Nez Percé gal to run his drinks.

"The rustlers rented a pasture and paid the man who owned it eighty dollars a ton for hay. They figured to sell off the steers a few at a time through the winter.

"Bill let the rustlers do all the work. After a while he went down to the house of ill fame where the rustlers spent their spare time."

Mr. Lee chuckled as he recounted developments. "The rustlers had lots of spare time. They were sellin' a steer a week just to stay even with their bill.

"Anyhow, Bill waited on the back porch and when one of the rustlers come by, headin' for the privy, Bill conked him with an ice mallet.

"Then he went upstairs and drilled another rustler in bed. Nothin' fatal, just plugged him in the backside with a little thirty-two.

"The third rustler had been in the parlor boozing and passed out on the floor. Bill rolled him up in the carpet and let him wake up in the pokey. The sheriff put the third rustler in Bill's custody when he sobered up. Bill put him to work carin' for the steers. He stayed in Virginia all winter livin' easy. The rustler did the work and they sold off the beef a few at a time. Made a big profit.

"In the spring all the cattle had been sold. Bill sent the money, minus his fee and expenses, to the farmer in Cache Valley. Then he herded the rustlers down to the pen in Deer Lodge. He left 'em there doin' five to ten and went home on the train."

Despite its amusing aspects, Mr. Lee's story about Kanaka Bill only increased the forebodings I had about the man. I asked, "Do you think he really handled those rustlers as easily as those fellows claimed?"

Mr. Lee drained his cup. "Probably not. But Bill's so good he scares me. They told another story about him. An emigrant kid stole some sheep that belonged to a Salt Lake big shot. When Bill caught up with him, the kid was herdin' the sheep right out in broad daylight. Bill come down on him a-horseback. When he passed the kid he just bashed him in the head with a horse pistol. Left him lyin' there with his brains in the trail.

"Bill drove the sheep back to where they come from. Finally he sent the owner a bill for sheepherdin' plus a coyote bounty. Feller paid it, too."

Although I was very tired when I tried to sleep that night the form of Kanaka Bill kept looming up in the firelight. In my dreams I tried to shoot him. But my gun either misfired or the slugs rolled out the barrel and fell on the ground. Every time the horses stirred I sat bolt upright clutching my revolver.

Mr. Lee observed one of these starts and said, "Hey, you're gonna shoot off a toe throwin' down on shadows. Kanaka Bill ain't been close to you since Brown's Hole. But he's got you so spooked you're seein' him behind every sagebrush."

"You're the one who told me the stories." I tucked the revolver under my coat and lay down again.

Bob Lee said, "Yes, and when those rustlers on Diamond Mountain found out Kanaka Bill was in the country and lookin' for me, they threw me out. We backed off from each other at gun point. They're that scared of old Bill."

"You make it worse all the time," I said. "Are we just going to keep running until Bill throws a net over us?"

"No. We're on the border of some of the wildest country in the West. These are the Book Cliffs we're headin' into. It's rimrock, ledgerock country with canyons a half mile deep. The brush is so thick on the flat tops you could lose a buffalo in it. Bill's not comin' this way. My guess is that he could make a try for us down around Cisco or in the Henry Mountains. He'll be rememberin' how slick that Virginia City pickup worked. See, Tom, we know Bill's methods but he don't know ours. And if he doesn't finally give up and throw off our trail he could get the last surprise of his life."

"You're not afraid of him, are you?" I asked.

"Not man to man. But I respect that man. I've seen him work." Mr. Lee tossed a chip onto the fire. "Come on, let's get some sleep."

A man can get used to almost anything. And without realizing it, I was getting used to running. We rolled our beds before daylight, ate some breakfast, and were on the move again within the hour.

I was learning to endure the cold, too. I had been cold most of the time since leaving Evanston. When we took Yancey into the Indian woman's cabin the first thing I noticed there was how hot it was.

It was a clear morning and the wintry sun shone down on us with some warmth. We were skirting the edge of a big sagebrush flat and noticed lots of deer sign.

I said, "Half the deer in the world must winter between here and Brown's Hole."

"Yep. They're about gone in some places but this is just like the old days. I expect we're gonna see some deer hunters, too."

We traveled across country, avoiding the deepening canyons and riding out the long ridges that rose gradually toward the south. In places we could see far out to the southeast. Mr. Lee said we were looking into Colorado. But it all looked the same to me, broken country with grayish-brown cliffs that layered off and resembled bookshelves.

There were dark green splotches of juniper and pinyon pine. I saw pink rock faces that blushed vermilion in a few places. The deer browse was up to our horses' shoulders. We often saw deer watching us from patches of shade or bounding away to reveal their creamy rumps.

The deer hunters' camp was back in the brush. It was located on the edge of an open swale where a spring bubbled forth. The spring water nurtured the surrounding meadow.

Earlier we had found a well-used trail. And because it led in the general direction we were going, Mr. Lee decided to follow it. It led us to this camp.

"We might as well go in, Tom. Maybe we can find out if any strangers are nosing around."

A wild-haired little boy met us at the edge of small meadow. He was clearly of mixed blood. But he gave us no chance to question him, for he fled back into the camp as we approached. This precipitated the wild barking of a couple of dogs and the self-important trotting around camp of some shaggy horses.

Mr. Lee stopped and called out, "Hello, the camp!"

A huge man, easily six feet six, emerged from one of the tents. "Hello! Come in and tell us the news."

We dismounted and led our horses into the camp. "Bob Lee," said my companion, extending his hand to the towering man of the camp.

"Monty Nickel." The man was in his mid-thirties. He had a thick brown mustache, heavy brows, and eyes that crinkled at the corners from sun and good humor. He said, "Hope you boys will stop awhile with us. We eat venison three times a day. But it don't appear that we're gainin' on 'em. Hope you come huntin' work. It's my camp, so I take the top quarter. We split the rest even up. Furnish your own outfits. Our women do the cookin'." Nickel laughed and his white teeth flashed. "And cookin' is all they do, if you take my meaning."

I stepped forward and shook Mr. Nickel's huge hand. He regarded me, smiling. "You look like hard times, mister. Might be we could fix you up with some moccasins. Them boots of yourn don't look too solid—if you don't mind me sayin' it."

"No, sir. They've been wet a lot."

There were two canvas wall tents with stovepipes jutting through their roofs. Around them were three Indian-style wickiups with dirt banked around them for winter. The ground was littered with bones and scraps of wood. Several sets of large deer antlers hung from crotches in the trees or lay tangled on top of the wickiups. Hanging from a pole on the edge of camp were the carcasses of a half dozen mule deer.

An Indian woman, gray and bent, emerged from one of the wickiups. She stared at us while the boy we had seen first backed into her black skirts and tried to hide.

"That's Emily's mother," said Nickel. "She's full-blooded Ute. She's the best skinner in camp. No holes in any hide she jerks except bullet holes." Nickel called, "Emily, you and Rebecca come on out and meet our guests."

No sooner had Nickel called than two women emerged from the canvas tents. One was an Indian with a smiling, plump face and wearing a buckskin dress trimmed with red and white beads. The other woman, called Rebecca, was a stunning blond with large blue eyes and fair skin. She had a fine figure that was enhanced by her clean shirtwaist and fringed skirt. Mr. Lee and I stepped forward and introduced ourselves.

Monty Nickel said, "Meet Emily Nickel and Rebecca Nickel, two of the finest wives a man ever had."

Neither Mr. Lee nor I so much as blinked. But Mr. Lee did assume that our host was a Mormon and he said, "I've always respected the Mormons. Salt Lake City is one fine town . . ."

"Whoa, partner," Nickel interrupted, "we're not Mormons. I don't hold with organized religion. No, sir, it just happens to be my good luck to have run onto two fine women who love me and like each other. Religion has nothin' to do with how we feel about each other."

I didn't know what to say to a man with two wives. But I couldn't fault Mr. Nickel. He was feeding his family and not hurting anyone. I didn't care a damn how many wives he had.

We were told that there were two other men in the camp. Both were out hunting deer and would not return before dark.

Nickel led us into one of the tents where there was a cookstove and large table. We sat down at the table and were handed mugs of hot, fresh coffee.

Nickel said, "This is mainly a hide business. We sell meat, most of it jerked, up in the Basin. But hides are better pay and a lot less work. Although, the Lord knows, there is still plenty of hard work in the hide business."

Mr. Lee said, "I should tell you, Mr. Nickel, that my partner has just had some bad trouble with five Utes." He described the skirmish Yancey DeRoot and I had had in Jones' Hole.

Nickel listened, then said, "That don't sound right, beggin' your pardon, Mr. Lavering. The Utes don't hunt there very much. The game is there. But the pickings are a lot better and easier up on the slopes, out of that canyon. Everything that goes out of Jones' Hole goes horseback and it's just too much work. My guess is that you ran into some renegades. Maybe they were hiding out and tried to rob you when the chance came."

Later, as we tended our horses, Mr. Lee said, "What Nickel said about those Utes has put a thought to me. There's a place called the Strip west of here. Surveyors made a mistake and it's ground that no one can claim. There's no law and it's full of sharps and men on the dodge. Do you suppose that Chun Kwo got word in there and those Utes came huntin' you?"

"Could be." My heart sank. It seemed that everyone was out for our blood. A man on the dodge can't really trust anyone.

When the two hunters straggled in that night I regarded each one warily. Although they had been in the mountains for several months they might know we were wanted.

One of the men was a Ute Indian, dark and with thick black braids that gleamed on his light-colored buckskin vest. Unlike our attackers at Jones' Creek, this man, Mitch, was a jolly free spirit who accepted us immediately.

Johnny Murphy, an old-sod Irishman, greeted us with some formality. "Come to hunt with us, have you? Ah, I see. Well, there's room for all and no need to get hoggish. Isn't that so, Monty?"

"That's it." Monty grinned. "Share and share alike—after my cut's out. Now, what is it to be, men? A meal and on your way or will you throw in with us?"

My immediate inclination was to join Nickel and his two hunters. I had liked them on the spot despite my misgivings. But Bob Lee said, "It's a good offer and I'm tempted. Let us sleep on it. We'll tell you in the morning."

Nickel smiled his agreement and sent us to one of the wickiups, where we threw down our bedrolls. "Well, Tom," Bob Lee asked when we were settled, "what about doing some market hunting?"

"This isn't much," I said, indicating the shelter we were seated in, "but it sure beats sleeping under a boat. I say let's try it. I don't think Bill or Chun Kwo will expect us to be here."

Bob Lee smiled. "You're getting smarter. I agree with you, let's stay. But we'll sample the cookin' before we decide for sure."

The food was good, if plain. Monty Nickel was not exaggerating when he said they ate venison three times a day. In my time I have eaten a big herd of deer. But I remember that those mule deer we shot in the Book Cliffs back in 1882 were among the best. They were fat deer and even when the bucks leaned down after the rut their venison was moist and tasty.

The two Indian women jerked a lot of meat. Deer were packed in whole. The women skinned them, butchered the carcasses, then cut the meat into strips. Sometimes this meat was sun-dried on racks built for that purpose. But I preferred it when it was salted and then dried in chokecherry smoke. Mind, it didn't *look* tasty. After smoking, the meat became dark, twisted strips more nearly resembling charred pinyon knots than something to eat. But it sure went down well. To this day I keep a stringer of jerky hanging on my back porch so I can carry off a chunk as I pass by.

Rebecca was a cook more after a white man's heart. She made what Monty called "bone soup" from the knuckles and joints of the deer. A joint with some meat on it was preferred but a good soup could also be made from bare bones.

She would put several joints into a five-gallon kettle. Then she filled the kettle with water and, if she had them, added a dozen dry onions all cut in chunks. Sometimes she added yampa roots that Emily or her mother had dug. It took at least two days of simmering before this soup was really good. Often, however, we were all too hungry to wait that long.

Rebecca always trimmed the fat from our venison. Some deer fat is better than other but it's best to trim venison and drain it after it's cooked. I used to put cold chops in my saddlebags and eat them for lunch.

A lot of the jerked venison was taken to the Indian settlements at Fort Duchesne or Ouray and sold. We were taking around thirty deer a week and couldn't eat more than three a week.

Mitch customarily did the Indian trading although Monty sometimes went in with Emily. The Utes didn't trust whites unless they'd known them a long time. So it was wise to have one of their own around when dollars were involved. The hides sold at from fifty cents to two dollars each. Emily and her mother dressed some of the best ones Indian style and these brought five and six dollars depending on their size. The reservation squaws usually liked a big doe skin; it wasn't as thick as a large buck's skin but still made a fine piece of soft leather that was prized by the Indians.

Fresh meat brought us ten cents a pound when we could sell it to the Indian agents. The agents passed it off as beef and kept the difference the government paid them for beef to feed the Indians. I didn't feel anyone was really cheated because our deer made finer meat than "Injun beef."

It was early December when we went into the hunting business. The rut was on and this, coupled with snow higher up, had concentrated the deer. City people reading this may think that in the "old days" we just sat up in bed and slaughtered the game. Nothing was further from the truth.

Our days began a couple of hours before daylight. We'd get our horses in before breakfast and see to them. Later, at breakfast, Monty would decide where each man would hunt that day. We normally went alone and Monty tried to send us where we wanted to go.

But, not knowing the country, Mr. Lee and I hunted with the other men for a few days until we got our bearings. I hunted with Mitch, the happy Ute, while Mr. Lee went with Johnny Murphy. We also spent some days with Monty Nickel. He was one of the best hunters I ever knew. Although he hung around camp a lot he brought in more deer than any of the rest of us who beat the brush all day long.

Monty told me once while we rested on a deer trail, "The real work of hunting is making yourself go slow enough. To a deer, anything in a hurry is either scared or after him. So if you can't move slow, sit down. Let the deer come to you. Mitch can't do that. He puts his old gun over his shoulder and walks. Sure, he gets deer but he probably walks fifteen, twenty miles a day doin' it. I go half as far and get half again as many as Mitch does."

By midafternoon we began packing the deer in. Sometimes, however, the carcass would be hung overnight in a tree. About once every two weeks a black bear would be surprised on a deer carcass. But by the time we began hunting, the bears had pretty well hibernated. The few we got tasted like pork. The hides weren't too good. A spring bear skin is the best. A bear hide might bring from fifteen to thirty dollars. That explains why there aren't many bears in the Book Cliffs anymore.

Many people believe hunting leads a man into a base and savage way of life. Some claimed that if the wild game were destroyed, Indians and squaw men would have to take up farming or storekeeping. They would become domesticated and therefore be of more value to the community.

I'll admit the hunting life does not train a man to respect material things. All a hunter needs is a good gun, a knife, and his horse. He doesn't have to keep up with his neighbors with new buggies and teams. Hunting has a peculiar way of gentling down a lot of young men. Some of the kindest men I ever knew were old-time hunters.

I liked the life far more than did Mr. Lee. He longed for a good bed in a hotel with a bottle of whiskey on the table beside him and maybe a female there, too. Monty Nickel didn't like liquor in camp and Bob Lee resented that.

Lee was a good hunter, nevertheless. I have seen him drop three deer with three fast shots from his Winchester. He never got excited like a lot of fellows do. As a matter of fact, he really wasn't much fun to hunt with, he was so cool.

Mr. Nickel said my big rifle damaged too much meat and leather if I shot for the deer's shoulder. With my old single-shot Remington I had to aim for the neck. And, to begin, I shot very few deer. After two weeks' practice, however, I began bringing in as many buckskins as Mr. Lee did.

My ponderous Remington was slower but it had reach and I shot many a deer with it at four hundred yards. Target practice is all right but there is nothing like shooting a lot of game to teach a man marksmanship.

In the weeks I spent in the hunting camp I gained back some of the weight I had lost getting through Lodore. And most of that was muscle, not fat. Mitch brought me new boots and clothes in trade for the hides and meat I shipped.

One evening in late December Mr. Lee said, "You're lookin' pretty spruce, Tom. You should've been a free trapper."

I grinned at him. "This isn't a bad life. I like it a lot better than tending sheep camps."

Lee replied, "Don't get to enjoyin' yourself too much. There are men somewhere out there huntin' you. We've had a nice long rest here. But the longer we stay, the nearer some of 'em are gettin' to us. My skin is startin' to crawl when I step outta the wickiup in the mornin'."

I did not realize then how prophetic that caution of Bob Lee's was.

CHAPTER 12

Repeated snows during December forced us to move camp down from the high plateaus. We set up again on the edge of the badlands northeast of Green River, Utah.

The hunting there was not as good as it had been higher up in the Book Cliffs. The deer were widely scattered. They found cover in the pinyon-juniper breaks where it was difficult to hunt.

"Ah, Tom," Mr. Lee said after a few days of indifferent luck, "this is no pay and hard on men and horses. Let's move south and hunt sunshine."

I had become very fond of Monty Nickel and his two wives. And the other two hunters, Johnny Murphy and Mitch, were my friends. I said, "I know hunting is poor. But we haven't seen a single Chinaman—let alone Kanaka Bill. Let's stick here a few more weeks. Maybe they've given up on us."

Mr. Lee said, "Not a chance. This country worries me. It's too close to the railroad. The Denver and Rio Grande line runs south of here a few miles."

Mr. Lee thought we could be too visible. If we were seen a telegram would have the bloodhounds on our trail within twenty-four hours.

I said, "Let's tell Monty and the men about it, being hunted and all."

"What makes you think he won't turn us in?"

"I don't think he'd do that. He might run us out of his camp but he wouldn't double-cross us."

After supper that night Mr. Lee decided to talk to Monty and his two hunters. He said, "We got into trouble with a Chinese gambler up in Wyoming. Some of his hatchet men trailed us into Brown's Hole. There was shootin'. I think they may show up here lookin' for us."

Monty Nickel sipped his coffee, then wagged his huge head. "Knew you were in trouble the first time I seen you. I don't want the law comin' down on my camp. On the other hand, you two have been square and pulled your weight. Why, Tom here has turned into a mighty good rifle shot." Nickel rose and walked to the sheet-metal stove. He held his hands over it, rubbing them thoughtfully.

"Here it is, boys," he said. "We're quits. But I wouldn't turn Jesse James out in January. So you stick here, hunt with us till winter starts breakin'. Then, first of March, I want you gone. Fair enough?"

Bob Lee got up and shook Monty's hand, saying, "Couldn't ask for more. We won't bring trouble down on you. We'd pull out before."

And that is the way it was left. We continued to hunt deer and sometimes rode into the lower country and tried for antelope. It was business as usual. Business just wasn't very good. The antelope were even fewer than the deer and much wilder. But we took some and Mitch sold them for us along the D&RGW tracks. He brought in our supplies while the three women stuck to the camp. They cooked, sewed, and tried to make the rough life as pleasant as they could.

In late January a wet snowstorm blew in from the northwest. It plastered the breaks and the desert scrub with a white lather that froze hard once the skies cleared. We virtually stopped hunting. Except for quick trips into the pinyons for firewood, we stayed in camp. Monty and Bob Lee cast bullets and loaded cartridges while I split wood and practiced with my rifle and six-shooter.

I was never any great shakes with the handgun but even Mr. Lee complimented me on my rifle shooting. "You can sure make that Remington behave, Tom. If that Kanaka gets too close I'll have you take out his left eye at half a mile."

That thought, despite its being Bob Lee's well-intentioned compliment, was disturbing. Although I'd become a good rifle shot I wasn't practicing to hurt anyone.

One morning the sun finally came out warmly. The frozen snow began melting and water dripped from the pinyons in growing streams. I went out to the woodpile and began splitting wood. While I was working Rebecca came and stood beside me. No sooner had I split an armload than she carried it into one of the tents. She could carry the wood faster than I could split it. So she stood for a moment and watched while I swung the ax.

"A few lumps of coal would come in handy at night. I hate getting up in the middle of the night to put wood in the stove," said Rebecca.

"Yes." I paused, balancing the ax in my hands. "But this pinyon is ironclad and burns a long time. At home we had fir that split a lot easier."

"Tom, you should go home. Mr. Lee is not a good man." Rebecca knelt and gathered some billets of wood.

"Bob Lee has been like a dad. He saved my life."

"I'm sure he did. But wasn't he the one who put it in jeopardy to begin with?"

I worked hard at splitting, angry at Rebecca for what she was saying and angrier still at myself for listening.

Rebecca continued, "My father traded me off to a rich man in Salt Lake City. I was supposed to be his fifth wife! All my life I had been raised to obey my parents and to honor their beliefs. But I could not marry that old man. I knew that to marry him would be wrong—just as I know it is wrong for you to stay with Robert Lee."

"You're no one to talk. What's the difference between bein' a second wife and a fifth wife?" I stopped to rest and looked at Rebecca.

"It's love," she said. "Monty is a good man. This is as hard for him as it is for Emily and me. He didn't want it this way, it just happened. He couldn't help himself and neither could we. Monty might have been a good ranch manager or run a mining camp. But because of the two of us, he must make a living in this awful wilderness. But no one judges us here except ourselves. I would not have it any other way."

The reasoning of women was never quite convincing to me. But I knew Rebecca was right when she said Monty Nickel was a "good man." I wished I had the same feeling about myself.

My self-examination was interrupted by Monty, who left his tent and called, "We have enough wood for a week. Let's take our horses and go back toward the rims. There's some elk in the breaks and this snow might have forced 'em out into the open."

Inside of twenty minutes Monty and I were in the saddle and leading two packhorses. We headed north through broken country that eventually reached into the Book Cliffs. Monty led the way onto a low ridge from where we could see the surrounding area. Monty had an old pair of field glasses, so worn from use that the brass case shone through the black leather binding. He dismounted and put the glasses to his eyes.

For a long time Monty peered intently through the glasses. He said nothing but made occasional grunts and chewed at his mustache.

"See any elk?" I asked.

"Nooo." He kept the glasses to his eyes, barely acknowledging my question.

I stood beside him trying to see what he saw. But I saw only clumps of juniper and pinyon patched in against dun-colored cliffs. The snow was dazzling in the sunshine.

"What I see," said Monty at last, "is a fellow standing way back in them junipers yonder. And behind him I see what could be the hind leg of a pinto horse."

My insides turned to cold stone and I could scarcely breathe. Monty Nickel was looking at Kanaka Bill!

"Does he see us?" I whispered.

"I would say he has been seein' us for some time. Otherwise why would he be hidin' back there in the junipers?"

I threw the reins over my bay's head and prepared to mount.

"Whoa, son," Monty muttered.

My inclination was to make a run for the camp, alert Mr. Lee, and then make tracks. "There's no time to spare," I said. "He's on to us."

Monty replaced his field glasses in their leather case and hung them from his saddle horn. He turned to me and said, "I think that fella is waitin' for somethin'. He wanted us to see him, but to think it was because of our good eyesight and luck. He's up to something."

We mounted our horses and rode back toward camp. Monty said, "Keep a sharp lookout. From what you say, some of those boys are good shots with a long gun."

We reached camp without incident. Bob Lee received our news of the watcher in the trees silently. His only apparent reaction was a narrowing of the eyes.

At last I asked, "What should we do, run?"

Lee said, "I wish I knew how long he's been waitin' out there."

Monty said, "Hard tellin'. But we've all been on the lookout. I haven't seen a thing till today."

When Johnny and Mitch came in from their day's hunt we asked them if they had seen signs of anyone. Johnny had not but Mitch said he had seen a lone set of horse tracks earlier in the week.

"Why didn't you say somethin'?" Bob Lee demanded.

"Looked like a stray. No shoes; I didn't think it was bein' rode."

Our deliberations were interrupted by the three women, who set out a meal. We had venison stew and sourdough biscuits with gravy.

"Eat hearty, boys," said Monty. "This could be the last hot meal you get for a while."

After dinner Mr. Lee and I rolled our beds. We stuffed our few possessions into canvas bags preparatory to packing them on the horses.

As we worked Mr. Lee said, "I think Bill wants us to run. And we're going to accommodate him." Mr. Lee smiled. "But what do you say we run right at him? Let's surprise that old Highwyan."

A mumbled agreement was the best I could do. But before we left I wrote a note to Georgia Willets in Brown's Hole. I told her my difficulties had not yet ended. In fact, the end wasn't even in sight. But someday I would be back and I hoped she would wait for me. I signed my letter "Love, Thomas Lavering."

It was dark when we shook hands all around and left Monty Nickel's camp. Mr. Lee led the way, riding south. But when we were a half mile from the camp he turned back toward the north.

He asked, "Can you take us to where you and Monty saw the Kanaka?"

Although it was a dark night with patches of black clouds streaking the moonless sky, I said, "Yes."

Secretly, I wasn't that sure. Night changes a place, putting new gulches across your way and trees where there were none that afternoon. But I guided on the North Star and the hulking mass of the Book Cliffs that lay below it. Within two hours Bob Lee and I were standing where Monty and I had stood that afternoon.

"This is it," I whispered. "He was over there in those junipers." I pointed to where the man had been standing. Now, however, the distant stand of scrub trees was black on a black background. There was not even a pinpoint of firelight to guide us.

Mr. Lee raised a moistened finger. The wind was from the northwest. "Smell, Tom. Do you smell a campfire? Sometimes I can smell a cigareet at five hundred yards."

I sniffed the cold air, feeling a bit foolish. But there was a smell; not the pungent aroma of juniper and sage or the scent of cold dust. But something.

"I can smell it. What is it?" But the more I sniffed, the more confused I became. Eventually I wasn't sure that I had smelled anything.

"It was a smell," said Bob Lee. "A man has got to trust his intelligence. Maybe it's just how the Kanaka smells when he needs a bath."

We left the ridge and, keeping to the shadows, made our way to within a half mile of where I *thought* the man had stood watching. Before I could speak Bob Lee touched a finger to my lips. Then he whispered into my ear, "We'll leave the horses here and cut a circle out in front of us on foot. No talkin' from here on. If we come on their camp we'll shoot it up an' run off the horses. Stay close, but not too close. Remember, a man tends to shoot high in the dark."

With the stars for a guide and Bob Lee's pocket watch telling us how far we'd come, the two of us crept forward. I had on soft buckskin pants but each sprig of sagebrush that dragged across them sounded like an avalanche. A stone turning underfoot grated like thunder. But we moved ahead, stalking the man who had come hunting us.

After what seemed an eternity of creeping Bob Lee abruptly turned and faced me. He pulled me close, roughly touching my nose and then sniffing softly himself. I sniffed, too. There was something, a pungent, unpleasant odor. I had smelled it before. I sniffed, then racked my memory. Where had I smelled that scent before?

Then I remembered. Back home I had smelled that odor along the railroad grade. A gang of Chinese laborers had been working there. The smell came from their suen choy, a fermented cabbage. My father said the workers ate it at every meal. It smelled to high heaven.

With his lips to my ear Mr. Lee whispered, "Chinatown! They're in there. Wish I knew how many. Wait now and listen. Not a peep. That Kanaka Bill sleeps with one ear to the ground."

We waited in the dark with the cold pouring down from the cliffs and turning our blood to slush. I took deep breaths to keep my teeth from chattering.

It must have been midnight when we heard the voices. Sleepy men muttering in the cold. Perhaps changing a guard, emptying a bladder, or just stirring the pot for a midnight snack.

More silence and then a cough followed by an angry rebuke. Mr. Lee seized my hand, held up his Colt in the other hand, and pulled me along after him.

The lessons of deer hunting now came in handy, for we could slip through the sage and clawing trees without a sound. We were murky shadows floating toward a rendezvous with the man who coughed. Then we heard another man, one who snored. We moved closer. The red coals of a fire glowed. We were in the enemy camp.

I nearly bumped into a horse tied among the junipers. He was looking at me and wondering. I reached up and silently slipped off his halter. The horse moved away a few steps, then paused, curious. Mr. Lee and I crept on, feeling our way as much as seeing it. When we came on a tethered horse we untied it.

The camp was in a tiny opening among the junipers. I saw four shadowy forms lying on the ground around the campfire. Mr. Lee held up four fingers. I nodded.

In less than a second he had emptied his revolver into the sleeping camp. A man leaped to his feet, blasting wildly with a carbine. Mr. Lee shot him down. I stood poised, holding my revolver but not firing.

Bob Lee hissed, "Shoot, damn you!" He had holstered his six-gun and was now pumping .44 slugs from his Winchester. The camp was a tumult of ricocheting bullets and the surprised cries of frightened and injured men. I fired a shot into the campfire and heard the ball clang against a pot.

From somewhere outside the fire circle we began to draw fire. I heard the shots and saw muzzle flashes.

"Come on." Bob Lee grabbed me and pushed. We were running away, juniper branches whipping at our faces, rocks and the trunks of fallen trees reaching up to trip us. We ran hard, stumbling blindly and almost falling.

Our horses, dozing in the gloom, started as we ran up to them. "Whoa!" They stopped moving and stood quietly. Bob Lee's careful selection of our mounts was paying off again. With a lunge we hit the saddles and were off at a lope. The packhorses followed obediently at the end of their lead ropes.

It was almost like our flight from Evanston. We were running again, frightened yet relentless. At least *I* was frightened. After two hours of fast riding I began thinking: What if those men in the camp hadn't been after us?

Mr. Lee had said he was just going to shoot up the camp but I saw a man go down from one of Bob Lee's shots. Also, considering Bob Lee's skill, there were probably dead or dying men back there who never got out of their beds.

Each time the violence increased. I felt that Bob Lee was not escaping but, instead, leading us deeper into an unending morass. Would we ever get away? I leaned forward in my saddle, pushed weight into the stirrups, and galloped after my companion's dark form.

We stopped once and rapidly swapped our riding saddles for the sawbucks on the packhorses. In minutes we were away again, traveling at a mile-eating lope. Before dawn Mr. Lee began dismounting and leading the horses for a mile before remounting and continuing our flight. As the first blood-red streaks appeared in the eastern sky he finally called a halt.

"I make it almost fifty miles since we left our friends. We sure gave 'em something to think on, didn't we, Tom?"

"I hope that's the end of it. My guts are still in a knot." I was stretched out on the hard ground, my back resting against the twisted trunk of a pinyon pine.

"I'd like to think you're right. But that fella who was shootin' back wasn't one bit rattled. He put a couple past my ears. I didn't wait for a third try from that one."

"Do you think it was Bill?"

Bob Lee pulled his hat down over his eyes. "Maybe. But I wonder if Bill would've missed his second shot. Did you cut loose a big pinto horse?"

"No."

Either we had missed the Kanaka's horse or he wasn't in camp. Just knowing that troubled a man. Bill did nothing and still you worried about him.

Bob Lee said, "I think we stepped out of a trap. The Kanaka was probably layin' for us somewhere. Maybe he has more help than we saw. I think those men in that hideout camp were set to drive us into the open." Bob Lee spat. "I just wish I knew for sure. Don't I, though!"

I pulled a stick of deer jerky from my coat pocket. While I gnawed on it, Bob Lee spoke with pleasure about our surprise attack on the camp in the junipers. He clearly did not share my feeling that our latest escape was only a part of an ever-widening catastrophe.

"What now?" I asked.

"I want to get into the Henry Mountains. I heard there's a ranch down there, a safe place. It's run by an Englishman, Henry Buhr. Buhr takes a man for what he is, not what he's been. We can rest up at Buhr's—before we make for the border."

"The border?" I asked. This was the first mention Lee had made about leaving the country. I said, "I thought we were going to winter in California or Arizona—where it's warm."

"It's warm in old Mexico, too. And they're not so particular down there."

"Mr. Lee, are we ever going to stop running?"

Bob Lee pushed back his hat and glared at me. "Stop anytime you want, Tom. You're a man. But if you stick, you stick on my terms."

At that moment I yearned to be free of both Kanaka Bill and Bob Lee. But I was also unsure of myself. I said, "Just asking. It's coming February and we're still on the dodge and still sleeping on the ground."

Bob Lee replied, "You better ask Kanaka Bill about that. He's callin' the turns." And with that he tipped his hat back down over his eyes and fell asleep.

Pulling my coat close around me to ward off the cold, I fixed my eyes on the distant buttes. The waiting was worse than the running. We had unsaddled the horses and staked them where they could nibble the sparse, dry grass. Ahead lay some of the most inhospitable of western land. High mesas and deep canyons cut from the rock by rivers like the Green, Colorado, and Dirty Devil. I had learned about these places from Monty Nickel, who called them the "slickrocks"—a trackless wasteland, thousands of square miles and no water you could drink.

Monty had said, "It's no place for honest men. A hellhole they call the Sinbad and Robbers' Roost. It's all rocks and rattlesnakes."

While Bob Lee slept I lay huddled against the tree and kept watch. Watching was second nature now. We were always expecting a man with a gun to rise up from behind a rock and start shooting. In addition to a money belt, Emily Nickel had made a holster for my revolver. I now carried the gun on my belt—the butt slanting forward on the left hip for a cross draw.

I had practiced, too. I was nowhere as fast as Bob Lee. But he'd said I was fast enough. Then he had laughed, saying, "Now all you got to do is learn to hit what you shoot at."

As I lay there I reached inside my coat and lifted the old gun from its holster. Emily had done a fine job. The weapon slipped from the smooth leather as if greased. As I perfected my draw I kept my eyes on a small white rock about fifteen feet in front of me. The secret, Mr. Lee had explained, was to draw and fire immediately. He'd said, "Concentrate on the target, not your sights. Learn to make your hits as the gun is coming up."

In the hunting camp I had learned to hit tin cans thrown into the air. To do that you only had to wait until the can reached the top of its arc. At that instant it was stationary and fairly easy to hit. The real test was to hit the can two or three more times before it landed. I didn't believe it could be done until Bob Lee did it.

As I practiced my draw Bob Lee awoke and lay there watching me. Seeing him, I felt a bit foolish and holstered my Colt.

"Go ahead," he said, "you're gettin' pretty handy with that old cannon. Just don't expect me to lie here asleep when someone's wavin' a gun around."

I was surprised by his remark. "I never pointed it at you."

"Course not. But I know you're gettin' edgy. This runnin' and not knowin' gets hard on a man. Maybe you'll break, then rub me out and give up."

I stared at Bob Lee. "What ever made you think a thing like that?"

He smiled. "What ever made you think of cuttin' your losses?"

Much as I was ashamed to admit it, even to myself, that thought had occurred to me. I felt ashamed and then angry that Bob Lee had been able to read my innermost thoughts.

I said, "Don't worry about me. I owe you a big debt and we're still partners, aren't we?"

"Yes, kid, we're partners. But partners sometimes think of their own skins first. I've been in too many tight places not to know that."

"Well," I said, "I've been looking out for us both while you slept. Let's keep moving. The horses need a drink."

Lee agreed and we had saddled and were heading south again inside of fifteen minutes. Our progress, however, became ever slower. Mr. Lee was following a faint trail but the tracks grew increasingly difficult to follow across the rocky ground.

In the bleak winter light the trail faded to a few light-colored scratches on the rock. Cattle had wandered on and off the trail and, to me, there was no telling which was the right route.

"Are we lost?" I asked shortly before dark.

Bob Lee glanced at me impatiently. "No, but like the feller said, 'I been confused a few times.' I never saw nothin' like this before. Men get through this but I ain't sure how."

We had followed numerous wrong turnings in the twisting labyrinth of canyons. Often I felt we were just riding up one blind gulch after another.

All that was being accomplished was to twist ourselves farther and farther into a rockbound maze. There was no assurance we could even find our way back. That night we made a dry camp under a rock ledge nearly a thousand feet tall.

High up on the reddish sandstone I saw some Indian markings. There was a big drawing of a man with disks in place of hands. And beside him was a boxy-looking creature that Bob Lee thought was a beetle.

"There's a feller wringin' his hands over a beetle," said Lee ruefully. "What's a little thing like a dozen mad Chinese and a Kanaka tracker compared to findin' a bug across your trail?"

I said, "I'm going to try to climb to the top of this mesa. Maybe I can find water and some better grass."

It was a waste of strength, for as I wandered at the base of the great stone fortress, I found that there was no way to its top. I hiked back into our dry camp about sunset.

"This place spooks me, Mr. Lee. There's no way to the top of this butte and I'm not even sure there's a way around it. The horses haven't had a drink since first thing this morning."

"That won't kill 'em. They can go till tomorrow night without it hurtin' 'em. The weather is cool and they ain't workin' hard."

In the morning we set out again. Mr. Lee followed the scratches he took for the marks left by shod horses. There was little grass. Here and there a twisted juniper writhed up from a fissure in the rocks. A few desert shrubs clung to the ledges high above us. But the forage in the canyons was insufficient to keep a rabbit alive.

Mr. Lee's mood grew increasingly black. Finally he said, "Let's stop here. I'll mind the horses while you scour around these ledges for water."

It was midafternoon when I set out. I climbed a dozen rock slopes to see if there was a natural tank of water hiding at the base of one of the cliffs. I found no water but in one hollowed-out place I found the skeleton of an Indian. He must have been lying there for a hundred years. The bleached bones shattered at my touch.

Not only had I found nothing but I had difficulty just finding my way back to Bob Lee. Once I found him I said, "Didn't find anything but a dead Indian. He's been there since Noah."

I looked at our good horses. They were standing quietly with their heads hanging. They looked poorly. I guess we all did. We were lost in the slickrock.

CHAPTER 13

On our second morning in the slickrock we had just enough water left to make us each a cup of tea. As we finished the last of that I asked, "How far do you guess we're into this place?"

Mr. Lee said, "I don't know. We backed up and switched over so many times I lost all track. I made a mistake, Tom. I come into this godforsaken place on hearsay. What we need is a guide."

For the first time I could remember Bob Lee sounded truly discouraged. "What did you hear?" I asked, trying to apply what Lee himself had taught me.

"There's supposed to be three trails into here. The one we tried to find from Green River and two others from the south and west. There's not much water. But there is some seeps back in caves under the ledges. But you couldn't even find one of them."

I replied, "We could try going back the way we came. The horses could find the way and we could take more time looking for water. They'll be in tough shape if they have to go all the way back to that last spring."

Lee smiled through the stubble on his worn face. "Guess you're practicin' what I been preachin'. That's good. You go back down this canyon and look for water. I'll look around here, just keepin' our horses in sight."

I agreed and, shouldering my rifle, set off down the canyon. As I walked I examined the sheer rock faces rising above me. Somewhere there had to be a way up. There was supposed to be grass and water on top of some of the mesas. At that moment grass and water were more valuable than the money belt sagging around my waist.

After I'd gone about two miles the canyon widened into a small valley. It was a barren place where only greasewood and thorny desert shrubs could exist. There was no grass. But as I studied the surrounding cliffs I saw what might have been smoke stains on one of the rock cliffs. Perhaps,

I guessed, there was a cave up there where men had camped—a cave with water.

In fifteen minutes I stood below the smudged ledge studying it for a possible approach. As I poked among the broken boulders below it a white-rumped antelope ground squirrel dashed for cover. If that lowly rodent could make his living here, I decided, I should at least be able to find a cave.

I began looking more carefully at the forbidding cliff. It wasn't as smooth as it had first appeared from a distance. There were many fissures and irregularities among the ledges. Here and there bushes clung to the rock walls. Then, amid some boulders the size of wagon boxes, I found a peculiar treasure. Although bleached and badly decomposed I found lying on the ground a pile of horse manure.

It might have been left by a stray that later died in this graveyard. But the manure was significant enough to make me look further. My search was rewarded. Behind another rock lay the shattered remnants of a whiskey bottle. The broken glass was partially covered with windblown dust but it was still sharp and bright. Someone had been here not too long ago.

My search was renewed in earnest. Soon I found some scratches on the rocks. It was not a trail, just a winding way up the rock wall. By walking along roughened creases, then stepping onto ledges, I found the cave within ten minutes. Inside I found ample signs of previous occupants: empty cans and bottles along with shreds of old newspapers and charred bones. It reminded me of entering a strange home and feeling uncomfortable because no one was there.

Horses had been kept in the rear of the cave. A seep there trickled down through the massive rock overhead to fill a small tank. The tank had been scraped out, then lined with flat rocks by the hand of some man. But because there were ancient Indian drawings on the rocks, plus some much more recent and obscene artwork, I could not definitely date my benefactor. The water was sweet and very cold. I drank my fill while feeling guilty about our thirsty horses back up the canyon.

Before leaving I examined the cave thoroughly. Half buried in soft earth at the back of the cave I found some charred canvas that had been partly unearthed by rodents. Pulling it from the sandy soil, I found that it was a half-burned express pouch, the kind railroads and banks used to carry money. There was no money in the pouch but there were some paper binders banks use to fasten stacks of bills together. Obviously I had stumbled upon the hideout of some of the Robbers' Roost outlaws.

Being alone there made me apprehensive. But before leaving I examined the area around the cave's mouth. On one side there were many whitish marks on the rock. Horses had somehow been coaxed up onto a ledge four feet above the cave's entrance. From there they had been driven or led up the side of the cliff to the top of the mesa. It was only a way, not a trail. In places the horses had to step across an abyss to reach the next ledge. Some ledges were hardly wide enough to accommodate a single horse while on others a team could have passed with ease.

I lingered just long enough on the mesa top to see that despite its desolate and windswept appearance there was grass. I also found a tiny spring. Heaven!

While descending I looked down the hundreds of feet onto the rock-strewn valley floor. I saw there the broken bones of horses that had slipped and fallen.

Mr. Lee was forted up in some rocks overlooking our camp when I returned. He was smoking his pipe and looking about as glum as I ever saw him look.

"I found it!" I yelled when he waved to me.

"No! Water? Grass?"

"Plenty. And better yet, I found a cave where we can hold off Kanaka Bill and the Chinese Army if need be." I told him about the cave and the evidence for calling it an "outlaws' cave."

Within the hour we had packed and were en route to the cave. At first Mr. Lee was reluctant to move into the bandits' cave. He said it was bad tactics, like retreating onto a peninsula without having the Navy around to take you off. In the end I convinced him that the cave was a place we could both defend and be safe from ambush. There was good grass on top of the mesa and the horses needed a rest.

"We could fort up here for a week," I said. "The rest will do us all good. There's a little deer sign up there, too. If we can get a deer we'll have plenty of fresh meat."

"Whew!" Lee exclaimed. "Aren't you sick of eatin' deer meat? Back in Nickel's camp I thought I'd gag on the stuff."

Before leaving the hunting camp we had purchased some bacon, dried beans, and a few other staples. Mr. Lee could have the bacon and I'd eat fresh venison.

After a couple of days in the cave I learned that wintering in one can be miserable. The smoke never left the place without first filling the premises. Our eyes were red and watering from smoke and we smelled like wild Indians after cooking and trying to keep warm over an open fire.

The coolness of the rocks turned icy cold by early morning. Our bones began to ache. Also, because Mr. Lee insisted that two horses must always be kept in the cave for emergencies, the cavern's overall aroma grew increasingly foul.

Mr. Lee dug up the cave's dirt floor looking for outlaw treasure. He did find a ten-dollar gold piece and a token from a saloon in Butte. But that was the extent of the booty. I preferred taking the horses up onto the mesa and spending the days there.

The mesa top covered about a section. There was grass, sage, and scattered junipers. The view from up there was unobstructed. I could see the Book Cliffs nearly a hundred miles away and even farther off, but to the south, the La Sal Mountains' snowy caps gleamed. More important to us was the fact that we could see anyone coming into our vicinity.

Mr. Lee insisted that we make careful observations. He wished aloud that he had taken Monty Nickel's field glasses. The constant need for watchfulness and its associated worries appeared to be bothering him more than it did me. And it bothered me plenty.

One morning he said, "I wish those outlaws had been men enough to leave a bottle of whiskey behind." Mr. Lee got edgy without whiskey.

There was no rest in the cave, only waiting for the unknown. Years later I heard a survivor of the Wild Bunch say, "When you're on the run every pissant crawlin' under your blanket at night sounds like a posse." I know the feeling.

Tending the horses did help pass the time. After once coaxing our horses up the slickrock to the mesa top they never again balked. It became our practice to leave a pair on the mesa overnight. First thing in the morning I took the two we'd stabled in the cave overnight up to join their comrades. I'd turn three loose on hobbles and keep the fourth staked. We were never more than twenty minutes away from full flight.

I rode the catch horse around to the overlooks when I inspected the approaches to our hideout.

At times Mr. Lee stayed in the cave and slept while at other times he joined me on the mesa. He was having increasing difficulty sleeping nights. I think it was the lack of whiskey. He napped under his blanket when he came on the mesa. One afternoon I patrolled the overlooks while he slept. I was bored.

As I sat looking out over the empty miles I heard a shot. Sound travels a long way on the quiet southwestern air. The sound seemed to have come from the northeast, the direction from which we had come. But when I looked there, I saw nothing. Nevertheless, I turned around and cantered my horse back to where Mr. Lee was sleeping.

"I heard a shot way off yonder." I pointed north.

Immediately Lee was up. "Let's look," he said, and swung up into the saddle behind me. The big horse carried us to where I'd heard the sound.

We dismounted and I said, "Maybe it was a rock breaking loose and falling into one of the canyons." We often heard shale sliding on the slopes. Occasionally a boulder broke loose and thundered down into the abyss.

Still, I knew what I'd heard wasn't a falling boulder. So, while Mr. Lee stood on a point, listening and watching, I gathered the three other horses and tied them to junipers. He might decide to leave in a hurry.

Returning to Mr. Lee, I found him seated on a rock, his chin resting on folded arms. "You heard somethin' all right. I ain't heard anything myself but there was dust in the air out there a while back."

Lee pointed to a broken section of rocky terrain ten miles off. Try as I would, I saw and heard nothing. Then, after straining ears and eyes for a half hour, I did see something. A flicker of movement at the base of a fawn-colored cliff.

"See, there!" I instinctively checked the load in the breech of my long rifle.

"I see it." Mr. Lee stood. "It could be wild horses. But we couldn't see just one horse this far off. Whatever it is, it's movin' too fast to be herded cattle. That's mounted men over there!"

As if to prove his opinion, a second shot rolled out. There was no mistaking it. Mr. Lee said, "Looks like we're gonna have company."

"What makes you think they're comin' here?" I could not see the moving mass clearly enough to call its direction.

Lee said, "They're comin'."

Fifteen minutes later a horse suddenly ran over a rise in the rock two miles distant. The horse was packed but running loose. A rider next appeared and chased the packhorse down a canyon, coming in our direction.

"Still think we're not havin' company?" Mr. Lee asked.

I said nothing but continued to watch. As I did so the lone rider pulled up behind an outcropping of rock. He was only a mile off and I saw plainly that he held a rifle.

He had waited no more than ten minutes when two mounted men, riding abreast, trotted into view. I saw the rifleman take aim and then wait for his targets to come nearer. My stomach tightened. Then he fired five shots as fast as he could pump his Winchester's lever. I heard the bullets smack into the rock walls around the two pursuers. While the gunfire still echoed down the canyon the riders wheeled their horses and ran.

"There's a cool customer," said Bob Lee. "He might've been way ahead to just drop those two. They'll be back as soon as they get some help."

As we watched, the lone rider casually mounted his horse and rode in our direction. The packhorse, which had stopped and waited beyond the battle, fell in before him.

Mr. Lee said, "That saddle horse is travelin' on heart. Shame to use a horse so."

I said, "He's heading for the cave. He could have enough food and cartridges on the packhorse to hold out for a month."

Then, just as the lone horseman was passing under our vantage point, there were more gunshots. The saddle horse sat down in the dirt, whinnying. The rider barely jumped clear as the horse fell over on its side. The man jerked his rifle free of the saddle scabbard and dropped behind his dying horse. As he did so, four mounted men burst from a side canyon and charged down on him. There was a burst of shooting and one man fell from his horse. The packhorse went down, kicking. We saw bullets throwing up dust all around the besieged rifleman.

The posse had dismounted and were firing from behind boulders. They were nearly invisible to their intended victim. But, looking down, we saw them clearly. They all had rifles and were aiming and firing carefully.

"That boy had better give up," said Bob Lee. "He ain't got a chance."

"Maybe we ought to help him," I suggested.

"Nope, that's his war. Let him fight it."

As the fitful gun battle continued the two men who had been initially turned back again appeared. This time they were moving on foot and took a flanking position on the lone gunman's right.

"They'll get him now," said Bob Lee. "He ain't got enough rocks to hide behind."

I hoped the man would surrender. Anyone could see that with both of his horses down and being badly outnumbered, he was finished. Then I saw something else. The two men who had just moved in on the right were dressed in black.

"Mr. Lee, those two are Chinese!"

"Are you sure?"

"Sure!" I could see a queue hanging down one man's back. "Look at the pigtail on that one." I slid my long rifle out over the rocks and cocked it.

Even as I fired I heard Mr. Lee say, "Pour it to 'em. They're really lookin' for us."

This was the first time I had ever aimed my rifle at a man. I could have shot them all, just like a buffalo hunter casually picking off a milling herd. But I could not shoot to kill.

Aiming carefully, I planted a slug a few inches from one man's head. He was peppered with fragments of rock and hot lead. He howled as he rolled away from his cover and I saw his face. It was contorted with fear. I fired again and the man jumped up and ran. He had not gone two steps before Bob Lee dropped him.

"They're fish in a barrel, Tom. Plug 'em. Don't fool around!" Even as he was yelling at me I saw Bob Lee shoot and send the second Chinese sprawling and clutching his belly.

Firing more quickly, I sent bullets whining by the heads of the remaining possemen. I wanted them to clear out before Bob Lee could shoot them down.

He saw what I was trying to do. "Damn you, Tom! Do that again and I'll shoot you!" Bob Lee began firing rapidly at the lawmen scampering out of sight into the side canyon.

Mr. Lee meant what he had said. I raised my rifle and sat up, watching him and the scene below. And as I sat there the memory of his threat sent a cold chill through me. I think it was at that moment, with the sounds of the gun battle still ringing in our ears, that I realized I was truly alone. Bob Lee might have saved me but he had also used me. If I was ever to be free of this bloody business I would have to do it alone.

I said, "I'm going down and see if that fellow needs help."

Mr. Lee's face retained the fierce set that I'd first seen just before the bunkhouse fight. He glared at me, then said, "Go ahead, I'll cover you from here." Then he turned and looked down at the battle scene.

As I slowly made my way off the mesa I reminded myself of a new danger. The man I was going to help was probably an outlaw himself. I must be as careful of him as I now knew I would have to be of Mr. Lee.

The man was sitting in the back of the cave when I entered. He was young, just a few years older than I, with thick brown hair and a week's growth of beard. Strangely, he was wearing a well-tailored suit that was now in bad repair. His white shirt was stained and he had lost or thrown away his collar and necktie. He wore ankle-length dress shoes with pointed toes and high military heels. The shoes were dusty and scuffed. This man looked like a young banker who had suddenly taken a trip into the badlands.

"Howdy, friend." The man smiled but did not move. His right hand was stuffed deep into his jacket pocket.

"Hello yourself. Are you hurt?"

"Just my pride. Those fellows jumped me about fifteen miles back. I don't know where they came from—specially the Chinamen. All of a sudden there they were, on my tail. They must be bandits."

There was an amused twinkle in the man's eyes when he called his pursuers "bandits."

I said, "Those Chinese weren't bandits, exactly."

The man smiled, saying, "Whoever they were, they were not friendly. This ain't friendly, either. But I've had a sawed-off forty-four aimed at your belly since you come in. Now set aside that rifle and show me if you're otherwise heeled." He produced a big Colt revolver from his pocket and aimed it at me. The gun's barrel had been cut off short and the hammer was of the slip variety. All the man had to do was let his thumb slide from the hammer and I'd catch a .44 slug.

"Look, mister, it was my idea to help you. There's two of us, Bob Lee and me. We're hunters, not sheriffs or anyone wanting trouble." As I spoke I unfastened my belt buckle and carefully slid my holstered revolver off my belt and onto the ground. "That's it," I said, "no more guns."

"Good!" The young man stood and walked over to me. He was nearly six feet tall, lean and graceful. He said, "I'm Sam Doran the railroad man." He grinned.

"I'm Tom Lavering. I'm a ranch hand and part-time hunter."

"What do you hunt?"

"My partner and I have been hunting deer and antelope in those roan hills north of here. Before that we worked for the Honeybee outfit west of the Salt Lake."

Doran slipped his revolver back into his coat pocket. "I was passing through the country lookin' over routes for the railroad. Don't think they'd come this way. But it never hurts to see for yourself." Doran was smiling, almost laughing at his ludicrous story.

He continued, "Now I'm afoot. You been keepin' horses in here?"

Before I could answer there was a slight noise. Doran whirled to face Bob Lee. His hand was jammed into his coat pocket again. Mr. Lee carried his carbine in his left hand while in his right he held his revolver. The two men faced each other; neither man smiled.

"Mr. Lee," I said breathlessly, "this is Sam Doran. He's got a hideout gun in his pocket!"

"It's cocked, too," said Doran, smiling.

"That so?" Bob Lee didn't smile. He said, "That's a poor way to thank the men what saved your neck."

"Well, sir, that's right, but there are so many outlaws in this district a feller can't be too careful. Now, if you'll put up your gun I'll take my hand out of my pocket." Doran's smile faded. "Otherwise we might kill each other."

Silently Mr. Lee lowered the hammer of his revolver. On his face was an expression I had never seen before. But I recognized it. Bob Lee was a little afraid of Sam Doran.

But I also saw that Doran wasn't taking Bob Lee lightly, either. There was something sinister about Doran. Perhaps it was combined in his looks and the tone of his voice. He was not afraid and he was dangerous.

As Mr. Lee holstered his revolver Doran let the hammer of his revolver click down softly. Doran said, "A good choice, friend."

Doran continued, "Glad I didn't have to ruin this suit. Had it tailor-made up in Seattle last month. Pity to treat it like this." He brushed dust from the lapels.

Mr. Lee said, "Yes, it's hard to get blood out of cloth like that."

Ignoring that, Doran said, "I understand you're partners; pretty far off your range, ain't you? Huntin' here don't amount to much."

"We're movin'," said Mr. Lee. "I heard there's plenty of deer down in the Henrys. Thought we'd see for ourselves."

"Uh, uh." Doran nodded and leaned against the cave wall. "Well, we take a man's word down here. Would you sell me a horse?"

"No." Bob Lee was frowning and sizing up Doran at the same time.

"I see." Doran frowned, too. "I can pay very well. I'll prove it if Tom here will help me carry up my outfit." Then Doran's face took on a wolfish look. "I can also guide the two of you out of here; point you in any direction you've a mind to go. That posse's gonna be back with help in a day, maybe sooner. Make up your minds, gents."

Leaving my guns behind, I went down to where Doran's packhorse lay in the dirt. Under the canvas pack cover I found two duffel bags, neither heavy, and a nearly new camping outfit. There were cartridges in cardboard boxes and, surprisingly, six wine bottles wrapped in straw.

When Doran unpacked in the cave we saw that they contained French wine. He snapped the neck from one of the bottles against a rock and handed the sharp-edged container to Bob Lee, saying, "It's been shook. It'll be better when it's had a chance to rest. But have a snort anyway."

Mr. Lee took a long swallow from the bottle, then handed it to me. I had never tasted French wine before. It had a musty taste and burned on the way down.

"Bought this out of a sportin' house in Price. Twenty-five bucks a bottle," Doran said.

Mr. Lee gave a noncommittal grunt. I knew he would have preferred whiskey. The two men eyed each other. Our situation was explosive and, unless a miracle occurred, there would be trouble if we stayed together in the cave for long. When the wine bottle was emptied Sam Doran tossed it out of the cave's mouth. And, as I expected, Bob Lee exploded the bottle with his Colt before it struck the ground.

Although his lips were white Doran grinned and said, "Nice trick."

Mr. Lee raised his eyebrows at Doran's choice of the word "trick." I started to say something calming but thought better of it. I didn't want to find myself between two vicious dogs.

We cooked dinner and Doran enhanced our poor fare with bottles of fancy sauces, jars of pickles, and tins of fruit and jam from his camp supplies.

Mr. Lee observed, "You live high, Mr. Doran. You must have been planning this trip for some time."

Doran didn't reply but passed us a jar of hard candy. "Have a mint," he said. "I think we'd better get together on this business of a horse."

"No sale," said Mr. Lee.

"None needed," replied Doran. He took a cigar from a fragrant cedar box and passed the box on to us. Then he said, "By the time you find your way out of here, those fellows we smoked today will have killed you a couple of times over. Folks don't much care what happens in the Roost; just so long as it don't go beyond here."

"All right," said Bob Lee. "I'll make you an offer. You take us through here and point us for the Henry Mountains an' I'll provide a good horse. But once we split the horse goes with us."

Sam Doran quickly agreed and we spent the rest of the evening drinking wine and getting our packs rearranged. There was more gear now than the single packhorse could carry. All of Doran's fancy groceries were buried at the rear of the cave. We threw away our few non-essentials and loaded the rest into canvas panniers.

The two men, still observing their brittle truce, agreed it would be foolish to leave the wine. They proceeded to drink it. Each man took a bottle and retired to his bed with a cigar. But they remained wary. Mr. Lee could have finished all the wine. But he nursed one bottle until we all turned in. He would not be shot in his cups; he was too smart for that.

For his part, Doran smoked more than he drank. As he smoked he talked. "You know, two of them fellers was Chinamen out there today. Never saw that before. They stay clear of the law. I think that pair was lookin' for two men that shot up a fan-tan parlor up in Wyoming. I heard they took the bank with 'em."

CHAPTER 14

Doran's mention of our robbing the Fan-Tan Parlor drew blank looks from Mr. Lee and me. Seeing them, Doran grinned. "It's fine with me, boys. You're just a couple of deer hunters as far as I care."

"And you're the chief right-of-way engineer for the Denver and Rio Grande!" Bob Lee took a puff on his cigar.

"When that title suits me," replied Doran. "But mostly I'm a man of independent means and I'm turning in."

Without saying it we all silently agreed that what a man really did for a living was his business. Curiosity could be dangerous. We all turned in, each one of us alone with his thoughts.

As I lay there I thought about the events of the past few months. I remembered Chun Kwo, ferret-sleek and smiling at the suckers entering his casino. Then I recalled the fear on his face when Bob Lee and I robbed him. I remembered my horror at seeing the old Chinese lady lying on the floor in a pool of blood.

I tried to contrast that nightmare with my happy memory of dancing with Georgia Willets at the Thanksgiving dance. These events had no connection yet they were bound together in a growing tragedy. Yancey DeRoot had helped me and been destroyed as a result. Monty Nickel took us in. In the Book Cliffs I was a free hunter and felt safe and more relaxed than I had in several weeks. Still, Rebecca Nickel knew something was wrong and urged me to free myself of Robert Lee.

That had to be done. I had liked Mr. Lee, even revered him. Nonetheless, the path he was leading us down could only end in disaster. And I could do nothing, for the immediate alternative to Robert Lee was Sam Doran. And Doran was the most dangerous man I had ever met.

In the morning I fell in behind the other two men as Sam Doran led the way into the sandstone wasteland. I have not returned to that desolate region in over thirty years but, even today, its cruelties recur in my nightmares.

There was no water. Our beautiful horses grew gaunt and haggard from the lack of that and decent forage. As we rode, their shod hooves rattled and scraped up one slickrock chute and down another. Doran must have been in this rocky jumble many times to have found his way through it with such relative ease. I watched him by the hour. He rode easily, his incongruous "city" hat pulled down over his eyes.

Once when we were alone Mr. Lee whispered to me, "Notice that he packed that duffel bag on his saddle? Do you think he's got the loot from his last job in there?"

I replied, "He told me it was a clean shirt and some fresh underwear." But few men take such care of their clean linen. I had also guessed that Sam Doran was carrying a bag full of money.

If our suspicions were correct we had found a guide but increased the size of the posse chasing us. I wondered if there were even worse man hunters on our track than Kanaka Bill.

I said to Mr. Lee when we paused to rest the horses, "Do you think Bill would take a payoff? Maybe if we left him some money he'd take it and go home."

Mr. Lee snorted, saying, "About two-thirds of the sheriffs will grab a bribe. But Bill don't need the money. He does this because he likes it. An' a man that likes his work is usually good at it."

At dusk we made a dry camp in a hollow at the base of a great sandstone ledge. We poured a little water from our meager stock into our hats and let the horses drink. They were still sucking and slopping their tongues around long after the water was gone.

"We'll strike a seep about noon tomorrow," promised Doran. "There's some grass and wood, too. We can have a fire."

The last statement was Doran's way of saying that we were going to spend this long winter's night in the cold. About midnight Bob Lee got up and began clumping around.

He said, "Damn! My feet are froze. Couldn't you have found us a better spot than this to camp in?"

"Sure," said Doran, "if you two had robbed a fan-tan parlor in the Hawaiian Islands. Then we could've slept on the beach and drank coconut-milk punch to keep cool. Tomorrow we'll have a better spot."

"Let's not go callin' turns you don't know nothin' about," said Bob

Lee. "All Tom and I want is to get through this damned place so we can hunt in the Henry Mountains."

Doran mumbled, "Uh, uh."

Before daylight I had another disturbing thought: Sam Doran was surely as interested in the contents of our money belts as we were in his carefully guarded canvas bag. I sat up shivering in my thin blanket. Occasionally I got up and walked around but that apparently made Doran nervous, so I stopped it.

Because there was no grass for the horses we had tied them all to a lariat stretched between two rocks. In the gloom I saw Bob Lee sitting up in his blanket and watching the horses. He probably was thinking that Doran might try to steal a horse and abandon us.

But Doran made no such attempt. And as the first weak light of a winter dawn crept down the ledge, we prepared to leave. For breakfast each of us chewed on a piece of venison jerky and had a sip of water. At least when it's winter in the slickrock a man isn't too thirsty.

"I'll bet this is a furnace in the summer," I said.

"By August," said Doran, "the rock is heated clear through. It never cools off, even at night. The only place I was ever in that was hotter was Chicago in the summer. We'd taken some cows to the stockyards and was waitin' for our pay. I spent half of mine on cold beer."

"What did you do with the rest?" asked Bob Lee.

"Bought me this Colt's forty-four an' had it smoothed up by a first-rate gunsmith. With a gun like this and a lot of practice a man don't have to tend other folks' cows."

It was afternoon before we reached the hidden seep of water Sam Doran had promised. After the chilling night the sun had warmed the sandstone wastes and made us thirsty. The horses drank greedily and when they had finished we staked them on an adjacent patch of dried grass.

Doran said, "We'll camp here. It's early but the horses want a feed and more water. We can make up the time tomorrow."

"Ain't we about out of this place?" Mr. Lee asked.

"I been savin' the best for last." Doran grinned but did not explain.

We spent another long night but here we had water, grass for the horses plus firewood for ourselves. Each of us took his turn replenishing the fire and keeping watch. No one slept much, partly from the cold and partly from mutual distrust.

At daylight we were riding again. As the sun rose we saw towering in the distance the four great peaks of the Henry Mountains.

"There you are, boys," said Doran, pointing southwest. "Those are the Henrys."

"Then why are we headin' away from 'em?" Lee snapped.

"There's a little problem of the Dirty Devil to cross. It's a devil, I'll say. Mean canyon and a stream of water so dirty it should be plowed. This time of year, though, crossin' will be easy. It's the canyon. I only know one place to cross. Follow me, gents."

Doran rode on. He seldom stopped to rest the horses or let them snatch a few mouthfuls of the sparse grass we occasionally passed.

This also provoked Mr. Lee, for, despite his faults, abusing horses wasn't one of them. Once he said, "Hey, Doran, let's give the horses fifteen minutes on this grass."

"They ate all night. If they're the horses you been claimin' they are, they can go a damn sight farther than this." Doran slapped his mount with the reins and the weary horse picked up the pace.

Mr. Lee didn't reply but I saw the angry set of his shoulders. He rode behind Doran, herding the packhorse between them as we descended a narrow, rocky gorge.

This was the "best" that Doran had been saving until last. To reach the river the white-eyed horses almost sat on their haunches and slid down the steep gorge. Only the scratches left on the rocks by other horses induced me to follow Doran.

I followed him, inching myself crab-like down the steep trail, bracing my feet as best I could. For two hundred yards we slid more than we walked.

At last, however, we came tumbling and stumbling onto the banks of the Dirty Devil River. In winter it was only a foul-looking desert creek with a silted bed. Doran warned us that some of the dried mud flats concealed quicksand. We crossed the river easily and then began struggling up the canyon on the other side. Somewhere along the way my horse threw a shoe.

Bob Lee was furious with me for not noticing and retrieving the lost shoe. "What did you think, that there'd be a blacksmith waitin' on the riverbank?"

"No, sir, I didn't notice. I checked his shoes this morning. But I was having trouble on those rocks myself."

"All right, damn it, start thinking how you are gonna get that pony across the desert and into the mountains. He'll bust his feet on these damn rocks."

"I'll walk partway." I was miserable and yet I felt the guilt wasn't completely mine. The horses' shoes were all worn.

"Lay off the kid," said Sam Doran. "We'll make it into Hanksville easy. You can get your horses shod there."

"Our deal was the Henrys, not Hanksville," said Bob Lee.

"Hanksville's the only place I can get horses. In fact, there will be two good ones waitin' there for me."

Sam Doran reined in, then turned his horse to face Bob Lee. He rolled a cigarette, casually lighting it before speaking. "There's friends in Hanksville. You rest there a day and then go to the Henrys or hell—that's up to you. But I taken you through the badlands like I said. You'd still be in there if it wasn't for me."

Hanksville, when we reached it just after dark, was a tiny collection of mean shacks under a few spindly trees. The leaves had long since fallen from the trees and their branches seemed to claw up at the darkening sky.

Mr. Lee and I waited in the shadows beyond the village while Doran rode in to appraise the situation. He was gone for over an hour and when he returned we could smell whiskey on his breath.

Doran said, "It's O.K. There's a woman here who will fix us a hot meal and give us a dry bed. Tom can get his horse shod in the morning. It'll be a hundred dollars apiece plus any supplies you take."

I didn't have to see Bob Lee's face to know how angry he was. "Was you gone all that time just havin' a drink and figurin' how much we was good for?"

"These folks earn every penny they get. You won't need to worry about a trainload of Chinamen comin' down from Price five minutes after you leave town."

Then Sam Doran led us into Hanksville, Utah. We ate in the kitchen of a small home on the village outskirts. The woman said hardly a word but kept by her stove frying steaks and chicken along with plenty of spuds and onions. Doran had a quart of whiskey beside his place, which he shared with us, pouring shots into our coffee cups.

A scraggly-looking middle-aged man was introduced as Eph Pease. He was the woman's husband and took station beside the table. We told him what was needed and after each item Pease said, "Yessiree, we'll get her."

For dessert we were served deep-dish apple pie covered with thick, rich cream. I had three helpings, saying, "As long as I'm paying a hundred dollars a night I might as well get filled up."

Later, as we finished our coffee, we heard a door open and a feminine voice. The lady asked for "Johnny" but Doran grinned and said, "That's me." He got up and hurried into the parlor.

After Sam left, Mr. Lee said to our host, "What can you do in that line for us?"

"Oh, I'm sorry, sir. That lady's an old friend of Mr. Doran's. She's not what you might think, not at all."

"I think what I want to think," said Lee, scowling.

Hard and lumpy as my bed was, I found sleeping in any kind of bed an almost forgotten luxury. Our host, Eph Pease, had to shake me awake the next morning.

"Better get up. The wife has breakfast about cooked. I got your horse shod overnight. Matter of fact, we checked 'em all. They need new shoes all the way around."

Bob Lee grunted. "Can you get 'em done for us?"

"Yes, sir. Take a while, though. Can't get you out of here till sundown. Lessen you want to leave 'fore dark."

"Will we be bothered here?" I asked.

"Noo," Pease hemmed. "We had some news in the night; not good. No, sir, not good at all. But I think you'll be fine here today. Just stay inside. I could get you a bottle. Say the word."

Saying the "word" in Hanksville meant that our enforced visit there cost us over four hundred dollars. I decided the money wasn't in being an outlaw but in working for them.

Sam Doran was seated behind a plate full of ham and eggs when we went in for breakfast. As she had at dinner, the woman stayed by her stove, silently cooking. She hardly turned her face to look at us. I think we frightened the poor creature half to death.

"What's this bad news?" Mr. Lee asked, sitting down.

Doran replied, "There's some men in the district we don't know. They've got guns and good horses. No one's been bothered, they're keepin' to themselves."

"How many?" Mr. Lee asked.

"Don't know, maybe six. Two of 'em are Chinamen."

"You know the Kanaka?" asked Bob Lee. "Is he with 'em?"

"Kanaka Bill?" For the first time since I'd met him, Sam Doran showed surprise. He asked, "Is he after you? I've heard of him but never seen him."

"We worked with him last fall. Tom saw him out in Brown's Hole last November." Mr. Lee cut off a piece of ham and stirred it into his eggs.

"Eph!" Sam Doran beckoned and our obsequious host hastened to his side. "Kanaka Bill may be with those fellers. Tell what you heard last night."

Our host looked at the floor and twitched uncomfortably. "Feller come in last evening, after you boys turned in. Can't say his name. He was in a hurry. Traded horses and left quick. Anyhow, he said he'd heard of these strangers in the country. Said there'd been a shootin' scrape in some huntin' camp up near Cisco. Guessed these strangers was mixed in that; he didn't know for sure. But he said there was men killed. He said that was for sure."

My thoughts immediately called up Monty Nickel's camp. When we left it, the camp had been near Cisco. "Who was killed?"

"Don't know." Eph wiped his mouth. "Feller said it was like the regulators' work. They hid in the brush till sunup, then shot everyone who came out to pee."

Mr. Lee continued eating but listened carefully. For my part, I couldn't eat another bite. I got up to go outside.

Sam Doran stopped me. "Don't go out till Eph says so. It's light now. We'll just stay in today, catch up on our knittin'."

I sat numbly at my place, waiting until Eph said it was safe to go back to our shack. When we were alone there Mr. Lee said, "We might've expected somethin' like that. I wonder if they shot the women, too."

Surely they would not kill women. Then I recalled the night we shot up the camp. Bob Lee had gunned down everyone in sight, or tried to. There had been no time for introductions. Still, I remembered Pease saying, "Men was killed."

"We should go back there and help them," I said.

"Like hell!" Bob Lee rolled over and sat up on his bunk. The muscles in his shoulders were bunched, ready to fight. "We're stickin' together now; split up and they'll get us sure. How much money you got left?"

Without counting it I guessed, "Fifteen hundred, more or less. Why?"

"We ought to leave the country. South America, maybe Australia."

I said, "I was never sold on going to Mexico."

"Mexico's not far enough now." Bob Lee began pacing the floor. "We got to get where they're never gonna find us."

I asked, "Where is that, exactly?"

The older man looked at me, his face worn from weeks on the dodge and now pale with worry. "I don't know, Tom, not for sure. I got to think, take things a step at a time. Stick with me?"

"Got to." I hoped there was more conviction in my tone than I felt. Bob Lee was a Jonah. But so was I.

By late afternoon we were ready to travel. One by one, Eph led our horses into his decrepit barn and saddled them. We knew there were also two other horses there. Sam Doran was leaving with us, promising to show us the Henry Mountain trail before we parted company.

Soon after sundown there was a knock at our door. Bob Lee opened it, holding his cocked revolver against the boards, ready to shoot. But it was only our craven host.

He said, "All clear. Your horses are ready. Sam's waitin' in the barn."

As we prepared to leave, Eph grinned, looked at the dirt floor, and said, "We didn't figure on you boys stayin' so long. Glad to have you, understand, but it was longer."

"Hell's bells, we was only here twenty-four hours," snapped Lee.

"We taken a big risk havin' you boys. Glad to, but we got to live here."

"How much?"

"Fifty." It was the first time I'd heard Eph Pease say anything positively.

"Tom, shell out." Bob Lee reached into his shirt pocket and threw some bills and change on the dirty bunk. I counted out twenty-five dollars and tossed them beside his.

"Thanks, boys," said Eph, grabbing the money and stuffing it into his pants pocket.

Mr. Lee tucked his rifle under his arm and brushed by our host. "Think nothing of it," he said. I followed him in silence.

The horses were standing in the barn, saddled and tied to posts and rings along the walls. I noticed Sam Doran's animals. Even under a light pack and a stock saddle it was plain that the two animals had been carefully selected for fast traveling.

Sam himself was standing beside a pole stanchion dressed in heavy denims and a new mackinaw coat. He was smiling that peculiar smile I'd first seen in the cave.

Something warned me: Watch out! But I ignored the thought. I followed Mr. Lee to our horses and began untying them. A lantern had been hung conveniently above our horses' heads. Beyond its circle of yellow light Sam Doran's form was indistinct.

Suddenly I knew. I whirled, trying to put the horse between me and Doran. Sam scarcely moved while I was grabbing for my gun and trying to run, all at once.

Doran shot through his mackinaw pocket. For a moment I thought he'd missed and the horse had kicked me. The barn's dirt floor flew up and hit me in the face.

Something was splattering. Damned horse, I thought. Then I realized it was my blood running out and splattering, not the horse. I was still drawing my revolver while the barn exploded: horses whinnying and pulling frantically at their ropes, gun flashes and pandemonium.

Sam Doran put a bullet in the neck of Bob Lee's horse. In the instant while the horse was falling Bob Lee shot Sam Doran three times in the chest. And when Eph Pease peered in around the corner of his barn Lee shot him between the eyes.

The horse I had been preparing to ride was dancing nervously on his tether. His big hooves flicked past my face and I dragged myself away. I continued dragging myself until I reached a corner of the barn, where I sat and watched the blood run from my leg. It surprises you to see how much blood there is in a leg. I don't know how long I watched it bleed until Bob Lee came and stood over me.

"He got you, huh, Tom?"

"Right leg, pretty bad."

Lee was bending down with a piece of cord and a stick in his hand. I thought of myself doing the same thing for that Ute Indian back in Jones' Hole. I felt ashamed for having doubted Bob Lee. Here he was, saving my skin again.

"Now, partner," he said, placing the stick in my hand, "let up on the pressure every half hour or so. If you don't, you'll get gangrene and lose your leg anyway."

Then, with the same bloody hand, he jerked open my coat and the shirt under it. "You won't be needin' this." Bob Lee ripped the money belt from around my waist and tossed it across his shoulder.

I looked at Bob Lee. "Toby Gates took my place, didn't he? Before he showed up I was your choice to ride a horse into Chun Kwo's."

I tried to raise my revolver. But the gun was too heavy and it fell into the straw beside me. Bob Lee ignored me. He was busy rifling through Sam Doran's clothing, taking his money belt and pocket change.

Next, Lee took his saddle and saddlebags off his dead horse. He put them on Doran's horse, apparently deciding it was the best of the remaining mounts. Then he left, leading our packhorse and his remaining bay. I heard the hoofbeats as he galloped out of Hanksville. Fortunately for me, he left my horse and Doran's packhorse.

My leg was beginning to feel as if a hot spike had been thrust into it. But despite the loss of blood and, now, the pain, my head cleared. I began assessing my chances. Whatever Eph Pease had been, he'd surely had more friends in Hanksville than I. Doran probably had friends there, too. But I had no one. I was broke and a common criminal to boot.

I told myself: You've got to get out of here! Then, much as I didn't want to, I pulled my pants partway down and looked carefully at my wounded thigh. What I saw made the arrow cut I'd received in Jones' Hole look like a pinprick.

Doran's bullet had hit me halfway between my right knee and the groin. To my great fortune the slug had gone all the way through without hitting either bone or one of the big arteries in my thigh. The wound was on the upper outside part of my leg. Seeing that, I knew I could still ride. I had to ride.

Finding a bucket of water, I rinsed off my leg. Then I took the cleanest of some horse-collar pads and cut them into large squares. I would make compression bandages from them. My leg would not stand much weight but by using a pitchfork for a staff I got around. It was easy enough to untie Doran's packhorse but climbing into my own saddle was agony. I could not hold my right foot in the stirrup. The blood began leaking out of my pant leg and into my boot.

For a while I rode with my right leg hanging down. But eventually the pain from that became so bad I nearly fainted. I remember swaying in the saddle and clutching the saddle horn to keep from falling off.

It was very cold; maybe that helped me. But finally I had to stop and almost fell from my horse. I judged that I had been riding for about three hours. But I had ridden so slowly because of the pain that Hanksville could not have been more than ten miles behind me.

I lay down on the rocky ground and let the two horses graze while I clutched the reins and lead rope. Although I wanted to stay there forever

I knew I must keep moving. I wanted to reach Monty Nickel's camp and find out what happened to my friends. I also wanted to know about Yancey DeRoot. The hunting camp was the only place where I might find help. I knew, however, that if I didn't find some means of easing the strain on my wounded leg I couldn't ride another mile.

After thinking it over it appeared that a combination sling and splint, hung from the saddle horn, might give my leg the necessary support. As I hopped around the big bay horse hanging on to him for balance, I grudgingly thanked Bob Lee. Had he not chosen a steady animal I could not have escaped.

My long-barreled Remington rifle became useful in a new way. I fastened a length of rope around the grip. Another, shorter, length was tied behind the front sight and a bowline knot added to the rope's free end. Finally I passed the upper rope from the gun barrel down through the loop on the bowline then back up to the saddle horn.

With this rig I could raise or lower the suspended rifle and give just the right amount of support to my leg, my foot being rested on the lower rope. As might be imagined, there were many painful problems with this lash-up and I adjusted it countless times before my wounded leg was comfortable.

Nevertheless, on the night I was shot I rode nearly thirty miles and camped at daylight in the San Rafael Valley south of Green River, Utah.

CHAPTER 15

Somehow I unsaddled the two horses and staked them on a patch of grass. My leg was extremely painful and I was weak from loss of blood. I crawled under a juniper to rest and examine the contents of Sam Doran's pack.

The big canteen I found under the canvas cover was full of slush ice. But from there on his pack was a treasure trove. Not that I found any money; Mr. Lee had carefully removed all of Doran's cash from his corpse.

But there was fresh food plus tins of fruit and corned beef. Doran had four bottles of Bourbon whiskey and I poured a part of one on my wound. Then I dressed it with clean bandages made from his linen.

In a carefully wrapped parcel I found a Smith & Wesson double-action .44 revolver and four boxes of ammunition. Packed with the gun was an open-topped Mexican-style holster and a gun belt filled with cartridges. The Smith was the most beautifully made weapon I had ever touched. The double action was silky and the trigger pull crisp. I immediately replaced my cap-and-ball with this new weapon.

Finally I spread Doran's woolen blankets and fell asleep under them. By the time I awoke the sun had moved far to the west. And it was all but hidden behind heavy clouds that were sprinkling snow across the sage and aromatic rabbit brush.

From what I remembered of my conversations with Doran, he'd said the river ford was just below the town of Green River, Utah. Like most men on the dodge, however, I had an instinctive fear of getting too close to civilization. My plan was to stay south of the town, cross the river, and then ride overland to the northeast and find Nickel's camp.

For many young men of my day, riding a horse was as easy as walking. But riding with a bullet wound in the leg is another matter. I never realized how many muscles, tendons, and joints are involved. My whole body ached from the unaccustomed strain. If the horse broke into a trot the pain was excruciating.

I hid up all day on the San Rafael. It was snowing hard enough to cover my trail from Hanksville. So my chief worry was about being seen around Green River. Except to move the staked horses to fresh grass and get something to eat, I didn't budge until sundown. I forded the Green around midnight. And by sunrise I had put twenty-five miles between me and the river.

By midmorning I had reached some lonely buttes. I took shelter at the base of one, staking the horses once more. I poured more of Doran's whiskey on my leg, pressing the wound as I did so to keep it draining. I knew I'd be doomed if I got an infection.

My greatest asset was to be young and healthy. The months of living in the open had hardened me for my ordeal. In four days I rode over one hundred miles with my leg in a makeshift sling. On a cold afternoon in late February I finally reached Monty Nickel's last camp.

There wasn't much left. The tents had all been burned and charred fragments of canvas hung limply from their blackened poles. Magpies squawked indignantly as they fluttered up from refuse strewn about the camp. The remains of a horse lay where it had been shot, the halter and tie rope still fastened to the skull.

"Hello, the camp!" I called. "Tom Lavering, coming in!" I stopped beside one of the wickiups that had a thread of smoke rising from its roof. I was about to call again when Rebecca Nickel raised the canvas that hung over the door and peered out at me.

"Tom! It is you!" Rebecca hurried out, setting aside the ax she had armed herself with.

"You won't need an ax to fight me off." I handed her the packhorse's lead rope. Then she held my horse while I unfastened the rifle sling and climbed stiffly out of the saddle.

"You're badly hurt!" she exclaimed. "What happened to your friend?"

"I got shot four days ago. My 'friend,' Bob Lee, robbed me and left me for the coyotes afterward."

Rebecca appeared exhausted. There were dark circles under her eyes and fine lines of worry and fear tugging at her mouth. I thought she might weep but she blinked back the tears and smiled at me.

She said, "Come on, let me help you."

I put my arm around her shoulder for support and limped into the wickiup. The smoke inside hurt my eyes and it took a moment before I could see. Then I saw Emily Nickel lying on a cot. She was propped up and although her eyes were open I wasn't sure she recognized me.

"Emily," I asked, "how are you?"

Emily nodded her head slightly and made it clear she felt terrible.

I sat down on a low bench. "What happened?"

"A few days after you left we were raided." Rebecca described how horsemen had galloped into the camp firing revolvers into the tents and wickiups. Monty Nickel was shot as he tried to drag one of the raiders from his saddle. Mitch and Johnny were both killed by a sharpshooter stationed at the edge of the camp.

Rebecca continued, "Emily's mother took her grandson and tried to run away. Two of the men rode her down. She and the little boy were badly trampled. They both died that night."

"Who did this?" I asked.

"The leader was a big man, clean-shaven but swarthy. He looked a bit like a Mexican. But he spoke differently, sort of a singsong. Some of the men with him were Chinese; the rest were white."

I said, "The leader may have been a Hawaiian. Was he riding a big pinto?"

"Yes, he must have been Hawaiian. And he rode a big pinto horse."

I did not tell Rebecca that Kanaka Bill's raid had been in reprisal for the raid Bob Lee and I staged on his camp. But I did say, "They were after us. I'm sorry I wasn't here to help you."

Rebecca said, "It wouldn't have mattered. They were so cool and efficient. We didn't have a chance. Emily was shot by one of them with a shotgun as she hid in her tent." Rebecca looked meaningfully at me and shook her head. She was telling me that Emily Nickel was dying.

Even as we talked Emily drifted between sleep and consciousness. Soon she would fall asleep and never awaken. I would have felt better if she had cursed me and blamed me for this catastrophe.

I asked Rebecca, "How did you escape?"

Rebecca was sitting with her forearms resting on her knees. She was staring at the dirt floor and did not look up as she replied, "I didn't get away. The leader, the Hawaiian, wanted to cut my throat. But one of the other men talked him out of it. He said, 'She's trash, Bill. Like the rest of 'em. But if we kill a white woman people are bound to find out.'

"Bill finally decided the man was right. So I was *only* beaten and then raped by everyone." Rebecca's emphasis on the word "only" was bitterly ironic.

Following the attack, and when she had recovered somewhat, Rebecca walked all the way to Cisco. Cisco was only a couple of railroad shacks on the Denver and Rio Grande tracks. The man there wired a message requesting a doctor but none ever arrived.

Rebecca said, "Perhaps he told them they'd be treating an Indian woman. I also think the railroad is sympathetic to anyone who even appears to be tracking bandits." She nodded toward my leg. "Banditry must be painful."

Weary and heartsick as she was, Rebecca Nickel worked with gentle efficiency to dress my wound. "You have done remarkably well, Tom. The wound is clean. This drainage is normal. But you must rest and give it time to heal."

Being laid up gave me lots of time to think. My first inclination, after my leg healed, was to get as far from Bob Lee, Kanaka Bill, and this part of the West as I could. To the law I was unimportant, just one of hundreds of half-forgotten desperadoes whose names gathered dust in police files. By moving to a new place I could adopt a new name and start living all over.

Then I thought of Yancey DeRoot. Was he dead? I could never forget Georgia Willets or Rebecca, who tended my wound. Neither woman had judged me; instead, they had given me their loyalty. Surely, I reminded myself, these friends were entitled to as much loyalty as I'd given Bob Lee—who had betrayed me. I could not just ride away from my mess. I vowed to recross the Book Cliffs as soon as I could and learn what had happened to Yancey DeRoot.

Bob Lee was also on my conscience. He had been trained to kill for the Union and was commended when he did it. After times changed, Bob Lee did not change with them. Like so many warriors before him, Bob Lee should have died on the last day of the last battle. As his criminal accomplice, I now felt responsible for the damage I had helped him inflict.

I told Rebecca, "Bob Lee isn't so much a bad man as he is a dangerous man. His rules are different than ours."

Rebecca said, "Have you the right to judge him, Tom? Won't he destroy himself?"

I said, "In time. But I am the only one who can find him. I have to try to stop him."

"Oh, Tom! Leave that up to Kanaka Bill. He's obviously an expert at this rotten work. From what I see, you're not, and I don't think you enjoy it."

As my leg healed, Emily Nickel's body crumbled. Rebecca and I took turns sitting with her. Finally she could no longer eat even the thin broth we made for her. In Emily's last hours there was little we could do but sit beside her and hold her thin hand.

Emily died early in the morning. Rebecca held her in her arms; a white woman embracing an Indian as if they were sisters. In a way, they were sisters; both had loved the same man. They had been willing to share him and the hard life such love required.

We buried Emily beside her family. Standing beside the grave, Rebecca said, "Emily wasn't a Christian. Her people were not offended because Monty had two wives. I think she lived a better life than many Christians. She did not deserve to be murdered."

That afternoon I mounted my horse for the first time in two weeks and rode to Cisco. From there I sent a telegram. Then I rode back to camp, arriving in time for supper.

"How is your leg?" Rebecca asked as she ladled stew from a pot.

"It still aches. It drained some, too. But there wasn't any pus. I'll be able to travel in a few days."

"Good," said Rebecca. "I want to leave soon, too. I'll go back to Salt Lake City and look for work. In time some of my family might accept me again."

Two days later I traded my cap-and-ball revolver to the railroad agent at Cisco for a one-way ticket to Salt Lake. I also sold him Sam Doran's fine horse for two hundred dollars. I gave half of the money to Rebecca.

She had ridden the horse down from the camp. At Cisco I said to her, "I hope you won't mind if I leave you here. Hanging around the railroad might be dangerous."

"I understand, Tom. Good luck! You have a good heart and a good head. Trust them. I shall pray for you."

"Thanks. It might help."

A few days later I was seated high in some ledges that overlooked the San Rafael Desert. The early-spring sunshine was warm on my face and I occasionally nodded. The ache in my leg was almost gone. It still hurt to walk or ride but I could do both.

The landscape I was watching was the same one I had ridden through on my flight from Hanksville. And, on this morning, it was almost as empty as it had been a few weeks earlier. Only the moving dot of a horseman in the distance was new. I watched the rider approach with feelings that ranged from anxiety to relief.

When he was within a mile of me I limped down to where my horse was tied. By riding down a gully that lay at right angles to the rider's course I could intercept him without first revealing myself.

I let the man pass by a few yards before calling, "Hello, Bill. You're right on time."

Kanaka Bill stopped his horse but did not turn to face me. "Hello, kid. What's on your mind?"

"The same thing that's on yours—Bob Lee."

"A sportin' gent in Wyoming offered two thousand for Lee. You only worth a hundred."

"I know where Bob Lee is," I said.

"Only Bob Lee really knows where he's at." Bill sounded disgusted. "Maybe he's up there behind a rock, gonna shoot ol' Bill in the back. Don't try foolin' Kanaka Bill."

"We fooled you so far. But now I'm ready to help you."

"You one friend I don't need, kid. Maybe I shoot you and get rid of a double cross." Bill's hands rested lightly on his saddle horn but even so I was apprehensive. He had beaten men far more dangerous than I.

"You can have the reward. Bob Lee should be brought in. I'll help you, then take my chances. Anything's better than being hunted; even being dead." I continued, "Maybe you'll get Bob Lee. But he could get you first. I saw him kill Sam Doran and he's a lot faster than you'll ever be. He almost got you back there above Cisco. The next time he won't miss. Let's go after him together."

Bill said, "I don't need no wet-nosed partners."

"I wouldn't partner with you on a bet. But I'll hunt with you. I'm not gun-shy and I know Bob Lee. That's worth plenty. Now what do you say? Let's work together and catch Mr. Lee. When we've got him I'll come in with you and surrender. But no tricks."

Kanaka Bill reined his big horse around to face me. He was smiling. "Hokay, no tricks. Which way you think he's headed?"

"South. He was talkin' South America before we split up."

Bill said, "I never seen South America."

"We can catch him before he gets down there." I rode my horse beside Bill's pinto. Sitting stirrup to stirrup, we stared at each other. We didn't like one another but we understood what we had to do.

Bill said, "You lost weight, kid."

"It's been a long winter." I tapped my horse with the reins and the horse stepped forward. Kanaka Bill and I set out in curious combination to search for a retired army sergeant called Robert Lee.

We rode steadily and by midafternoon reached a rise of ground that laid the panorama of the Henry Mountains before us. "Henry Mountains?" It was the first question Bill had asked since we left the gully in the San Rafael.

"Yes. Never been there but I've seen them before." I avoided telling Bill any more than necessary. But I guessed that his mind was racing far ahead of mine. It would be a miracle if I could control the dangerous chain of events my telegram had set in motion.

We camped that night on the Dirty Devil River. The stream was up and not so placid as I had remembered it. Bill showed me how to skin cactus and put it in a pot of the river water. The cactus settled the mud. But even with plenty of coffee beans in it the water still tasted awful. I contributed some bacon to the night's meal. Bill handed me a pouch filled with a mixture of dried berries, fat, and pounded meat. He called it "pem'can." I silently called it something else but I ate a handful anyway.

I was still eating my meager supper when Bill rolled up in his blankets. "Sleep fast, kid. I never caught no one in my bed."

I soon learned what he'd meant, for in a few hours we were riding again. Bill insisted on moving by the light of a waning moon. The man remains in my memory as a mysterious being but I did learn one thing about him—he was relentless. All his efforts were focused on the man he was hunting.

We barely spoke on our long ride toward the Henry Mountains. But the day was fresh with streamers of wind-driven clouds in the blue sky. On another errand and with a healed leg, I could have enjoyed the trip. The mountains rise abruptly from the floor of a dry plain. Only a scattering of low scrub breaks the mountains' spectacular appearance.

The three tallest peaks are all over ten thousand feet and have snow on their summits for nearly half the year. This isolated mountain range is nearly forty miles long and a dozen wide. It is the range of wild game, livestock, and, for many years, wanted men.

The Buhr ranch, which Mr. Lee spoke of as a possible hideout, lay at the northern end of the mountains. The first time we halted was when Kanaka Bill paused to examine the ranch with his field glasses.

The ranch buildings were clustered at the base of the mountains and looked out over the vast plain. The only signs of life were widely spaced groups of bony cattle and shaggy horses.

Bill lowered his glasses. "Not exactly Diamond Head. But they know when a jackrabbit come within ten mile." Bill paused, musing for a moment, then said, "Go on in, kid."

"What do you mean?" Just the thought that Bob Lee might be at the ranch made me apprehensive.

"You got to go in," said Bill. "There's no way to sneak up on that place."

"What am I supposed to do? Lee will smell a rat."

Bill replied, "Sure, but he'll smell this first." He pulled a pint of whiskey from his saddlebags. "You take this. It'll just wet his whistle. Tell him you want to travel with him again."

"He'll know I'm lying. The last thing he did to me was steal my money."

Bill grinned. "This time he'll steal your whiskey. The last thing he did to me was put a bullet past my nose and plug two of my deppities. One died."

Bill hitched his bulk around in the saddle so that the Winchester carbine he carried across his lap was pointing at my belly. He said, "Go in, kid. You'll think of something to say."

Bill then instructed me to stay at the ranch if Bob Lee was there. He would come in late that night, after Lee had drunk the whiskey, and make the capture.

The scheme was too bald and simple to fool Bob Lee. But if I refused to cooperate Kanaka Bill would shoot me. And I could not forget that I had come to settle a score with Mr. Lee. So, repulsive as Bill's scheme was, I had no choice but to follow it.

Although it was set in a wasteland the Buhr ranch looked prosperous. A large house stood beneath several big cottonwoods that also gave shelter to some outbuildings and corrals. A large irrigated hayfield fronted the buildings. The fenced stacks that remained after a winter's feeding testified to the hayfield's productivity. This was the kind of place I hoped to have someday.

I found Mr. Buhr and two of his men in a corral. The cowhands were breaking horses and had a rank-looking pony snubbed to a post in the center of the corral. Because he had asthma Mr. Buhr was known as "Wheezing Buhr." The rancher was seated on the top pole of his corral when I rode up.

"Mr. Buhr?"

"Correct."

"I'm Thomas Lavering from California. I spent two years on the Honeybee ranch west of the Salt Lake."

"Well, Mr. Lavering, that is hardly cause for rejoicing."

"I'm looking for a job."

Henry Buhr panted but when he'd got his wind he said, "If you have ridden all the way from the Great Salt Lake"—he paused to catch his breath—"and not found work between here and there, you're a poor hand indeed."

I thought if Bob Lee had been by and Buhr had given him this cold welcome, he'd be minus those buck teeth. "No, sir, I'm a good hand. But I don't like the winters up north. So I've been hunting for the market and moving south by stages. I'd make you a good hand with horses or cows."

Buhr replied, "Hardly a week goes by that I couldn't hire some drifter. And to hear them talk you'd think they were all top hands."

"I'm not a top hand but I'm good."

Buhr's cowhands glared at me while they saddled the rank pony. Their expressions made it obvious that they didn't want me for a partner.

But, for some reason I never understood, Henry Buhr said, "I haven't any riding jobs. I just put a good man on last month. He's old enough to be your father. I put him up in the mountains cutting timber and skidding it down to my mill." Buhr indicated a canyon south of the ranch.

I assumed he had a sawmill on the creek there. But the real news was that he probably had Bob Lee logging for him. Then, in his next breath, Mr. Buhr made it official, saying, "If you want to cut timber I'll put you on for two weeks. Ten dollars and found. Mr. Lee could use some help."

For an instant I was as breathless as the rancher. Then I managed, "Thank you, sir. I'll make you a good hand."

Buhr waved off my thanks, then fixed me with a cold stare. "From the look of you, young man, you have traveled far and fast to reach here. I don't need you. But I am offering you a chance to stop, rest, and aim your life in a new direction."

"Yes, sir. I'm obliged."

I turned my bay horse and rode toward the canyon. Bob Lee was up there. After all the waiting and worrying a showdown with him was racing to its conclusion. Henry Buhr had indeed aimed my life, whatever might be left of it, in a new direction.

The creek had been diverted near the canyon's mouth. Some of its waters were turned into a sluiceway that ended at a steam-driven saw-mill. Under a lean-to I found an old steam engine and a circular saw with a log carriage. Beside the mill was a pile of freshly cut logs. They had been big trees, ponderosa pines with thick, reddish bark. Each log bore the neat ax work of Robert Lee.

I left the mill and looked in at the tiny shack that stood nearby. No one was home, so I went in and built a fire in the stove.

Once the fire was burning well I went outside and looked for a corral. I found it near the creek. Bob Lee's bays greeted my weary horse with a friendly nicker. A pile of hay lay under a tarpaulin. I fed the horses generously, then returned to the shack, carrying my rifle and other belongings.

The shack had no windows but there was a candle stuck in a bottle on the crude table. I lit the candle, then sat down to wait in its flickering light. As an afterthought I took the pint of whiskey and placed it on the table. I hoped Bob Lee would see it as a peace offering.

Presently there was the thud of hooves and the grating sound of a log being slid across the ground. I went outside to face Bob Lee. But he wasn't there; only a team of horses stood beside the pile of saw logs. I approached them and found their reins neatly looped and tied to one of the hames. I had often seen Bob Lee fasten reins in just this way back on the Honeybee.

"Mr. Lee," I called. "It's Tom Lavering. I'm alone. Wanted to see you."

There was no reply, so I unhooked the team and led them to the corral. I unharnessed there and hung both sets on corral posts. Then I put the horses into the corral and fed them.

Bob Lee was waiting for me in the shack. He was sitting near the wall, half hidden in shadows.

"How, Tom." Although I had not seen him in weeks Bob Lee had not changed. I saw the same hard, flat cheeks which he shaved every morning. And the dark hair carefully swept across his frontal bald spot.

"Never expected to see you again. The way you was bleedin' back there in Hanksville I wouldn't have give spit for your chances."

"I made it back to Nickel's camp. Rebecca took care of me."

Lee smiled. "That's a nice bit to have take care of a man. How was they? Any truth to what that old varmint in Hanksville said?"

I replied, "It was all true. They slaughtered everyone but Rebecca." I wanted to tell Bob Lee that those good people had died because of us. But I did not, for I knew he would not agree, much less care.

He said, "Never heard a peep about it down here. Riders pass through here every so often. Seems like Kanaka Bill and his pals has pulled off the trail. I knowed they would." Mr. Lee kept glancing at the whiskey on the table, then said, "I haven't seen a thing till now when you showed up. What's your game, Tom?"

"You owe me fifteen hundred dollars."

"Do I now? You're riding a mighty nice bay horse. Santy Claus give him to you?"

I said, "That's right. Keep what the horse is worth and give me the rest."

Mr. Lee frowned, his eyes fixed on the whiskey. I said, "Excuse me, have a drink."

Lee smiled. "That English wheezer don't allow liquor. I haven't had a drink in a week."

"Help yourself." I handed him the pint.

Bob Lee took it eagerly, flipping out the cork and swigging a fourth of the pint in three gulps.

"Ah!" Lee grinned and tipped the neck of the bottle toward me. "Have a snort?"

I shook my head. "Go ahead. I'll try some after dinner."

Mr. Lee nodded and took another big drink. At that rate there would be none left very shortly. "Where did you get this stuff? It sure packs a wallop but it tastes a little off."

As Robert Lee sat there grinning, his face flushed with liquor, his features suddenly twisted. He clutched his stomach and pitched forward onto the floor.

CHAPTER 16

Mr. Lee lay writhing on the dirt floor with his hands gripping his stomach. For a moment I stared at him in horrified amazement. This miserable creature twisting at my feet could not be Bob Lee!

Lee's lips were contorted in agony and amidst his awful groans he uttered one word, "Bastard!"

"No!" I had never dreamed that Kanaka Bill would give me poisoned whiskey. I knelt beside Bob Lee and, grasping his shoulder with one hand, tried to shove the index finger of my other hand down his throat. But Mr. Lee had gone into convulsions and I could scarcely hold him, let alone force him to vomit.

I said, "It wasn't me, Mr. Lee. I swear. I wanted to get even but not this way. Kanaka Bill gave me that whiskey!"

On hearing Bill's name, Bob Lee's eyes widened. His last thought on this earth was that I had betrayed him. A moment later his body stiffened in a final spasm and he died.

I half sat and half collapsed on the bunk behind me. How long I stayed there staring down at Bob Lee's corpse I can't say. I had seen violent death all too often but I was totally unprepared for the sudden death of Bob Lee. The thought of finishing the whiskey and going out with him crossed my mind. I had not believed, deep down, that I would survive a showdown with Bob Lee. Only because I wanted to be alert and quick had I not had a drink of the whiskey with him.

Once my thoughts were collected I knew there would still be a showdown. But it would be with Kanaka Bill. The unrelenting deadliness of that lazy-looking Hawaiian was freshly seared on my mind. He had destroyed a man of Bob Lee's caliber without coming near him. I knew I was next on his list. But I did not know when, or from what direction, Bill would strike.

Reaching out to the guttering candle on the table, I pinched the wick between my fingers. The room was plunged into blackness. I could not be sure that Bill wasn't waiting outside.

I dropped on all fours and crawled to Bob Lee's corpse. The body was stiffening and growing cold as I ran my fingers over it. I found and removed his money belt. Fastening the belt under my own shirt, I crawled to the wall and began feeling for my saddle. I had dropped it there earlier with the long-barreled Remington hanging from the skirts.

Locating the saddle, I dragged it to the door, still moving on my hands and knees. I expected to be ambushed by Kanaka Bill at any second. The door creaked agonizingly as I opened it. When no bullet slammed through I clutched my saddle, stood, and ran to the corral.

The draft horses had been nodding over their hay and jumped when I approached them. They soon quieted, however. I led them and Bob Lee's bay horses to the open corral gate and pulled off their halters. Then, slapping their rumps with the halter ropes, I sent them galloping down the trail toward Buhr's ranch.

My own horse stood looking at me. At least he had had a good feed and some rest before I put him on the trail again. I saddled him and then stepped aboard.

We both jumped when a crash of gunfire exploded near the canyon's mouth. Kanaka Bill had been waiting. I lifted my horse into a run. Running a horse uphill was contrary to all my principles and training—except the principle of self-preservation. Kanaka Bill had guessed wrong but I might not be so lucky the next time.

There were no more shots, only the heavy, rhythmic breathing of my horse and the clash of his hooves on the rocky trail.

In less than a mile the trail became too steep for running and I slowed him to a walk. After half an hour of walking the trail vanished under a crust of the past winter's snow. Eventually the crusted slush became too deep for my mount to carry me through. I dismounted and began climbing on foot.

It was coming dawn when I broke out onto the windswept crest of the mountain range. The snow wasn't so deep there. But after plunging over the divide and starting down I was up to my hips in the stuff. With my horse sometimes sitting on his haunches on the steeper slopes we floundered and slid down the mountainside.

Although it made traveling even more difficult I stayed in the timber and brush as much as possible. There was just no telling where Kanaka Bill might again appear.

It was midmorning before I reached the mountain's foothills. I led my tired horse into a patch of oak brush and loosened the saddle's cinches. I would have liked to unsaddle but dared not do it. A few seconds taken to saddle a horse might be all the time Kanaka Bill needed to get me.

As I rested and my horse grazed at the end of his reins, something Mr. Lee once said came to me. It was: "Never try to beat a man at his own trade." He hadn't even been thinking of Kanaka Bill's man-hunting efforts. But I wondered if Lee's advice wouldn't apply all the same.

I began to think along these lines: Bill's bound to catch up to me sometime. Maybe I'll have a better chance if I let him do it at a place and time I choose.

Of course, I hoped that Bill would settle for Bob Lee's corpse and forget me. Then I remembered Monty Nickel's ravaged camp and Bob Lee's horrible death. I had to get Kanaka Bill. I turned my horse to the north; we were going back to Robbers' Roost.

That is, we were going back if I could find my way across that water-scarce maze of broken rocks. The most frustrating thing about those badlands is that there are so few trails through them. A man may ride for miles only to find himself at a dead end and looking down into five hundred feet of sheer drop-off.

I reached the Roost country without seeing a soul. Then I missed my way several times and lost many hours to the ledges and blind canyons. I was two days in that wilderness before getting my bearings and finding the cave. I had subsisted on venison jerky and a canteen filled with water at a place misleadingly called Poison Springs. In two days my gallant horse had one drink from a mud puddle plus a few sips poured from my canteen into my hat. He ate wherever we found forage, which meant he ate very little.

The horse remembered the route back to the cave better than I. For the last few miles I gave him his head. When we reached the cave's approach he sprang up it and rushed to the seep-water tank.

There was no sign that anyone had used the cave since Mr. Lee, Sam Doran, and I left it weeks before. There were so many memories in that place. I could hardly believe that both Lee and Doran were dead.

I dug up the tins of food we had cached there and heated the contents of one. It was Spanish mackerel. I would have preferred a beefsteak and potatoes but I ate the smelly fish to the last morsel. Later I led my horse up the slickrock trail to the top of the mesa and staked him in good grass.

While he grazed I went hunting and shot two sage hens and a jackrabbit. Near the small spring I found a patch of yampa. I dug all the roots my hat would hold, then carried them and my game back to where the horse waited.

Once in the cave, I peeled the tubers and boiled them in an empty can. While they simmered I fried some grouse and rabbit. My mouth watered; this was my first square meal in several days.

I lived in the cave for over a week. And while I made frequent careful inspections from the overlooks, I saw no one. I had been able to plan a strategy for coping with Kanaka Bill. The only flaw in my plan was that Bill never appeared. All I accomplished by staying in the cave was to eat my few cans of food.

The first days of the desert spring did yield a few more edible roots but there were no deer on the mesa. I exhausted the supply of rabbits and sage hens in short order and by the end of the second week I was getting hungry. It was ironic that I carried a money belt filled with hundreds of dollars that couldn't be spent. I had no soap, let alone a razor, and felt like an unsheared sheep.

It was obvious that Kanaka Bill wasn't coming in after me. He would sit waiting like a curly wolf on the edge of this desert or in some other retreat. Then he would pick the time and method of attack.

"No, sir, damn him. He's not going to do that to me!" I was speaking to no one in particular. The thought of surprising Bill occurred to me. But I knew it would be very hard to surprise him, especially after catching him once back in the junipers. I also considered giving myself up. But even as I thought of it I knew I couldn't surrender. Kanaka Bill didn't want prisoners.

The next day I let my horse eat and drink all he wanted. I ate my last scraps of food and, as soon as it was dark, began making my way out of Robbers' Roost. It was nearly fifty miles to the nearest settlement, tiny Green River on the Denver and Rio Grande line. And, traveling at night and through rough country to boot, I was seventy-two hours getting there.

Sam Doran had told me about a particular store in Green River. He said the storekeeper minded his own business but kept flexible hours for certain travelers. I did my shopping at 1 A.M.

The merchant wasn't friendly but he was efficient. With a minimum of talk he filled my order for new clothes, boots, and a few groceries. I had exhausted my .44 ammunition in target practice and small-game hunting. I replenished that and bought a quantity of oats for the horse.

Long before daylight I was back in a simple camp at the base of a lonely butte. I guessed I must be growing owl-eyed from so much night work. As I lay there before a small fire I told myself that Bill had won the first skirmish and by default. I now decided to try to find him before he found me.

Posing as an out-of-work cowhand, I visited cow camps in the district. It was my practice to arrive just before suppertime, hand around a bottle, and swap news. In those days there were so many outlaws in that part of Utah that my reception was often cool. Some of the camps were probably run by part-time rustlers and such hosts were equally wary.

Still, in a few days' time, I talked to a dozen men who had ridden the local ranges for weeks. Not one mentioned seeing a big Kanaka on a pinto horse, let alone any posses. The only Chinese they'd seen worked in the town laundry.

At one camp the boss offered me a riding job. There was nothing I would have liked better than to take a job where the main worry was cows. I hated to refuse. But I knew that as soon as my attention wavered Kanaka Bill would strike. I left that camp without finishing my supper.

Although I changed my campsites frequently and only visited the town at night, I began attracting attention. There was nothing Bill would have liked better than picking me up from a small-town marshal. I decided to leave before that happened.

April had begun when I set out from Green River. The dry hills had turned green with fresh grass and the first wildflowers appeared. I was riding north, climbing the great escarpment of the Book Cliffs, then heading down the long ridges into the Uintah Basin. There was an Indian cabin near the Split Mountain gorge I wanted to visit. Had Yancey DeRoot miraculously survived?

All told, it was a long ride. But when I finally reached the cabin site, the fate of Yancey DeRoot was still a mystery. The cabin had been a typical weathered Indian dwelling with one room and a barren dooryard. This time it was like Monty Nickel's last camp. Nothing remained of the cabin but some charred logs. Even the ashes had been blown away.

I was several days finding the Indian woman who had lived there. She was down on the reservation and living in a ragged tent near Ouray.

At first she would tell me nothing. She blamed me for the loss of her cabin. Perhaps I was to blame, indirectly. So I rode to the trading post at the mouth of the White River and paid for enough supplies to half fill a wagon. The trader agreed to deliver the goods as I directed. Then I returned to the woman's tent and made her understand I was also buying her a cabin. She brightened at that news and we walked down along the Green River where several cabins stood under the big cottonwoods. I bought her a nice cabin there and the former owner threw in the pony that was tied to the back wall.

But not until I had helped her move and seen to the delivery of her supplies would the woman tell me about Yancey DeRoot. I don't care if a woman is Indian, Chinese, or lily white; any female who believes she's been wronged is the most vengeful creature on earth. And because this particular woman had some justification for her anger, my task was doubly hard.

Finally, however, she told me about Yancey. He had been shot in the chest but she was able to drain the wound. And once the fluid left his chest he began to recover. He was blind, of course. The woman had driven off Yancey's infection with herbal medicines and his fever abated. It was a long convalescence, normal for anyone but a miracle for a man Yancey's age. As she spoke it became clear that this simple woman had been won over by Yancey's goodness.

I do not speak Ute and the woman didn't speak much English. What with the limitations of sign language plus countless questions and re-phrasings it was many hours before I learned the full story.

It happened in March, on one of the first nice days of the year. The sun had warmed the front of the cabin and the woman took Yancey out to sit on the bench there. He hadn't been outside thirty minutes when she heard a thump on the wall and the echoing report of a far-off gunshot. Terrified, the woman peeked out the half-open door.

Yancey was lying on his side. It must have been a big soft-nosed bullet. It struck him square in the chest and came out his back, leaving a hole the size of a dollar. The woman dragged Yancey's thin body back into the cabin but, this time, there was no helping him. At an age I knew not, Yancey DeRoot's unhappy life had ended.

The woman put Yancey on the bed. That was where Kanaka Bill found him. Bill, on his now-familiar pinto horse, had ridden up to the cabin. Dismounting, he kicked in the door and entered with his rifle leveled and ready.

Bill told the woman it was bad medicine to help bad men. The big white chiefs did not like it. She should have reported Yancey's presence. (Bill didn't say to whom or for what reason, since Yancey wasn't wanted for anything.) Nevertheless, Kanaka slapped the old woman around, smashed her few possessions, then set fire to the cabin. When the cabin was engulfed in flames Bill mounted his horse and rode away.

"Which direction did he go?" I asked.

The woman pointed north. Kanaka Bill was going back to Brown's Hole. I cursed my stupidity. I had wasted time in Robbers' Roost and around Green River. I should have guessed that Bill knew I would return to Georgia Willets. That's where he was waiting!

Leaping to my feet, I left the astonished Indian woman sitting in her new cabin. In two jumps I hit the saddle and didn't slow the galloping horse for five miles. Bill was weeks ahead of me. I had some awful visions of what he might already have done to Georgia and the two Willets brothers.

It was a ride of seventy miles. But I don't remember much of it. Higher up on Diamond Mountain there were still snowdrifts. Sometimes I had to dismount and break trail for my weary horse. Despite the drifts and traveling by night I reached Brown's Hole and forded the Green by midafternoon of the following day.

The river was filling with logs and other debris of the spring runoff. Crossing it took the last of my horse's strength. I stopped by a meadow on the far shore and unsaddled. The horse took a grateful roll, then ate avidly for two hours. I lay under a tree and watched his gaunt flanks fill out. I couldn't miss Bob Lee but I sorely missed the confidence his presence would have given me. I tried to imagine what he would do now.

What I did was reckless. When my horse was standing quietly, his belly full, I saddled him and rode to Uncle Dick's store. It was late in the day when I arrived but the old sinner was there, sitting in a chair beside the counter. He looked the same as ever, not even appearing to have changed his clothes. The old man stiffened when I came through the door.

He collected himself quickly. "Well, now. Looky here! It's the kid what shot that hole in your hat, Isom!"

Isom Dart's black face was expressionless as he sat facing me. But his eyes wavered. We both knew I had beaten him in a no-holds fight. I could see fear in Dart's look.

I said, "That's something I'm here about. Give Mr. Dart the best Stetson you have. I owe him a new hat."

For a moment the two men stared, unbelieving. Then Uncle Dick, always eager to make a sale, cried, "Well, now! Isom, step up here and get your new hat 'fore this gent'man changes his mind!" Dick began placing hats on the counter for Dart to try. He eventually chose a five-dollar black Stetson that Uncle Dick was good enough to let me buy for seven dollars.

While my horse munched a bucket of oats I had Uncle Dick fry me a big steak. He and Dart sipped whiskey and watched as I ate the steak with two eggs and chased it down with a pot of coffee.

Until then Isom Dart had scarcely spoken. Finally, his new hat perched rakishly on his head, he asked, "Have a good winter?"

"I've known better."

Uncle Dick said, "You caused some commotion hereabouts, you and"—he paused—"you had a partner?"

"Right, I *had* a partner. He's dead."

Uncle Dick feigned shock. "No! Sorry to hear it."

Knowing that these men were most comfortable on the far side of the law, I took a gamble. I said, "Yes, that big Kanaka that was in here last year poisoned him. Bob never had a chance; died in my arms down in the Henry Mountains."

It was one thing to dry-gulch a man or knife him in an alley but poisoning was an outrage to these men. Poison was for coyotes and gophers, not men. Using it was a woman's trick.

Dart said, "Why, that son of a bitch. He was in here the other day braggin' on how he'd shot that feller off'n his horse. Said he took him in a fair fight an' got a dandy reward."

I shook my head. "Bill poisoned some whiskey. He never came within a mile of Bob Lee. Then he dry-gulched one of the best friends I ever had. Last month he hid behind a rock and shot Yancey DeRoot in the chest. Yancey never had a chance. He was blind and just gettin' over bein' shot by an Indian down in Jones' Hole."

Killing from ambush was familiar to the likes of Dart and Uncle Dick. But they deplored it when it was done by the "other side." They were the sort of men vigilantes and regulators left hanging from trees. I was counting on their fears of Bill's methods to help me.

I asked, "Have you seen where Bill is staying?"

Isom Dart replied, "Sure, he's been hangin' around down to Willets'."

I said, "I'm surprised the Willetses would trifle with a man like that."

Uncle Dick said, "No accountin' for what folks will do for a dollar. They got him sleepin' in the bunkhouse and takin' meals in the house with them. I would never believed it but it's Miss Georgia that's behind it. Sam was in the other day an' said it was Georgia made him take Bill in."

I frowned but inwardly I rejoiced. Georgia knew Bill was after me. By keeping him at the ranch she made him much easier to keep track of.

Dart said, "He's takin' life easy. If it's warm he goes down to the river and fishes. Sits there in a chair with a long cane pole stuck in the bank waitin' for some no-account fish."

Now I had what I needed to know. The Willetses were safe. Kanaka Bill certainly wasn't just sitting idly on the riverbank; he had something planned. While the two men rambled on I tried to guess what Bill's plan was.

Then I said, "Sounds like Bill is having a fine spring vacation. I'll just keep going and not disturb his rest."

I started toward the door. As I was about to open it Dart said, "I'd be careful. Bill's got a Chinaman on every hilltop. No one gets near that place without he knows it."

I paused at the door, thinking. Then I turned to face the two men. "Thanks. Maybe I'd better head down to Lily Park. Do some mavericking and maybe build an outfit of my own. Dick, sell me a couple of good lariat ropes." Then I added, "Broke the handle out of my ax the other day. Let me have a single-bit and a pound of big spikes."

The two men watched with open curiosity as I paid for my purchases and left the store. It was dark when I reached the ford on the Green River. For the second time in that long day my horse carried me safely across the swollen river. Bob Lee could certainly pick horses.

On the far bank I rested my horse, then led him upstream. It was still cold once the sun had set and walking got me warm again. Finally I mounted my horse and rode at a leisurely pace until the lights of the Willets ranch house came into view.

Although it was pitch dark with no moon I kept to the junipers and brush patches until I was a half mile upstream from the ranch. The river is wide and deep there with no fords for several miles in either direction. I settled down in a brush patch, fed my horse some grain I'd bought from Uncle Dick, and waited.

As the first lamps of morning were lit at the ranch I stood up. Then, making sure my horse was well hidden, I walked upstream. In about a mile I found a spot where several logs had become jammed in against the bank. Working with my new ax and a pole, I broke up the jam and saved three solid logs from the bunch that floated away.

When I had done this it was full daylight. I stopped work and, again moving through brush patches and the cottonwoods along the river, returned to my simple camp. I spent the day loafing while my horse grazed at the end of his reins.

I was watching a place across the river, below the Willets ranch house. The river formed an eddy there, drawing itself into a slow swirl at an indentation in the steep bank. If I'd chosen a place to bait fish I would have chosen that one.

Early in the afternoon a stocky figure appeared on the far bank. Although he was a half mile off I knew it was Kanaka Bill. I watched him while he baited his hooks and set out his long pole. Bill had a seat rigged for himself so he could sit with his back against a big cottonwood tree. After a while he appeared to be asleep. But I knew better. I was tempted to try drilling him with my Remington. But the range was a bit too long for certainty. And, much as I wanted to end it soon, shooting anyone from ambush, even Kanaka Bill, wasn't my style.

Kanaka Bill wasn't in Brown's Hole for the fishing. Apart from the odd trout that get lost in its muddy waters, there is only one fish in the Green River worth eating. That is the Green River whitefish, or "salmon" as it is sometimes called. I have heard of these fish weighing fifty pounds. But the ones Bill caught that afternoon ran five to fifteen pounds. By the end of the afternoon he had caught eight fish. When he stopped fishing he selected two of the largest fish and kicked the rest back into the water.

As soon as it was dark I went back upstream to where I had left the three logs. This time I was carrying the two lariats and the spikes I had bought from Uncle Dick.

As a kid playing on the Sacramento River I had made many rafts. It was therefore just the work of a few hours to build a crude but serviceable raft. Once it was finished I lined it downstream to a point near my campsite and secured it out of sight.

Back in my rough camp I took two previously cut five-foot poles and lashed them together at the tops. I tied in a crossbar at the lashing. Finally, I fed my horse the last of the grain, ate a can of peaches, and tried to get some sleep.

I dozed fitfully during the long and cold night. But when lights were lit at the ranch I was up and doing, too. After saddling my horse I fastened the five-foot poles, sawbuck fashion, across the saddle. Then I arranged my coat on the crosspiece and tied the wadded grain sack at the top. I put my hat on the wadded grain sack and stepped back to judge my handiwork. It was crude but from across the river it would look like a man riding through the trees.

When Kanaka Bill came down to fish that afternoon I replaced my scarecrow on the horse's back. My hands shook as I buttoned on the coat. This was my one chance. It had to work because Bill was too wise to ever give me another try. After tying up his reins I slapped my horse on the rump and sent him trotting back downstream.

As the horse cleared the thicket I boarded my raft and pushed it off into the current. I had added some old limbs to the raft for concealment and lay down behind them. My rifle and six-gun were placed carefully to hand in front of me. Thanks to having already floated the Green, I handled the raft easily.

Bill was sitting in his fishing chair. His face was shaded by that big hat he always wore. But even as I steered the raft across the river I knew Bill wasn't just fishing. He was waiting, his eyes searching the far shore. I froze as the current seized my raft and carried it into the big eddy below Bill's fishing chair.

Without warning Bill sprang to his feet and grabbed a rifle from beside the tree. I dared not move. The raft was turning in the eddy. I was thirty feet from Bill when he threw up his rifle and fired three fast shots. The muzzle blast was fearsome.

The shots were over my head; he hadn't seen me. I glanced across the river. My horse was running through the trees there, the scarecrow tilted back over his rump.

Bill saw me just as I raised up on the raft, my Smith & Wesson aimed in both hands. Bill flipped the lever on his Winchester.

He was too slow. My first bullet struck him over the right eye. I thought I hit him two more times as he pitched forward into the river.

Kanaka Bill's corpse floated beside my raft for a moment, then disappeared into the turbid water. I knelt on the raft, shaking. Then I stuck my pole into the water and steered to a hasty landing on the far shore.

I found my horse grazing quietly within a half mile. The scarecrow was still hanging over his rump. But a sensible horse like that one didn't let things spook him. He scarcely looked when I reclaimed my coat and threw off the poles. Bob Lee could sure pick good horses.

I rode out of Brown's Hole that same afternoon. I kept riding, clear across Wyoming, following the spring north until I struck this range in Montana. I have lived here ever since.

For a long time I considered returning Chun Kwo's money. I also considered sending for Georgia Willets. But as time passed and I became a peaceful rancher, I did not do either.

About the Author

In his varied career, Frank Calkins has been a magazine editor, a newspaper columnist, a big-game hunting guide, and a Utah State Game Warden. He is the author of two non-fiction books, *Rocky Mountain Warden* and *Jackson Hole,* and one previous Double D Western, *The Tan-faced Children.* He lives on a five-acre enclave in a national wildlife refuge in Jackson Hole, Wyoming.